THE REJECTED
Mail-Order Bride

"*The Rejected Mail-Order Bride* is a tender, faith-filled book about overcoming life's difficulties and finding love in unexpected places. With its tenacious heroine and loyal hero, Rose and Harl's story drew me in from the first page. Sure to please fans of inspirational historical romance."

Kellie VanHorn
PW bestselling author and 2023 ACFW Carol Award winner for Short Novel

"This historical romance, *The Rejected Mail-Order Bride,* is a delightful story of redemption. Greta Picklesimer weaves a brave tale of a woman escaping her past only to find a new path among Kentucky hospitality."

Terri Heunaber Bentley
Author of *For Love of Family*

THE REJECTED
Mail-Order Bride

LOVE IN THE KENTUCKY HILLS – BOOK TWO

GRETA PICKLESIMER

AMBASSADOR INTERNATIONAL
GREENVILLE, SOUTH CAROLINA & BELFAST, NORTHERN IRELAND

www.ambassador-international.com

The Rejected Mail-Order Bride

ISBN: 978-1-64960-517-7
eISBN: 978-1-64960-559-7
Library of Congress Control Number: 2024932286

Cover design by Karen Slayne
Interior Typesetting by Dentelle Design
Edited by Katie Cruice Smith and Megan Griffin

Scripture taken from the King James Version (Public Domain).

Ambassador International titles may be purchased in bulk for education, business, fundraising, or sales promotional use. For information, please email sales@emeraldhouse.com.

AMBASSADOR INTERNATIONAL
Emerald House
411 University Ridge, Suite B14
Greenville, SC 29601
United States
www.ambassador-international.com

AMBASSADOR BOOKS
The Mount
2 Woodstock Link
Belfast, BT6 8DD
Northern Ireland, United Kingdom
www.ambassadormedia.co.uk

The colophon is a trademark of Ambassador, a Christian publishing company.

For my father, Mitchell Picklesimer, Sr.,
One of my favorite storytellers.

Chapter 1

1871

Harl Adams loaded the last of the feed for the livestock from Grant's Mercantile into the back of his wagon. Turning, he bumped into Cletus Tooth, who was mumbling something to himself. Tooth didn't slow his pace or apologize. Instead, he threw a small photograph case at Harl's feet and kept walking.

"Hold up there, Cletus," Harl said. "You dropped something."

"I didn't drop nothin'," Cletus spat over his shoulder.

"What's got you in such a state?"

Cletus spun around and marched back to Harl. "Her—that's what," he said, jabbing his finger at the case Harl held.

Unlatching the tiny clasp, Harl looked at the delicate black and white image of a young woman. Shaking his head, he looked at Cletus.

"*That* don't match *that*," Cletus said, emphasizing the statement by jabbing his index finger first at the picture and then in the air toward the train depot.

"Were you meeting someone?"

"Was I! Been talking to her through letters."

"I didn't know you could read and write."

"I can't. My neighbor Paul Richardson's been writing them for me and reading them to me."

"Oh. And you were meeting her at the depot?"

"Ha, not anymore."

Harl furrowed his brows.

"You mean to tell me that you saw her and left her standing there alone?"

Cletus shook his head as he backed away. "Go see for yourself. You won't believe it. Rose ain't no rose."

Turning, Cletus rushed back out into the busy street.

Harl turned toward the depot that was located next to Grant's Mercantile. Holding the case open, he turned the corner onto the platform. There, standing alone, was a short, stout, red-headed woman in a green coat and matching dress. She was nervously twisting a white handkerchief in her gloved hands while standing next to a trunk. Her face was beet red; her brows were pinched; and her mouth was pursed into a scowl.

Harl stepped cautiously over to her. "Rose?"

She turned toward him. "Mr. Tooth?"

Harl shook his head. "No."

"Oh, I knew it. How typical," she said, crushing the handkerchief in one hand and straightening the matching green hat with long pheasant feathers with the other. "I must look a mess."

"No. You look fine."

Opening her purse, she pulled out a small leather case and opened the delicate clasp, shaking her head as she looked at the photo. "I never should have answered his advertisement."

Harl stepped beside her and peered at the black and white picture of a man in a Confederate uniform. It was a younger version of Cletus Tooth. Looking at the photo case that Cletus had given him, Harl handed it over to her, lifting his brows as if to question her.

She looked at it and scoffed. "I didn't have a more recent photograph to send. I thought once he met me . . . " Her voice trailed away.

"There's a resemblance there," Harl lied. She took the case, closed the clasp, and thrust it into her purse.

Holding out Cletus' photograph, she said, "Would you be so good as to return this to Mr. Tooth for me? I have no need of it now."

Harl nodded. "Do you have relatives here in town?"

"No, no one."

Harl thought for a moment. He couldn't just leave her standing alone on the platform. "Would you like me to drive you over to the hotel? There're no more trains for the night."

Her shoulders sagged. Twisting the handkerchief again, she said, "I don't have any money. Mr. Tooth paid my way here. Said I didn't need any money. I left everything to come here."

Large, cotton-like snowflakes began falling around them as the afternoon light dimmed.

"Well, you can't stay here all night. Come on. I'll give you a ride to the hotel."

"But I don't have any money."

"My treat. Besides, it's just for one night. We'll get you back on the train in the morning, and you can head for home."

Rose twisted the handkerchief angrily. "What will my father say when he finds out I've been thwarted in love?"

Harl gestured for her to follow him.

"Wait, my trunk!"

Harl turned back and hefted the trunk up onto his broad, muscular shoulder.

"Oh my," she said. "Isn't it too heavy for you?"

"Not at all."

When they reached his wagon, he placed the trunk in the back and helped her up onto the seat. He climbed in on the left side, took up the reins, released the brake, and told the mules to walk on.

The Moore Hotel and Restaurant stood a couple of blocks down from the train depot. Even so, Harl felt it was his duty to help this new stranger and get her safely to the hotel.

At the hotel, Harl jumped down and helped Rose off the wagon. Inside, Garlin Moore stood behind the ornate oak counter reading the guest ledger. He straightened, keeping his eyes on the ledger as he turned it around when they approached.

"One night or two?" he asked, taking a key from a row of boxes in the wall behind him. Turning, he gasped when he saw Harl. "Oh, oh!"

Harl chuckled and held out his hand. "It's not like that. *She* will just need a room for the night."

"Of course," Garlin said. "We have a lovely room overlooking the pond out back."

Rose cut her eyes to Harl.

"She'll take it." Harl placed a coin on the desk, and Garlin snatched it.

"Last door on the right. I'll show you," he said, walking around the desk.

"I'll bring your trunk in," Harl told Rose.

Harl dusted the snow off it before lifting the trunk out of the wagon. The snow was coming down in large, wet flakes and covered the backs of the mules. He hefted the heavy trunk inside to an anxiously waiting Rose.

Garlin led the way up the stairs, followed by Rose and Harl. At the last door on the right, Garlin placed the key in the lock and opened the door.

"Here we are," he said, gesturing Rose into the large room.

Rose stepped into the room and looked around. The walls were decorated with pink roses on white wallpaper. A white porcelain washbasin stood against the wall by the dresser and fireplace. A table and chair were placed opposite near the full-size bed covered in quilts.

"Oh, this is lovely!" she exclaimed. "Reminds me of my room back home."

"Where's home?" Harl asked, placing the trunk down next to the dresser.

"Chelsea, Michigan."

Garlin Moore's mouth dropped open. "You came all the way from Michigan to Harrisville? Whatever for?"

Rose opened her mouth, but Harl cut her off by waving his hand. "That's not important right now. Let's just say that reason has come and gone."

Garlin shrugged. "I hear it's cold up there in the winter."

"Yes, it does get very cold. We have snowstorms. I even came through one getting here."

"It will be cold tonight. Let me start a fire for you," Garlin offered.

"Thank you."

Harl looked out the window. "If you're all set here, I better be going."

Sticking his hand in his pocket, he withdrew it and offered it to Rose. She shook his hand as he pressed something hard and round into her palm. She gasped.

"Garlin here has the finest restaurant in town. Why not go down and get yourself something to eat? I'll see you in the morning about the train fare."

Licking her lips, Rose smiled. "Thank you, Mister . . . I don't even know your name."

"Harl Adams."

"Rose Henderson. Thank you for your help today. I don't know what I would have done without you."

Harl's lips hiked up on one side, giving him the appealing trait of a crooked smile. "My pleasure."

Harl hurried from the hotel. When he reached his team, the snow was coming down in icy torrents. "Come on, boys, let's get home."

Chapter 1

The next morning, Rose poked her head out from under the covers. She shook all over. She gazed over at the grate in the fireplace and saw that the fire had died down to glowing embers during the night, leaving the room bitterly cold. She crept out of bed, shivering, placed her bare feet into her boots, and pulled a shawl out of her trunk. She knelt before the fireplace grate and crisscrossed two large pieces of wood on top of the gray ashes. Using the poker, she found a few glowing embers under the ash. She pushed them toward the wood and waited for it to catch fire.

Rose rubbed her arms through the shawl while her breath came out in little clouds. A crate to her left caught her eye. It was filled with newspapers. She read the masthead of several of the papers— *The American Bugle*.

"Well, I have a specific job for you, *American Bugle*," she said as she tore the paper in half once and then in half again. Crunching up the strips of paper, she placed them near the embers. Hungrily, they ignited; and in a few moments, the logs began to burn. At last, she had a cozy fire going. Rose rubbed her hands together and felt the glow of the fire on her face as her body began to warm.

She stood. Gazing about the room, she spotted the white basin and pitcher. The handle of the heavy pitcher was cold to her touch.

She tipped it over the basin, but nothing came out. Rose placed her hand inside the pitcher and pulled it out quickly.

"Ice!" she hissed. She replaced the heavy pitcher carefully into the basin and moved to her trunk as one side of the shawl slipped off her shoulder.

She pulled the green gown and a fresh pair of white stockings out of the trunk, along with her corset and pantaloons. She took off her nightgown and boots and donned her front-closure corset, stockings, pantaloons, and gown. She brushed her long, red hair and pinned it up on top of her head in a pleasing fashion. When she was fully dressed, she sauntered over to one of the two windows. They, too, were iced over. Rose rubbed her fist against the glass of one window until she had a circle large enough for her to see out.

What she saw surprised and pleased her. Long, thick ice covered the trees and shrubs, which bent under the weight. She sucked in her breath.

"Oh, how lovely."

But when had the snow turned to ice? Stepping away from the window, she caught her image reflected in the mirror over the dresser and smiled to herself. She was a good-looking woman, even though she was larger than most. Any man should be pleased to call her his own.

She tossed her green wool coat over her arm, donned her hat, and picked up her purse. She opened the door to the room, and stepped into the hallway. The hearty smell of bacon tickled her nose. She followed it to the restaurant, where she found Garlin Moore serving a handsome couple at a table near the door.

Looking up, Garlin smiled. Setting down the silver coffeepot he held over an empty table, he gestured for Rose to follow him.

"Here we are," he said, pulling out a chair a few tables away from the couple, who were lost in conversation.

Rose sat at the small, round table draped with a white linen tablecloth. Garlin brought over the coffeepot.

"Coffee?"

"Yes, please."

Turning over the plain, white stoneware cup, Garlin poured her a drink.

"The creamer and sugar bowl are on the table."

Rose stirred in two heaping spoonfuls of sugar and a good amount of cream.

"I love the thought of coffee, but I really don't care for the taste," she explained. "It's the warmth I want."

"Oh." He chuckled.

"May I see a menu?"

"I'm afraid all we have this morning is what I can fix in the kitchen. Cook couldn't make it in with the ice storm."

"Oh? So, you are doing the cooking?"

"Yes," he said, ducking his head. "Oh, but I'm a good cook."

Rose smiled. "I'll have whatever you recommend."

"Coming right up."

After a few minutes, Garlin returned wearing a clean, white apron and carrying a plate. Setting the plate before Rose, she inhaled deeply and closed her eyes.

"This smells delicious."

"Wait 'til you taste the sausage gravy."

She surveyed her plate of sausage gravy, bacon, sausage, buttered toast, and scrambled eggs.

"I was going to make the eggs over-easy; but the yolks broke, so I scrambled them," he explained.

"I'm sure they are very good, and I prefer my eggs over-hard," she said, picking up her fork.

She dug into the eggs, swirling them around in the gravy before tasting them.

"Oh yes, this is good gravy, Mr. Moore."

"Well, I'll leave you to it," he said, smiling as he retreated.

When Rose finished, she looked around the room. The couple who had been seated when she entered had left. She was alone. Garlin walked over and picked up her empty plate. "What time will you be leaving this morning?"

"That depends entirely on the train schedule."

"Oh, there's no train today. At least, I haven't heard any yet. Usually, one's here by six a.m."

"No trains!" Rose shrieked. "I simply must return home. "

"Well, unfortunately, it looks like you won't be able to today. Hopefully, there will be one available tomorrow."

Rose's eyebrows shot up, and her mouth dropped open.

Garlin dropped his eyes to her purse on the table. Digging through her purse, she pulled out a small coin and handed it over. He tucked it into his vest pocket. "Don't worry, though. The ice will probably be gone by day's end, and you'll get on one tomorrow and head for home."

"Oh." Rose shut her eyes. "I hope so—though my father will be sorely disappointed when he finds out what has happened."

"Well, don't dwell on it right now," he said, picking up her plate and returning to the kitchen.

Rose stood, pulled on her coat, picked up her purse, and then walked out the door. "I simply must get back to Michigan. "

Standing in the doorway of the restaurant, she surveyed her surroundings. The street was covered in thick ice. No one stirred on the street, but warm light illuminated shop windows.

"Maybe the train depot owner will know something," she said to herself, stepping out onto the icy street. As soon as her right foot touched the ice, it slipped out from under her; and she fell to the side. A popping sound came from her right ankle. She landed heavily on top of the ice.

"Goodness gracious!" Garlin exclaimed from behind her. "Are you all right?"

Rose rolled over and peered at the man. "Help me up, quick."

Garlin, still dressed in the white apron, bent down and offered her his hand. Taking it, she braced her feet against the ground as Garlin yanked her up.

"Oh, my ankle," she cried when she tried to put weight on her foot.

"Did you break it?"

"No, I don't think so. I twisted it; but oh, it hurts." Tears began to well in her eyes. What a mess! No money, no way to get home, and now an injured ankle!

Holding onto Garlin's offered elbow, Rose hobbled back into the restaurant.

"I'm so sorry," she said.

"Whatever for? You couldn't help it that the street was all ice."

"I was going to go to the train depot to check when the next train would be."

"Well, let's get you up to your room. I'll send word to Dr. Johnson that you possibly sprained your ankle and ask him to have a look."

"Thank you."

Back in Rose's room, Garlin brought in a chair and placed a pillow on it. "Do you want to sit here by the fire or by the window?"

"By the fire."

He arranged the chairs facing each other near the fire. "I'll grab a book for you to read while you recuperate."

"Thank you."

He hurried out of the room and quickly returned with a book in hand "I'll bring up a tray when it's time for lunch," he said, closing the door behind him.

It was just over three hours later when Dr. Robert Johnson arrived in Rose's room with his medical bag. Garlin Moore followed close behind, carrying a tray with Rose's lunch. Garlin stepped out the door as the doctor placed his hand lightly on Rose's ankle, which was hidden beneath her gown. She grimaced. The doctor examined her ankle, moved it a bit, and sighed.

"It's not broken. It's just a bad sprain," he said. "Where did this happen?"

"Outside on the icy street," she said as she shifted her gown down around her feet on the floor

"She was going to check the train schedule," Garlin chimed in through the door.

Dr. Johnson looked at her and gasped. "There won't be any trains for a few days until this ice melts."

"If it melts," Garlin added from the hallway.

"In the meantime, do you have any friends here in town you could stay with? A hotel is fine, but it's no place to recuperate."

Rose's mouth turned down into a frown, and she scowled. "No. Well, I thought I had found a friend here, but he left me standing on the train platform."

"Well, well," the doctor said. "I didn't mean to upset you."

"It's all right."

"May I come in?" Garlin asked.

"Yes, come in," Rose said, adjusting her skirts lower.

"The only people she knows are you, me, and Harl Adams," Garlin informed the doctor.

"And Cletus Tooth," she mumbled under her breath.

"Cletus?" the doctor asked, looking from Garlin to Rose.

"It was all set. We had written to each other for a few months. I was going to be his bride as soon as I stepped off the train, he said. But he never came for me. I guess I've changed a little since my photograph was taken."

"Well, don't fret about that right now."

"Come to think of it, the Adamses would be a good family to stay with. Hazel Adams is a good cook; and her daughter just got married to our town's preacher, so they would have room for you out at their place," Garlin said.

Rose's brows knit together. "I can't just go busting in on a family I don't know."

"Well, we could make you as comfortable as we can here," Garlin said.

Dr. Johnson shook his head. "You have a hotel and restaurant to run. You can't be running up and down the stairs for a sick patient."

Garlin looked at Rose. "You're not that sick, and I could send one of the chambermaids up to look in on you. Then when the ice melts, we'll get you on a train headed north."

Rose's brows pinched together. She licked her lips and touched her face as she looked at the fire. She shook her head. "I left everything to come here and marry Mr. Tooth."

"I'm sure we could scrape together some money to get you on a train," Garlin said.

"My father will be so disappointed when I get home. He thought his little bird had finally flown the nest and now this. How will I explain Mr. Tooth's rejection of me?"

"Let's not worry about that right now," the doctor said. "Let's get you better first."

Rose twisted her handkerchief. "I could just strangle that man."

"That won't help matters," Garlin said.

Relaxing her face, she said, "Thank you so much. You both have been very helpful."

"My pleasure," Dr. Johnson said, standing. He grasped the handles of his medical bag.

Garlin nodded. "I'll send the chambermaid up to check on you."

"And I'll send word to the Adamses that you fell. They may want to offer you hospitality," the doctor said with a tip of his hat. As the two men left the room, Rose settled into her chair by the fire as she tried to figure out how she was going to get home.

How quickly everything had changed! Just a couple of days ago, she had been a hopeful bride on an adventure to meet her groom. Now, she was alone in a strange town with no friends and a sprained ankle. Her father would surely be upset, and she would probably die an old maid.

Rose allowed the tears to fall as she began to sink into self-pity. As the wind howled outside, Rose dozed off to sleep, dreaming of strangling a certain former bridegroom.

Chapter 3

Harl was tending the livestock at his family's farm when Aaron Williams, sitting on the bare back of a mule, rode up to him.

"Message for you," Aaron said, handing Harl a folded piece of paper.

Harl scowled as he read it. "I knew I should have just brought her home. Ma wouldn't have minded."

"Brought who home?"

Harl glanced at Aaron. "You working in town now?"

"Yep, ever since Teacher got married. I been at the livery stable."

Harl nodded. "Just a minute," he said.

Harl took a few long strides over and into the house, where he found his mother setting the table for breakfast. He held up the paper.

"What is it?" she asked, pulling her hand up to her neck. "Bad news?"

"No. Well, not really. Just a neighbor in need is all."

Mama took the paper from her son's hand and read it.

"Sounds to me like she could use some good, ol'-fashioned help. You want to go fetch her?"

"I'd like to, but I wanted to ask you first."

"Why, sure. Go get her."

Harl smiled. "It won't be too much on you, will it? Having her recuperate here?"

"Not at all. 'Sides, it will give me something to do now that Catherine and Clair are living in town."

"Thanks, Mama." Harl bent and kissed his mother on the cheek.

His mother smiled as her son turned to go out the door.

"Wait! At least have your breakfast first."

Harl spun back around. "You got enough for another mouth at the table?"

"Of course, I do."

"Mind if I invite Aaron Williams to sup with us?"

"Not at all. I'll set another plate."

Harl opened the kitchen door and motioned for the big, black man to come to him. Aaron rode the mule over to the porch. "Are you hungry?"

"Sure am."

"Come on in. Mama's got the table set for us."

Aaron smiled, climbed down, and threw the reins around one of the square pillars on the porch.

"After we eat, we can go back into town and pick up Miss Henderson."

After they finished eating, Aaron helped Harl hitch his mules to the wagon.

"I'll let Mr. Moore and the doctor know you're comin' for Miss Henderson," Aaron said. "You want me to meet you at the hotel?"

"No, I can manage her and her trunk by myself," Harl said, carefully climbing onto the wagon seat.

Aaron nodded and then turned his mule back toward town.

Harl carefully eased his team of mules over the icy road. He drove slowly and purposefully.

"The first thing I'm going to do when Miss Henderson is well enough is make sure that Cletus Tooth apologizes to her and does the right thing by her," he said out loud as he listened to the cracking of the ice under the mule's hooves and the wagon wheels. "He ought to have apologized to her when he saw her and paid her ticket back home. Now, she's stuck here where she doesn't want to be."

The drive into town seemed to take hours. Harl was not a man who liked to wear a pocket watch, so he had no idea how long it actually took. The last thing he wanted to do was to hurry the team and have one of them slip and break a leg.

In town, Harl guided the mules to Moore's Hotel and Restaurant through the deserted street. He turned the mules so they were perpendicular to the entrance of the hotel.

"Well, I was wondering when you'd get here," Garlin Moore said, opening the door to the hotel.

"It's pretty icy. I didn't want to hurry the mules and have them break a leg in the rush."

"No, of course not."

Harl set the brake and climbed down.

"Aaron Williams came by here a few minutes ago and let me know you was coming," Garlin said. "She's all ready for you. You sure it won't be an imposition having her at your place? I mean, she is welcome to recuperate here. I could send a maid up to check on her every so often. Besides, with this ice storm, we aren't busy."

"It's all right. Mama could use the company with Catherine and Clair gone."

"And as soon as this ice breaks up, and a train can get through—and she's well enough to travel—you'll put her on a train headed north."

"As soon as she's well enough to travel, I'm going to get that skunk of a man, Cletus Tooth, to apologize to her and buy her a ticket home."

Garlin nodded. "Well, come on. Let's get her and her things in the wagon."

Harl followed Garlin up the carpeted stairs of the hotel to Rose Henderson's room at the far end of the hallway.

The hotel owner knocked softly at the door.

"Come in," Rose said.

Garlin opened the door. Harl peered into the room over Garlin's head. Rose sat wearing the same dress she had worn when she had met Harl at the train station. Her feet were tucked under her gown. A lone brown boot lay under the chair across from her.

"I'm so sorry. My foot is too swollen to get it back into my boot," she said, tucking her dress around her swollen ankle.

"That's all right," Harl said. "Can you walk?"

"I can try," she said. She stood and wobbled. Harl raced to her side and grasped her arm to steady her.

Rose flushed as Harl gripped her arm gently. She seemed to relax after a moment, and Harl quickly let go.

"Thank you," she whispered, looking up into his face. He reassured her with a crooked smile.

Taking a step, she grimaced and grabbed the back of the chair.

"Here, let me help her," Garlin said. Moving to her side, he held out his arm. She grasped it and reached down for the boot.

Harl picked up her trunk and placed it on his muscular shoulder. Balancing it, he walked toward the open door.

"Now, lean on me and don't use your bad foot," Garlin said from behind him.

"Oh!" Rose cried. "I'm not sure I can do this."

Harl set the trunk down in the hallway. "Here, Garlin. You take the trunk, and I'll help Miss Henderson."

Garlin hefted the trunk. "Nothing I haven't done plenty o' time before," he said, groaning under its weight. "What do you have in here? Rocks?" He chuckled at his joke as he peered over his shoulder at Rose.

"Yes, but just one," she admitted.

"You have a rock in your trunk?" Harl asked, sounding shocked as he moved to her side.

"Yes, it's my favorite from my parents' farm. It used to sit in our front yard with the roses. I thought if I brought it here, it would be like bringing a piece of Michigan with me—a new start with something familiar. I guess it will be going back with me, though."

Harl smiled kindly and offered his arm.

"We already tried that," Garlin said, shifting around to face them. "Just you never mind. Let her get situated."

She hobbled on her good leg. "Ow!"

"Here," Harl said, sweeping his muscular arms under her.

"Oh," she gasped as he picked her up.

"Now, if Mr. Moore would be so kind as to go before us with your trunk, we could get on home and back to Mama."

Garlin turned abruptly and headed for the stairs. Harl followed close on his heels.

The hotelier set the trunk in the back of the wagon. Taking a handkerchief out of his back pocket, he mopped at his sweaty brow.

Harl placed Rose on the frozen ground beside the wagon with her arms still wrapped around his neck and the uninjured foot bearing her weight.

"Hang on here," he said. Rose grasped the wagon with both hands as Harl lifted her up and onto the wagon seat. He climbed over her and sat down.

"Oh my," she said.

Garlin patted the rump of one mule and waved to Harl. "Let me know if there's anything you need," he said.

"With this ice? I probably won't be coming into town anytime soon."

"But what about the train?"

"That'll come," Harl said, releasing the brake. He jiggled the reins and spoke to the mules to walk on.

Rose waved back to Garlin standing on the boardwalk just outside of the hotel and restaurant entrance watching them. "Thank you, Mr. Moore."

"Not a problem at all," he called back.

Rose turned back to Harl and fiddled with the strings on her purse. She opened her mouth several times and almost started a sentence before clamping it shut. Finally, she said, "I'm so sorry for this imposition."

Harl chuckled and glanced over at Rose. "No imposition about it. Ma and me will have you up walking in no time, and you'll get on that train headed back home. Everything will be fine. You'll see."

Harl drove the wagon slowly over the icy streets. As they passed Rev. Harris' house, he pointed it out. "That's where our town preacher lives with his new wife, my sister."

"Oh, how nice. They have a very lovely home."

Catherine and her daughter, Clair, waved to them from the other side of the house as Harl and Rose passed.

"What are you doing outside on this ice?" Harl asked, slowing the mules to a standstill.

"We're getting icicles!" Clair exclaimed, holding out a large icicle in her mittened hand.

"More like knocking them off the roof," Catherine said, holding a broom. "And who is this?"

"Catherine Harris, I'd like you to meet Miss Rose Henderson. She, ah, fell on the ice, and she has nowhere to go while she recuperates. Ma and I agreed to take her in until she's back on her feet and able to catch a train home."

Catherine cut her eyes from Rose to Harl and smiled. "Oh, how nice."

Harl scowled. He knew what his sister must be thinking—that here was the woman for him. He'd had his fill of love lost, thanks to Nellie Hampton and Emma Whittaker. Both women had run off and married someone else after he had confessed his love to them. He understood Nellie running off. She was as changeable as the wind. But Emma had been the town's schoolteacher before his sister was hired. She was a stable, sensible woman—or so Harl had thought. Women were trouble—trouble that he didn't need.

"We'll be seeing you," Harl said, shaking the reins. The mules resumed their walk.

"That's the school," he said, pointing out the white clapboard building right next to the preacher's home.

The ice under the mules' feet crunched and cracked as they walked. Rose gasped at the sound of a particularly loud crack and grabbed Harl's forearm.

"Isn't it too dangerous for your mules? What if they slip and fall?"

He chuckled. "Don't you worry. These mules have sure footing. They aren't going anywhere, as long as we don't get too pushy with our speed."

Rose removed her hand from Harl's arm.

After a few minutes, she asked, "How far is it to your home?"

"See that orchard up ahead?"

Rose looked to where Harl pointed. Row after row of ice-draped trees met her gaze. Ice clung to the trees and cascaded down to the ground.

Harl watched Rose survey the orchard.

"How lovely," she said, "what kind of trees are these?"

"Apple trees."

"But won't the ice kill the trees?"

"I'm hoping not. All I can do is hope and pray that the Lord'll see them trees through this ice storm."

Rose sat back and folded her arms across her chest. "Oh, you're a Christian then?"

"Yes, why? Aren't you?"

"No, I'm not. My father forbade Mother and me from going to church. So, we didn't go. Father used to work on Sundays. Got the jump on the competition, he said, by keeping his blacksmith shop open on Sunday. I never went to church until I turned twenty."

"Why twenty?"

Rose bit her lip. "Well, I met a man when I was twenty. He was a Christian and invited me to go along with him. We planned to marry; but someone prettier and thinner came along, and he changed his mind about me. Ever since then, I haven't wanted a God Who would allow someone like that in my life. I see no reason for Christ, anyway. It's all hogwash."

Harl slowed the mules and craned his neck for a better look at his passenger. Was it really true that here in this wagon was a heathen of sorts—someone who didn't believe in the Lord and said so blatantly? What had happened in her life to make her risk damnation and eternal flames instead of living life filled with the promises and blessings that Jesus brings? There was more to this story than what she was telling. He wanted to get to the bottom of it and help her see that Jesus died for her sins and stood with open arms to welcome her to a Heavenly home when this life was done.

"You know, Rose—" Harl began, but she cut him off.

"Is this your orchard, then?" she asked, changing the subject.

"Yes."

"Well, even though it may kill the trees, it's lovely. My parents planted several apple trees on our property. Nothing like this, though."

As they entered one of the rows of trees, Rose reached out a gloved hand and broke a long icicle from one of the branches.

"Don't do that. You might hurt the tree worse than it's being hurt right now."

Rose dropped the icicle off the side of the wagon.

"I'm so sorry. I wasn't thinking. It was just so pretty. I couldn't resist."

Harl scowled and nodded.

"Did you plant all of these trees?"

"No, I didn't."

"Oh? Who did?"

"My great-grandfather, Ezra Adams. He planted most of them. My father and I planted the rest before he died in the war."

Harl looked out at the trees as he thought back to that fateful day when his father had been shot as they were heading to enlist for the war. His father had been shot by a Southern sympathizer. Even though his father had been shot dead right in front of him, that hadn't kept Harl from signing up for the Union infantry. Even after all these years, it hadn't stopped the nightmares, the headaches, or the memories.

The passenger beside him was saying something about the apple orchard. "My goodness! And it's been in your family this entire time?"

Harl nodded and then shook his head to clear it. He pointed to the farmhouse as it came into view when they rounded the last tree in the row.

"There's home," he said.

Rose turned her eyes toward the homestead.

"What a lovely place."

Harl grinned. "In spring and summer, Mama has roses that grow up the pillars."

"Yes, I can see their icy, skeletal remains still clinging there."

The two-story home was nestled into a clump of bare tulip poplar trees.

A well stood in front of the house, which sat across from a gray, weathered barn.

Harl drove the wagon alongside the ice-covered steps. "I'll take you in and then come back for your trunk."

He climbed down and walked around to the side on which Rose sat. She leaned down; and in one fluid motion, he scooped her up, turned, and carried her up the steps.

At the top of the steps, Harl's mother flung open the door. Seeing Harl carrying Rose, she then rushed to the table in the middle of the yellow kitchen and pulled out a chair.

"It's about time you two showed up! I was starting to worry," his mother exclaimed.

"Sorry, Mama. I took it slow on account of the ice."

"I knew you would; but still, I had begun to worry."

"I'm afraid that was on account of me," Rose offered sheepishly. "I couldn't walk on my foot."

"Oh, honey, I'm not blaming you. I was just afraid those mules would have slipped and broken a leg or somethin'."

"You know as well as I do that those mules are as surefooted as anything that could pull the wagon," Harl replied indignantly, returning to the room carrying Rose's trunk. Harl set the trunk down and turned to go back out the door. But before he did, he remembered his manners and turned back to introduce the women. "Miss Henderson, this is my mother, Hazel Adams."

"Sit down; sit down. Let me run and get a pillow for your foot," Mama said to Rose as she rushed from the room. She returned momentarily with an embroidered pillow. "Here we are." Mama turned a chair and placed it opposite her guest. Directing her gaze at her son, his mother said, "Go on and tend to them mules."

Harl stepped out onto the porch and back into the wagon. The ice cracked and popped under the weight of the mules' hoofs as they walked toward the barn. He was relieved to get back to work instead of staying in the house with the women.

After Harl left, Rose lifted her foot and placed it on the pillow.

"Oh, that feels much better." She sighed.

Mrs. Adams watched her son drive away and closed the door. "Now, you just relax, and I'll put the food on the table," she said, turning back to her guest.

"Thank you so much for your kindness, Mrs. Adams," Rose said, pulling off her gloves and shimmying out of her coat.

"Pish posh. Don't think anything about it. We're always glad to help a neighbor in need."

"I'm not very much of a neighbor. I'm from Chelsea, Michigan."

"Michigan! Whatever caused you to come down all this way?"

Rose cast her eyes down to her lap, where her folded hands rested on her purse. "I came down to marry Cletus Tooth. I had answered his advertisement for a wife. We wrote back and forth for a few months," Rose said, lifting her eyes.

"And he left you at the train station to fend for yourself?"

"Yes," Rose whispered, casting her eyes down again.

Mrs. Adams turned back to the stove and poured gravy into a small white pitcher. Then she carried it to the table and set it down in front of Rose.

"Well, now, there's nothing to feel sorry about. I can see you're hurting. It was for the best that the Lord saw fit to not allow Cletus to meet you at the station."

Rose looked up. "Why is that?"

"He's a scoundrel—that's why. He busted up the school when he didn't agree with the teacher—my daughter, Catherine—over something."

"Oh," Rose said, her eyebrows pinched together. "Well, his letters were beautifully written. I never suspected anything of the sort."

Hazel set a large platter of roasted potatoes in front of Rose. "I hope you're hungry. But we'll wait for Harl. He should be in soon."

Sitting down opposite her guest, Hazel smiled. "Well, it looks like the good Lord saved you from an ill-advised marriage."

Rose studied Mrs. Adams' face. "I don't believe Providence had anything to do with it. It was a foolhardy thing for me to do, anyway. I never should have read his advertisement for a wife. I never should have answered it either."

"Well, what's done is done. Soon as this ice melts and you are healed up, we'll get you back on a train headed home."

Rose bowed her head as tears spilled from her eyes. "I can't go back there."

"Oh, honey, I'm so sorry. What's wrong?" Hazel asked, leaping up and coming around the table to take Rose's hand.

"Don't ask me. It's too terrible. I'm so ashamed."

"All right. Well, whatever it is, don't you think on it. If you don't want to return home, you don't have to."

"There's no home to go back to," Rose said, blowing her nose into a handkerchief she kept in her purse. She placed the used handkerchief in her lap and wiped her fingers across her eyes. "I'm so sorry."

"Don't be sorry, honey. You don't need to talk about it if you don't want to."

"Thank you. You've been so kind to me."

The sound of Harl's boots on the porch steps caused Rose to turn toward the door and remove her foot from the pillow. He bounded into the house.

"Right on time," Hazel declared.

Harl smiled at his mother and cut his eyes to their guest. "How are you feeling?" he asked, seating himself at the head of the table.

His mother went to the stove to bring the rest of the food to the table. She placed the cast iron covered dish on a round piece of wood on the tabletop and then took her place across from Rose. Folding her hands, she tucked them under her chin.

"Harl, will you say grace?"

Rose's mouth dropped open as she glanced from bowed head to bowed head.

Harl closed his eyes and folded his hands in front of him. "Dear Lord, we thank You for this bounty. Thank You for bringing Miss Henderson to us. Help her ankle to heal, Lord. In Jesus' name, amen."

Mrs. Adams looked up and smiled at their guest. "Here, pass the potatoes to Harl."

Rose obeyed.

"Harl, would you do the honors of carving the roast?"

"Mama, your roasts always turn out so tender. All I need is a fork to pull the meat apart. Pass your plate," he said to Rose.

She held her plate while he placed plenty of the tender meat on it.

"You have a lovely farm and orchard," Rose said to Harl.

His face grew red, and he smiled sheepishly.

"It's his pride and joy. Don't know what I'd do without Harl taking care of the place. I'd probably have to sell and move into town."

"Don't talk like that, Mama. You'll always have me here taking care of things. Besides, this place is in my blood."

Mrs. Adams sniffed and rubbed her nose with the linen napkin. She replaced it on her lap. "I'm glad to hear it."

Rose glanced from Harl to his mother. The corners of her mouth lifted. *If only Father and I could get along like this. Why was he so dead set on my marrying someone before I could leave the nest? Couldn't he see I would be happy finding my own beau instead of having one forced on me—one who was as sweet as pie when Father was around but who insisted on taking my elbow in his vice-like grip anytime we went for a stroll around town?*

"Miss Henderson? Is anything wrong?" Mrs. Adams asked.

Rose's eyes fluttered back to meet the older woman's gaze. She had been staring at a spot on the yellow paint just above Hazel's head.

Rose shook her head. "No, there isn't anything the matter. Please call me Rose, Mrs. Adams. Miss Henderson is much too formal."

"All right," the older woman replied, "but you must call me Hazel instead of Mrs. Adams."

"Thank you." Turning to Harl, Rose lifted an eyebrow. "How about you, Mr. Adams?"

"It's Harl. Plain Harl. With you staying with us, we might as well be on a first-name basis."

Harl could feel the heat rising from under his collar. It crept up his neck and cheeks and settled at his ears. Maybe the newcomer wouldn't notice. Glancing at the lovely red-headed woman seated next to him, Harl met her eyes staring back at him. He jerked his head back to stare at the thinning contents of his plate. She had seen him.

Why was it that anytime he started liking a girl—well, woman in this case—his neck, face, and ears gave him away? Nellie Hampton had caused him to go red in the face whenever she was around him. She loved to tease him by telling him she wouldn't be seen being courted by someone with such big, awful hands as he had. Harl didn't think his hands were all that large, but what Nellie said had stuck. Many a girl giggled when he walked by them in the schoolyard. After they had graduated from school, Harl had asked Nellie to the church picnic, but she had said she'd already been asked to go with Edgar Richardson. In no time, those two were hitched.

Then there was the schoolteacher, Emma Whittaker. She had been assigned to Harrisville School after the old schoolmaster, Elder Craton, died of influenza a year after Harl graduated. The new schoolmistress had caught his eye in church one Sunday.

After the service, he was determined to talk to her and introduce himself, but the town's bachelors had buzzed all around her, vying for her attention. If he was going to get a chance to talk to her, he'd have to make his move. Drawing air into his lungs, he pushed his way through the crowd, excusing himself as he moved forward until someone stuck out a foot and tripped him. He fell headlong into the schoolmistress, knocking her down in the process. To make matters worse, he landed on top of her.

Scrambling to his feet, he pulled her up with him. "I'm Harl Adams," he said, taking her hand and shaking it vigorously. "And I would be pleased to walk you home. That is, if you'll let me?"

Emma let out the slightest of giggles and wiped a tear from her eye. "I must say, Mr. Adams, that you are determined. I would be pleased to have you walk me home."

Thus began their courtship. Things were going really well, and Harl decided to ask for her hand in marriage when her spinster aunt in Louisville fell deathly ill. Emma, who was from Louisville, headed home to care for her aunt, while Harl waited impatiently for her to return.

Weeks turned into months apart. Emma wrote often. Harl tried to keep up with her correspondence letter for letter but felt the news he had to share was monotonous. Even so, he pressed on writing how much he missed her, news about the town, the farm—anything to keep receiving her letters.

After a few short months, Emma's letters changed. She wrote of how happy she was back in her hometown and of their need for qualified teachers. And she never mentioned anymore that she missed him.

The next time a letter arrived from her, she wrote about a surprise encounter with an old school chum she'd had a crush on during their school days. It was her last letter to him.

Months later, word reached him that she had gone off and gotten married to said school chum. Harl was heartbroken. He moped around the house for days after hearing the news that his sweetheart had married someone else. His heartbreak soured him against ever opening his heart to love again, thus abruptly ending his attempts to have a woman notice him.

Coming back to the conversation at the table, Harl noticed that Rose had finished the food on her plate. Leaning down, she rubbed the ankle of the sore foot and moaned softly.

"Your ankle hurting you?" Mama asked.

"Yes, very much. It does throb so."

"Would you like to lie down?"

"I would love that."

"We'll put her in my room. I'll sleep upstairs," Mama said.

Harl nodded. Standing, he scooped Rose up into his strong arms and carried her to his mother's room across the hall from his. His mother ran ahead of him. She threw back the covers on her bed as Harl set Rose down on the bed and left the room.

"Do you want to lie down or sit up for a while?" Hazel asked.

"I'd like to lie down."

Hazel fluffed the pillow for her head, placed one under her ankle, and adjusted the covers over her. "I'm sorry you are feeling so poorly."

"Thank you," Rose said, reaching out a hand.

Hazel took it and patted it. "You just rest. I've got a chamber pot under the bed. You just call if you need anything."

"I will. And thank you again."

Hazel shut the door. Heading back to the kitchen, she found Harl seated, picking at some dry skin on one of the calluses on his open hand.

"What do you think, Ma?"

"What do I think about what?"

"Miss Henderson—er, Rose?"

"I think we done the neighborly and Christian thing by inviting her here. I think she's a dear, sweet woman."

"She isn't a Christian."

"Don't you worry about that right now. We'll just let our lives shine for Christ, and maybe that'll bring her around."

"I need to go tend to the livestock. You need anything right now?"

"Not a thing."

As Harl left the kitchen, Hazel set about cleaning up the kitchen. Considering her son as she watched him out the kitchen window, she found herself wondering whether their injured guest would end up causing trouble for their little household.

Chapter 4

Out in the barn, Harl absentmindedly brushed down one mule and then the other. He stared at the hayloft as he worked in the chilly air.

"She came all this way just to be cast aside," he said, smoothing his hand over the mule's rough winter coat. "What do you make of that?"

The mule snorted as it munched hay.

"Exactly my thoughts, too," Harl said, patting the mule's withers. He draped one arm over the mule and looked back toward the hayloft. "Lord, I know it's been rough on Miss Henderson—Rose—this last day. Please use it to help her find You in all of this. Help her to want You. And touch and heal her ankle. In Jesus' name, amen.

"Well, the least we can do is give her a home until she's well enough to travel," he said, moving to the stall where the Jersey milk cow, Brownie, stood.

Placing the short, three-legged stool next to the cow and a pail under her, Harl straddled the stool and sat down. Removing his gloves, he rubbed his cold hands together and blew into them, trying to warm them up before squeezing an udder. The cow turned its head and looked at him as he worked. "Not quite warm enough for you, Brownie? I tried to warm them up, but the air is so cold."

The cow swished her tail and caught Harl on the side of his head. Swiping his face with the sleeve of his coat, he laughed. "Fair enough, Brownie." He quickened his pace. Soon he had a full pail of milk.

Placing the pail out of reach of the cow's swishing tail and back legs, Harl replaced the stool to its place on one side of the stall. He put his leather work gloves back on and unfastened the lead from a nail in the wall. He tugged on the rope around the cow's neck and led her outside behind the barn. He removed the rope and pointed to the herd. "Go join your friends. There's a good girl." He patted the cow's rump and watched as she ambled toward the rest of the herd.

Climbing up into the hayloft, Harl opened the door that faced the back of the barn and the pasture beyond. Using a pitchfork, he threw hay down to the waiting cattle. "I bet you'll be glad when springtime comes and you get to eat fresh grass again."

The contented cattle mooed softly. After throwing several pitchforks full of hay to the waiting cattle, he shut the door.

"Oh, Lord, what am I going to do about Miss Henderson?"

Climbing down the ladder, Harl wrapped his coat about him tighter. Shutting the door of the barn behind him, he headed back to the house with the fresh pail of milk.

Mama stood over the stove stirring something in the Dutch oven.

"Mmm, smells good, Mama. What are you cooking?" The warm aroma tickled Harl's nose and warmed his senses. He placed the milk on the side cupboard and removed his hat, gloves, and coat. He placed the gloves and hat on a shelf by the door and hooked the collar of the coat on a peg under the shelf.

"I thought I'd make us some vegetable soup," Mama commented with a smile. Several empty Mason jars stood next to the milk pail.

Harl placed his hands over the hot stove and rubbed them together. "Sure is cold out there. Got any coffee brewing?"

His mother nodded her head toward the gray enamelware kettle on the back of the stove. "It's from breakfast," she explained.

"Beats nothing."

"Pour me a cup, too."

Harl took down two large cups off the shelf above the cupboard and poured the thick black liquid into each.

"I've got fresh milk here. You want a little bit of cream in yours?"

"That sounds good. Go see if our guest would like some."

Harl shuffled to his mother's bedroom door and tapped softly.

"Yes?"

"Would you like a cup of coffee?" he asked through the closed door.

"That would be lovely."

"Do you take cream?"

"Yes, and sugar please."

Harl returned in just a few minutes. In one hand, Harl held Rose's cup of coffee doctored with plenty of cream and sugar. In the other, he held his cup.

"May I come in?"

"Yes, I'm decent."

In the room, Harl handed her the cup of coffee. She drank deeply. "Mmm, just the way I like it."

"Feel like some company?" he asked, wrapping his hands around his cup. He smiled down at her, and their eyes met.

The cup in Rose's hand shook. Dropping it onto her lap, the coffee spilled out. Harl grabbed Rose's spilled cup with his free hand. Placing both cups on the bedside table, he rushed out of the room.

"Ma, we need a rag. Miss Henderson dropped her cup."

Mama whisked a feed-sack dish towel off the counter and handed it to Harl.

Harl rushed back to Rose's room and began blotting her dress with the dish towel. He could feel the heat rising in his face.

"Oh no. Here, let me," Rose exclaimed, waving her hand and grasping the dish towel. "I'm so sorry. I don't know what came over me." She finished blotting her dress.

Harl turned his eyes to Rose's face, which was red.

"Yes, I would like some company once I change out of this dress. Could you get your mother for me?"

Harl hurried out of the room, glad to escape the awkward situation, and went to find his mother.

"Ma? Rose needs you."

His mother dashed past him and into the room. She closed the door behind her.

"I don't know what came over me, Rose said.

"Let's get you out of this dress. We'll get you a fresh one and let this one soak in the wash tub."

"I'll get my trunk." Rose placed her feet on the floor and pushed off the bed. Her sore ankle betrayed her, and she fell to the floor.

"Oh dear! Harl!" Hazel called.

Momentarily, Harl burst in. Spying Rose on the floor, he gasped and reached out his hands to her. "Here, let me help you up." He swept his arms under her and gently placed her back on the bed.

Hazel rummaged through Rose's trunk and pulled a navy blue dress out of it.

"Here, we'll put this on. Harl, shoo."

Harl walked out of the room and shut the door.

"Now, don't you worry about your dress. I'll put it in the wash tub and get it soaking with some of my lye soap. It will be as good as new in no time."

"Thank you."

By the time Mama came out of the room, Harl had managed to fill the wash tub half-full of water as it sat on the stove.

"Think this will be enough water?"

"That'll do just fine," his mother said as she placed the dress into the tub and pressed it down beneath the warming water as Harl watched. "Get me that bar of lye soap, please."

Harl reached her the soap. She began to scrub at the coffee stain.

"There now. Let's let it soak."

Harl looked toward Rose's room. "Go on. Keep her company."

Harl returned to the room and pulled a cane-bottom, straight-backed chair from the corner of the room to the foot of the bed.

"So, tell me about yourself, Miss Henderson."

"What would you like to know?" She rubbed her hands together, one over the other.

"Where did you come from again?"

"Chelsea, Michigan."

"What kind of place did you come from?"

"It's a lovely village. Not at all as large as this town."

"What did you do up there?"

"I was a milliner and seamstress." She brushed a stray strand of red hair away from her face.

"Hatmaker. Well, now that's something. We've got a couple of seamstresses in town, but I don't know of any milliners."

She continued to rub the tops of her hands and sniffed the air. "My, what smells so good?"

"Mama's making vegetable soup for our dinner."

"I should be out there helping her do something instead of just sitting here."

Rose started to toss the covers back, but Harl put out his hand.

"Now, hold on. There's no cause for that. You need to get to feeling better before you go skirting around the kitchen. Besides, we don't want you falling on the floor again."

Rose smiled. "You're right. I don't want to hurt my ankle worse than what it is. I just wish there was some tangible way for me to repay your kindness."

"All in good time," Harl said and then chuckled. "Maybe you could do up a hat for Mama."

Rose's eyes widened, and her smile spread. "I will. That's a great idea. If I could just reach my trunk . . . "

Harl jumped up and moved the trunk over beside the bed.

Clearing his throat, he stepped out into the hallway and shut the door behind him.

His mother was humming as he walked into the kitchen.

"Have a good visit?"

"Yes. Fancy a hat?"

"What? No. Why?"

"Well, don't be surprised if you get one. Miss Henderson is a hatmaker and seamstress. She wants to do something nice for you. So, don't turn her down if she makes a hat for you."

"I'm happy with my plain bonnet."

Harl chuckled. Retreating to the table in the center of the room, he picked up the paper and began reading.

Chapter 3

When the soup was ready, Mama dished out a large helping into a bowl. Placing it, a spoon, and a napkin on a wooden tray, she carried it to her bedroom door.

"Here, Ma, let me get that door for you." Then calling through the door, Harl asked, "May we come in?"

"Yes."

Harl opened the door wide enough for his mother to enter with the tray and followed her inside.

"I brought you some nourishing vegetable soup," she said, arranging the tray over the bed covers.

Rose stuck a hatpin in the brim of the hat she was working on before setting it aside. Mama placed the tray down on Rose's lap.

Harl drew in his breath at seeing the hatpin stuck into the hat. Immediately, he was back on the frontlines of the war.

The man wearing a gray uniform in front of him had a bayonet sticking in his chest—his bayonet. He tried to pull it free, but it must have been stuck in a rib. Another man charged at Harl. He had just enough time to pull out his army-issued pistol and shoot the man in the face. The man screamed and dropped his weapon. His hands went to his bloodied face.

"Harl?" Someone was calling his name from somewhere. If he could just get to where that voice was coming from, he would be safe.

"Harl?" His mother called again.

Shaking his head, Harl turned his face toward the sound of his mother's voice.

"Are you having another one of your spells?" His mother asked quietly, placing her hand on his sleeve.

Harl hung his head and nodded.

"You want to go sit in your room?"

"No, it's passed now."

She rubbed his arm gently. "Well, now."

His mother's eye strayed to the blue hat with tiny pink roses on it sitting on the bed covers.

"What are you making over there?"

"I'm trimming a hat for you. I thought blue would go well with your gray eyes, and I love to embroider pink roses on all my cloth hats."

"Well, I do declare! That is very pretty."

"Would you like to try it on?"

"I would. You're an awfully fast worker if you got all them little roses done while I was making soup."

Rose bowed her head. "Well, I was making it for me—for my new life with Mr. Tooth."

"Oh, I'm sorry I brought it up."

"Why? You didn't know. I think it will have a better home with you than with me, anyway."

Mama smiled and placed her hand over her heart. Harl stood off to the side smiling at his mother.

Rose handed Mama the lovely hat. Mama hesitated and studied the woman before her.

"Well, go on," Harl urged. "Try it on."

His mother smoothed her hair. "I must look a mess working over a hot stove all day." She chuckled.

Rose cocked her head to one side. "You look beautiful."

Mama laughed. She placed the hat on her head and turned to Harl. "Well, how do I look?"

Harl smiled with pride. "As pretty as ever, Mama. You'll be the envy of the town."

His mother jerked the hat off her head. Looking wide-eyed at Harl, she said, "I don't want to be the envy of the town. That would be sinful. Maybe I shouldn't accept something so fine." She turned back to Rose and held out the hat. "It wouldn't be proper for me to have a hat when all the town's women don't have none except our bonnets."

"Hats aren't sinful, and neither is looking our best," Rose countered.

"Well, it was a nice thought," Mama said, holding out the hat.

"No, you simply must take it. How else am I to repay you and your son's kindness to me?"

"Well, if you insist, I'll keep it."

"I do insist you keep it. But will you wear it?"

Mama's smile warmed. "Of course, I will. It's too bad you'll be going home once you're well enough. You could have set up a little shop in town. It'd be a nice complement to the dressmaker shops."

Rose smiled and pulled the tray of food close to her again. She drew in the aroma of the hot soup. "This smells wonderful," she said as she sipped the soup. "Oh, just like my dear mother used to make on cold winter nights."

"I'm glad you like it." Turning to Harl, his mother said, "Come on, son. Let's let our guest eat in peace."

Harl and his mother returned to the kitchen. Mama placed the hat on the shelf next to the door. She then dished up large bowls full of soup and set them on the table.

When they finished eating, Hazel went to pick up the tray with the empty soup bowl from Rose's room.

"That sure is a fine hat you gave me." Hazel grinned at Rose.

"It suits your coloring," said Rose pleasantly.

"My what?"

"Your cheeks are pink, and the hat suits you."

Hazel nodded her agreement and then headed back to the kitchen to wash the dishes while Harl settled into the living room to read the newspaper. Once the dishes were done, she returned to the bedroom, where her guest reclined in bed. Rose gazed out the window at the foot of the bed and watched the snow falling down on top of the prevalent ice.

"You sure are good with a needle and thread. Care to help me mend some of Harl's work clothes?"

"Why, of course. I'd be pleased to."

Hazel grabbed several shirts out of a basket in the corner by the foot of the bed.

"Since Catherine and Clair left, I just haven't had much gumption. Having another woman around the house may be just what I needed."

Hazel picked up her sewing basket from the dresser and closed one eye while trying to thread the needle. After several tries, she sighed.

"My eyes just aren't what they used to be."

"Here, let me."

"Thank you," Hazel said, handing them over to Rose, who had the needle threaded in one swift movement.

"Here's yours. And here's mine," Rose said, opening a small clasped silver case with needles poking up through a leather holder. Rose threaded one of her needles and then set to work finding the hole in Harl's shirt.

Hazel nodded as she gazed at the little silver case.

"That sure is a pretty needle case you got there."

Rose glanced up from her work. "Yes, it was my mother's."

"And she didn't have need of it anymore?"

"No, she didn't. She's dead."

"Oh, honey, I'm so sorry. I shouldn't have said anything."

"No, it's all right. You didn't know."

"My mother died in an accident. She was thrown from the wagon my father was driving and killed."

"I'm so sorry. That must have been hard on you. How old were you?"

"It was just last year when I was twenty-two. Yes, it was hard. It's still hard."

"I understand," Hazel said. "My father died first. My mother died a few months later of a broken heart, some say. It never gets any easier, no matter how old we are, to lose a parent."

"Oh? Was he ill?"

"No, he was as strong as an ox. He just keeled over one day coming up the lane bringing the mail from town." Hazel looked up at the ceiling as she spoke.

Dropping her gaze back to Rose and then to her handiwork, she said, "You're very good at sewing. Why, you can barely see that there ever was a hole in that shirt."

Rose grinned. "Thank you."

Peeking out the door, Hazel called to her son, who was still reading the paper, "You know, when you get done with that paper, you might want to let our guest read it."

"Sure will, Mama."

Rose held the finished shirt across her lap and sighed. "You've both been so kind. I don't know what I would do if you hadn't taken me in."

Hazel finished sewing the shirt she was working on and then patted Rose's hand. "Don't you worry about it. We're happy to have you here. You just get better, so we can get you back on a train headed home—or to wherever you want to go."

Standing, Hazel walked out of the room.

Entering the living room, she found Harl rubbing his eyes. "Eyes bothering you?"

"A little," he said. "It's the strain."

"We'll have to go see Dr. Johnson once this ice melts. See if he can order you a pair of glasses."

"It's not that bad, Mama."

Harl stood and, tucking the folded paper under his arm, walked to his mother's bedroom doorway. Craning his neck around the corner, he viewed their guest, who held his shirt under her nose. *Was she smelling his shirt?* He knocked softly.

Rose jerked her head toward the sound.

Harl stepped into the room and handed her the paper. "Care to read some?"

"Sure, thank you." Her face turned a bright red as their fingers brushed against each other when Rose took the paper. They exchanged glances. Harl cleared his throat.

"It's our town's newspaper, *The American Bugle*. It comes out weekly."

"Not many places have their own newspaper, I suspect."

"It's been around for ten years now. It lists cattle, sheep, and grain prices, along with information about town happenings and advertisements for local shops and all sorts of thing. I enjoy reading it," he said, rubbing at his eyes with one hand.

"Your eyes bothering you?"

"Only when I read too long."

"Oh, here, sit down," Rose said, pointing him to the chair that his mother had vacated at the end of the bed.

Harl sat and glanced at the shirt in her lap. She smiled sheepishly and handed it to him.

"Ma and you get finished with the mending?" he asked, taking the shirt.

"Yes."

He turned the shirt over in his hands. "I can't even find where it was mended."

"There on the sleeve."

Harl studied the shirt sleeve and shook his head. "That's some mighty fine mending you done. It's almost as if the shirt was never torn."

Rose lowered her head, the color rising into her cheeks.

"Harl, go get me a chair," Mama said, entering the room, "so we can all sit around the bed and visit. Harl sprang to his feet and headed out of the door.

"He's a thoughtful son," his mother said.

Entering the room, Harl set the chair down by the bedside table. His mother swiped her skirts under her legs and sat down.

"I can't believe I came all this way just to twist my ankle. What a horrible thing that Mr. Tooth did deciding he didn't want me."

Harl and Mama exchanged glances.

"What made you want to write him when you saw his ad?" Mama asked curiously.

Rose's eyes began tearing up. "I had to get away. I couldn't stay in a place where my father was going to send me off to be the wife of his horrible apprentice."

"Now, now. Don't take on so. What was so bad about him?" Mama asked.

"He looked at me in a way that no woman ever wants to be looked at. It made my skin crawl. I once saw him whip another man's horse for not standing still when he was shoeing it."

"Oh."

"But I thought he left you for someone else?" Harl asked incredulously.

Rose reddened. "No, that was another man."

"That's why you don't want to come to the Lord? Because a man left you for someone else?" Harl asked.

"Harl!" his mother exclaimed through clenched teeth.

After a moment of awkward silence, Mama softly commented, "She's come through quite an ordeal. Maybe we should let her rest a bit."

"Yes, I think rest is just what the doctor ordered." Rose sank under the covers, tossing them over her. She turned her back to Harl and his mother. Mama nodded toward the door. Picking up the tray, Harl followed her out into the hall.

"Close the door. Let's let our guest rest."

In the kitchen and out of earshot, Harl whispered loudly, "She's not telling us something. There has got to be a reason why two men rejected her. Not to mention that her story is the opposite of what actually happened."

Mama held up her hand. "Now, the Christian thing to do is to just let her talk and tell her story without any interruptions from us. She'll eventually unwind it for us, and we'll hear the truth in her words. In the meantime, we need to be praying for healing for her body and soul."

Chapter 6

The next day dawned bright and cold. Rose rolled over and tried to look out the window, but it was frosted over with a glaze of ice. She pulled the quilts up under her chin as her teeth chattered. A light tapping sounded at the door.

"Come in."

Hazel peered inside the room. "It's colder this morning. Mind if I leave the door open so you can get some heat in here?"

"Not at all. I would appreciate that."

"I started a fire in the fireplace in the parlor that is next to my room—I mean, this room. It should be getting warmer in here soon. I'll bring you some coffee to warm you in the meantime."

"Thank you. That would be nice." Rose tucked the quilts under her body and shivered.

Hazel returned to the room with the coffee. Rose reached out a shaking hand and took the cup.

"Maybe you might like to sit in the parlor for a while? Or you could sit at the table and keep me company while I make breakfast."

"I think I would like to sit in the kitchen and keep you company."

Throwing back the covers, Rose set her bare feet on the floor. She had pulled off her stockings sometime in the night and tucked them into the trunk, which still sat by the bed. Her right ankle—what could be seen of it under her cotton, high-necked nightgown—was black and blue.

Hazel shuffled around to stand next to the bed. She offered her arm to Rose. "Ready? Now, just take your time and see if you can put any weight on it."

Pulling back, Rose crossed her arms over her chest, leaned toward the headboard, and peered out the door. "Is Harl here?"

"Sure, he's here, but he's out tending the livestock and won't be in for a while."

"Would you please hand me my underthings and dress? Let me put them on before he returns."

When Rose was dressed, the nightgown neatly folded at the foot of the bed, she took Hazel's offered arm and stood, placing all of her weight on her left leg. Biting her lip, she shifted her weight a little at a time.

"Ouch! I don't think I can bear any weight on that foot for now."

"Well, we've got to get you into the kitchen where it's warm. I'll help you. Lean on me."

Rose obeyed. She hopped her way to the kitchen on Hazel's arm.

Seated at the table, Rose asked, "When will Harl be back in?"

"Once he's done with the livestock, he'll come in. He had a quick bite before heading out."

"I wish there was some way to repay your kindness to me," Rose said, brushing back strands of red hair from her face. She wound her long braid into a bun and secured it with two combs.

"There is a way you can repay our kindness," Hazel said, busying herself at the side cupboard. Turning, she held a pan of wrinkly apples and a knife. "You can peel these and slice them. We'll have us a mess of cooked apples to go with the biscuits, eggs, bacon, and gravy."

Rose chuckled. "I would love to help. Thank you," she said, reaching for the pan.

Hazel turned the bacon sizzling in the cast iron frying pan on the cookstove as she talked.

"My daughter, Catherine, and her daughter, Clair, went to live with the town preacher after they got married last month. Got married over in Bell County up at Hogs Creek Baptist Church by one of her husband's preacher friends." She looked up at the wall behind the cookstove. "I forget what his name was. It was a beautiful wedding. When the ladies of the church heard Samuel and Catherine's story about growing up together and then finding each other again after so many years, you know what those ladies did?"

Rose stopped peeling and looked up at Hazel, who had turned around with turning fork in hand. "No, what did they do?"

"They decorated the church. They took pretty, white and pink silk ribbon and made bows. They hung a bow on every pew. I didn't think they needed to go to all that fuss, but Catherine seemed to like it. I brought them all back home with me. Thought I might make a quilt top out of them. They sure would make a pretty quilt."

The stamping of feet brought the attention of the women to the door as it swung open. Harl stepped inside the warm room and tilted his nose toward the ceiling.

"Bacon! Mmm, you know I love bacon after being out in the barn," he said, removing his black felt hat, leather gloves, and wool coat. He hung the coat on a peg by the door and placed his gloves and hat on the shelf above it.

Rose looked at the man standing before her and marveled at his pink cheeks. He smiled at her.

"I thought we'd have some cooked apples to go with our meal," Hazel said. As Harl reached into the pan, he pulled a small, shriveled apple up to his lips, took a bite, and nodded.

"They're still good—even after all this time."

"It helps that we can keep them cool in the root cellar," Hazel said. Taking the bowl of peeled apples from Rose, she slid them into a sizzling skillet, along with some pats of butter. "We are almost ready."

"I know I had something earlier, but a man works up an appetite working with the livestock."

"Well, sit down and keep Miss Henderson—I mean, Rose— company." Hazel began to hum as she worked.

Harl smiled at his guest as he approached the table, pulled out a chair, and sat. Rose fiddled with the edge of her sleeve and returned the smile.

"What was life like in Chelsea?" Harl asked.

"Oh, it was . . . " Rose stared at the ceiling.

How could she explain to this man all she'd been through over the last year? Her mother had died in a suspicious accident when she fell headlong off the wagon her father had been driving. He had said he was going too fast around a corner, but Rose wasn't so sure. Her mother had lain in state in their parlor for a day before Rose's father had "had enough," as he'd said. He had ordered the funeral director to nail the coffin shut and hurry it out to his waiting wagon. The whole thing had been a rushed affair.

It all seemed a blur now—all except for the cat eyes and trivial smile Widow Hampton had given her father as he followed the coffin out the door of the house to the waiting wagon. Rose had solemnly followed behind him.

In some sort of penance, her father painted his wagon black. After a few weeks of mourning, he took Widow Hampton for rides in the black wagon.

"How could you?" Rose asked her father.

"Your mother's dead. She isn't coming back. I want to get on with my life."

"You haven't given yourself enough time to grieve properly."

Her father raised his hand to her, his eyes narrowed and his mouth set. Rose ducked, knowing what she thought was coming next. Just as quickly, he lowered his hand.

"She's good for me. You'll see."

Snapping her attention back to the present, Rose looked at Harl, and the corners of her mouth raised. "It was good," she lied. "My father was one of the town blacksmiths."

"A skilled tradesman. That must have given you many hours of interesting conversations with him."

Rose swallowed and lied again. "Yes."

How could she tell this kind man that she thought her father had killed her mother just so he could court the Widow Hampton? What would that say about her? No, it was best just to remain silent as much as possible on the subject.

"Here we are," Hazel said, setting the food on the table. Seating herself, she nodded at Harl, who bowed his head.

Rose looked from Harl to Hazel, who was folding her hands in front of her and bowing her head as well. Rose scowled but did the same.

Harl cleared his throat. "Father God, we thank You for this bounty set before us. Bless the hands that prepared it. And thank You for bringing Miss Henderson to us. Heal her ankle, and I pray we can be a help to her. In Jesus' name, amen."

Rose lifted her head and gazed at Harl as Hazel began passing the food. "Why did you say 'Father God'?" she asked as she took the bowl of scrambled eggs from Hazel's hand.

Harl put down his fork, which was loaded with a piece of biscuit covered in gravy. "That's how I see God. Scripture tells us that Jesus prayed to His Father in Heaven. If we've accepted Christ as our Savior, then God is our Father. He's a Father for any believer." He resumed eating, almost reaching his mouth this time.

"I've never heard God mentioned as a Father, except to Jesus." She spooned out some eggs before passing the bowl to Harl, who scraped out the rest onto his plate.

"He is called Abba Father—like Daddy. He's our Daddy," Harl explained.

"I don't believe it. Show me."

"All right, I'll show you after we eat."

When the meal was at an end, Harl rose and went into the parlor. He returned to the table with a large black Bible. Thumbing through the Holy Book, he smiled when his finger landed on a page.

"Here in Galatians 1:3-4, the apostle Paul says, 'Grace be to you and peace from God the Father, and from our Lord Jesus Christ, Who gave himself for our sins, that he might deliver us from this present evil world, according to the will of God and our Father.'"

Rose leaned over and followed Harl's finger as he moved it down the page as he read.

"Have you never read the Bible?" Harl asked.

Rose shrugged. "Never had any need to."

"Maybe you might like to now." Harl slid the Bible toward Rose.

She shrugged and closed the book. "Maybe."

"Well, you can't read it shut," he replied sarcastically.

"I know, but I don't know where to start."

"I'd start in the New Testament in the book of Matthew. It tells of the birth of Jesus and about His life."

She opened the Bible and thumbed through it, landing in the Psalms. "I don't know where it is."

"Here, I'll show you," he said, taking the book back from her. He rubbed his eyes and then quickly flipped to the book of Matthew chapter one and handed it back over.

Rose placed her finger on the first verse and began to read silently to herself.

Content, Harl sat back and looked at his mother, who had watched the exchange. She smiled and nodded. "I got the slop bucket ready."

Harl stood and reached for the bucket on the floor near the stove.

"If you wouldn't mind, please gather the eggs, too." She handed him a small basket. "It's too slick for me to be out there right now."

Harl nodded; donned his coat, hat, and gloves; and went out the door.

"He's a brave soul," Rose observed.

"Let's get your foot up on a pillow, so it doesn't swell up. I'll get one out of the parlor."

When Hazel returned to the kitchen, Rose was poring over Scripture. Lifting the younger woman's foot, she placed it on the cushioned chair now directly in front of her as she sat beside the table.

"Coffee?" Hazel asked.

"Yes, please," Rose said without looking up.

Hazel prepared coffee for both of them and returned to her seat across the table from her guest.

Outside, Harl dumped the slop bucket contents into the pig trough. He patted and scratched his two sows behind the ears and chuckled to himself as he turned toward the chicken coop. The ice cracked under his feet as he walked, holding out his arms to keep his balance on the slippery ice. He held the egg basket tightly as he watched the chickens cluck and skid on the ice on his way toward the coop. At one end of the chicken coop was a small door held open by wire hooked to a nail. A wide board served as a gangplank for the chickens to run in and out of their house all day until Harl latched the door shut and put the chickens away for the night.

Inside, he worked quickly, feeling around in each nest for eggs in the darkened space. After plundering the eggs, he hurried back into the warmth of the house to find his mother and Rose seated at the table.

"It's just like reading a history book," Rose said, sliding her foot off the cushion and back under her skirt. "The first chapter is about the genealogy of Jesus. And then Herod killed all those babies because he was jealous of Jesus being born King of the Jews."

Mama hitched up the corners of her mouth and nodded.

Harl took off his work gloves and put them and his hat back on the shelf. He shrugged off his coat and hung it on the peg before picking up the basket of eggs and placing it on the side cupboard where the gray graniteware dishpans sat.

"I was planning on finishing reading the newspaper. Mind if I go retrieve it from your room?" Harl asked.

Rose smiled up at him and shook her head. She returned her attention back to the Bible.

"Well, I might as well stir up a cake for our lunch—what with all these fresh eggs," Mama said, rising. "More coffee?" she asked Rose.

"Yes, please."

Mama poured the coffee. Rose doctored the concoction with sugar and stirred it with a delicate spoon.

Tearing his eyes away from the paper, Harl asked, "Cake sounds good. What kind?"

"I was thinking pound or the 1-2-3-4 cake."

Rose licked her lips. 'I don't know what a 1-2-3-4 cake is, but I do love pound cake. My mother taught me how to make it before she died."

"Oh? It sounds like you were close," Mama said, getting out a large bowl from under the counter. She turned back to face her guest.

Rose closed the Bible and set it on her lap. "We were. I miss her so much." Rose's bottom lip quivered.

"Oh, honey," Mama stepped forward and pulled a clean handkerchief from her apron pocket and handed it to Rose.

"Thank you. My father was never known to be a reckless driver. And why he took the turn so fast, I'll never know."

Harl shot a glance at his mother, who returned his gaze.

"I just wish she was still here," she said, blowing her nose. "Maybe then, she could have talked some sense into my father about whom he chose to have me marry."

"So, you ran away?" Harl asked.

"Not really. I mean, my father knew I didn't want to marry his apprentice because of his bad nature. And then I found the advertisement from Mr. Tooth saying he was a tailor. It was going to be so perfect. I sent him my photo in its case, and he sent me his. I talked about working alongside him in his shop. It just wasn't meant to be, I guess."

"There never was any tailor shop," Harl said, his brows pinched together.

"Well, it's for the best. The Lord was looking out for you. It was a blessing that Mr. Tooth didn't decide to marry you," Mama said, turning back to the eggs and the bowl.

"I don't see how. I mean, I came all this way to get away from a hurtful man just to find another. Are all men so cruel?"

"I'm not," Harl said, leaning his folded arms on the table.

Rose glanced at him over her shoulder.

"As soon as this ice breaks up, I'm going to go get Tooth, bring him here, and make him apologize for sending you on a wild goose chase."

Rose chuckled. "Yes, this has been quite a mess, hasn't it? If he's all that bad, then I don't see how he would be willing to apologize to me."

"If Tooth knows what's good for him, he'll come apologize."

"If your father knew that his apprentice was a mean man, why would he have insisted that you marry him?"

Rose bowed her head. "I'm not sure he knew the kind of man he was. He just had my word for it. He wasn't there the day that I saw him whip that horse. I was bringing them lunch like I did every day. Albert Winters—that's his name—didn't see me enter through the backdoor, but I saw him. I screamed when I saw him strike that poor horse. He stopped. I told my father, but he didn't believe me—or didn't want to believe me."

"So, you ran away?"

"Not right away. I found Mr. Tooth's advertisement in a copy of a newspaper that came wrapped around a lamp I had ordered for the parlor. I never would have answered his advertisement if it didn't mention the part about him being a tailor. So, I wrote to him, telling him all about myself and sending him the photo I had taken several years ago."

"Photographs are expensive, aren't they?"

"One of my father's friends, the druggist, wanted to practice making photographs and needed models. So, he chose me, my mother, and my father. I posed by myself, with my parents, with my mother, and then with my father. My father paid him something, I'm sure."

"How long ago was that?" Harl asked.

"Several years. Well, you saw the photograph. Is it really so hard to believe that it's me?"

"There's a resemblance there."

Mama poured the batter for the pound cake into a loaf pan and slid it into the oven. "It's been a while since I've made a cake. I hope it turns out all right. I usually make pies and cobblers."

"I'm sure it will be fine," Rose said.

She shifted in her seat and rolled the bad ankle under her skirt. Pulling it up a bit, she said, "It looks a bit better."

Mama stepped over to the younger woman and peered at what she could see of her foot.

"I believe you are right. It's not as black and blue anymore."

Harl abruptly stood, turned, and walked to where his coat hung. Taking it down, he placed it on his head and donned his hat and gloves. "Think I'll go check the fence rows." He shut the door behind him as he left.

Chapter 1

After checking the fence rows to make sure no cattle had broken through, Harl hitched up the mules to the wagon and eased them out in the direction of Cletus Tooth's home. All the way, Harl chewed the inside of his cheek.

"Cletus, you need to come with me. You've got some apologizing to do," he said out loud to himself as he rested one hand on his hip. He rubbed his temple, trying to dispel his throbbing headache.

After a half an hour, Harl reached Cletus' home—if it could even be called a home. The ramshackle, one-story cabin listed to the right side. Cletus, dressed in dirty overalls and wearing boots, opened the door and stood on the icy, beatdown dirt just outside the door. Three good-sized hogs snorted in a pen in front of the house. Cletus held up his hand as Harl's wagon approached.

"I ain't done nothin' lately," Cletus called, holding his hands in the air.

Harl slowed the mules and drew them up short of the hog's pen. "I didn't say you did."

"Well, whatcha coming all this way out here fer?"

"You have some apologizing and explaining to do."

Cletus' mouth dropped open. "To who?"

"Miss Rose Henderson."

"Who's that?" Cletus scowled and rubbed his stubbly chin.

"You don't know?"

"No, should I?"

"It's the woman you left at the train depot the other day."

"Oh, her." He chuckled. "Don't need no fat wife. Wanted a skinny one like in the picture she sent me—and a young one, too."

Harl leaned back and pushed his hat back on his head. "Well, get your coat. I'm driving you over so's you can apologize for paying her way down here."

"I didn't pay her way down here," Cletus said, rubbing one hand under his nose.

"Well, then, how'd she get all this way? She doesn't have any money."

"Don't know. She wired me and said she was coming and to meet her at the train station. If I had known how big she was going to be, I never would have spent my time driving up to get her."

"Come on, get your coat. I'm not leaving here without you."

"I ain't got none."

"What?"

"A coat."

"Well then, bring yourself and climb on up here."

Cletus shut the door behind him and walked by the pen of hogs. He patted the head of one, which rewarded him with a snort. Climbing up onto the wagon, Cletus seated himself next to Harl. "All right, I'm ready."

Harl made a face when the putrid smell of Cletus' breath hit him. "Come on, then." Harl turned the mules around toward home.

As they rode, Cletus asked, "What am I s'pose ta say to her?"

"For one thing, you're going to confess you never were a tailor. What put it in your head that you needed a wife in the first place?"

"I needed me somebody to cook and clean and butcher hogs with. 'Sides, my friend, Paul Richardson, said I should have me a wife—that he'd put in the advertisement that I was a tailor, so's I could get me a pretty, little seamstress. He said that having a wife makes life easy. Why, they cook and clean and kill hogs and can shoot a gun and do other things." Cletus snickered. Harl shot him a look, and Cletus sobered.

"Ain't it too bad to be out?" Cletus asked.

"It's starting to break up. Won't be long before the railway will be clear, and we'll put her on a train headed north."

"Well, I don't know now. Seems like a waste to put all that womanly flesh on a train headed north. Maybe I could get used to having me a fat wife. As long as she cooks and can clean and butcher hogs, it might not be such a bad thing."

Harl's mouth fell open. "If you think for one minute I'm going to let you marry Miss Henderson, you have another thing coming. It's not like she is property."

"Didn't say she is. So, she come all this way with nothin' in her pockets, huh? Better check them pockets. They might be deep."

When Harl arrived back at his mother's house, he drove the mules up alongside the porch and set the brake.

"Come on. Let's go. If you're real nice and apologize convincingly, maybe Mama will let you sup with us."

Cletus' head shot up, and he cackled. "Don't mind if I do."

Harl jumped down and walked around to where Cletus stood on the ground.

"Follow me."

Harl opened the door and walked into the warmth of the kitchen, followed by Cletus. The pound cake rested on a platter in the middle of the table. Rose sat with her back to the door. His mother was working over the cookstove with her back to him. She turned and gasped.

"Oh, goodness gracious me! Cletus Tooth!" Mama shrieked.

Rose's head and shoulders whipped around.

"Well, howdy to you, too," Cletus said, stepping around Harl, who shut the door. "Sure do smell good in here. What's that you're cooking?"

Mama raised the wooden spoon she was holding as if it would shield her from the likes of Cletus Tooth.

"Never mind. Don't you have something to say?" Harl asked.

Cletus cleared his throat and stepped forward. Walking around to the opposite side of the table, he paused and gazed at Rose, whose mouth stood open. Mama moved around the table to stand by Rose.

Cletus combed his fingers through his rumpled, greasy hair and cleared his throat again. "I come to apologize to you for my behavior the other day. I never should have made that advertisement for a bride. I lied about being a tailor. Goodness, I can't even sew on my own buttons. I'm sorry you come all this way expecting a good, decent, respectable man, only to find me." He bowed his head and clasped his hands in front of him. He lifted his eyes, but not his head, and eyed the women.

Rose and Mama smiled. His head shot up, and he turned to Harl. "Good enough? When do we eat?"

Rose scowled, and Mama grasped the spoon with both hands, her eyes wide and mouth agape.

"What makes you think I'd give the likes of you anything to eat after your sorry performance?" Mama asked, cutting her eyes to Harl.

"Mama, I—"

Cletus pointed a boney finger at Harl. "He said you'd feed me if I apologized real good. You ain't givin' me nothin' to eat? In that case, I ain't sorry!" Cletus stormed out the door and down the stairs.

Harl went after him. "Cletus, you come on back here."

"I ain't gonna do it. You promised me vittles," he said over his shoulder as he cut through the barnyard.

"I didn't promise you any such thing. You come back here and let those women know you are sorry, or you'll not get a ride home from me."

"I don't need a ride. I'll walk. And I ain't sorry," he shouted, turning out of the barnyard into the back field and out of earshot.

Turning around, Harl walked back inside to face his mother, who was still holding the wooden spoon in front of her.

"You brought that man into my clean house," she said.

"Yes, Mama. I thought he was going to apologize to Rose."

"Well, that was quite a little show he put on for us. Now I'm going to have to scrub my floors again!"

"What for? His boots were clean."

"I don't want the thought or stench of him to linger where he stood. How dare he come here thinking he was going to get a handout if he performed well enough! Why didn't you tell me that was where you was going?"

"I didn't think it through."

"No. You didn't." Her scowl softened. "If you are done with your errands for the time-being, you might like to know lunch is almost ready." Turning, his mother marched back into the house and closed the door.

Harl jogged down the steps and climbed up into the wagon. He stood with his foot braced on the front board as he drove the mules back toward the barn. In the barn, he unhitched the mules and led them into their stalls. He brushed them down quickly and then headed into the house.

Lunch was on the table when he arrived.

"I can't believe you would bring that skunk of a man into my house!"

"I'm sorry, Mama. It won't happen again."

"Well, I'm so flustered, you'll have to do the honors of praying for our meal."

Harl gave the blessing.

"Amen," Rose said when he had finished, lifting her head.

She moved the Bible to the edge of the table as the food was passed around.

After the meal, Rose said, "I think I might like to go lie down for a bit."

Harl stood and offered Rose his arm. She smiled up at him. "Thank you," she said,

A pleasing warmth radiated from Harl where Rose's arm touched his. He smiled down at her and she up at him.

Taking their time, Rose was able to hobble back to the bedroom, where she sat on the bed and waited for Harl to leave. Only, he didn't leave. He propped his elbow up on the high chest of drawers and gazed at Rose.

"Something on your mind?" she asked.

"Yes. You said Cletus paid your way down here, but he said it was you who paid your own way. He said that you wired him that you were coming and when to expect you."

Rose's face turned pink as her mouth fell open. She gazed down at her hands in her lap and smoothed her dress, licking her lips. She placed both hands on the sides of her face and raised her head, smiling.

"He must have been addled. I came when he sent for me, and that is that. Now, if you don't mind, I'd like to get some rest."

Harl rubbed his clean-shaven chin. "Uh huh," he said, removing his elbow from the chest of drawers. He walked out into the hall and closed the door behind him.

In the kitchen, he squinted at his mother, who had her back to him as she washed the dishes.

"Had a good visit?"

"No, not really."

His mother spun around. "What? Why not? What happened?"

Harl moved closer to his mother and whispered, "I think she's lying about some things."

Mama's eyes widened. "What?"

"Cletus told me outright that she bought her own ticket and came down here. She wired to let him know she was on her way."

"Maybe he got it wrong?"

"I don't think so. When I asked her about it, her face went all red like she was embarrassed she got caught."

His mother gasped. "Why would she lie about something like that?"

"I don't know, but I'm going to get to the bottom of this story of hers."

Chapter 8

After Harl shut the door, Rose rung her hands. "Oh dear, oh dear. He knows," she breathed. "Oh, what am I going to do?"

Hobbling to her trunk, she threw the lid open and reached deep inside under her dresses and skirts and waistcoats to the bottom. Feeling the coolness of the metal shaft, she relaxed. "At least, that's still there."

Replacing the dresses, skirts, and waistcoats over her father's army-issued revolver, she hobbled back to the side of the bed. Throwing back the covers, she slid inside, feeling the coolness of the quilts against her burning cheeks. Soon, she was asleep.

Rose didn't wake when Mama tapped lightly at the door, flanked by Harl.

Mama opened the door a crack and peeked in at Rose's sleeping form. "We'll just have to ask her later," she said, shutting the door. "Now, don't you worry. We'll get to the bottom of this story."

"You keep an eye on her. I'm going to go check the herd and double the fence in the back forty. Don't want those animals breaking through again."

"All right."

After some time, Rose awoke. The sun was still high in the sky. She rolled out of bed and hobbled out into the kitchen, where she found Hazel reading the Bible she had left on the corner of the table.

"Oh, honey," Hazel said upon seeing her, "you shouldn't be walking on that foot. I'm glad you're feeling better, but I don't want you walking yet. It's too soon."

"I'm feeling much better, and the swelling is almost gone."

"Well, come sit down, anyway, and put your leg up. Here, let me arrange the chair for you."

Hazel rushed around the table and pulled a chair out for her guest. Rose hobbled over to it and sat.

"Thank you."

Hazel pulled out the chair with the cushion on it and placed it in front of Rose. She bent and helped the young woman place her leg on the cushion.

"Better?"

"Much. Thank you." She looked around the room, making sure to cover her ankle. "Where's Harl?"

"He's out checking the fence lines," said Hazel, settling down in the chair across from Rose. "Now then, let's have a chat. Harl told me what Cletus said and your reaction when he told you. Is there something going on that I should know?"

"Oh, that." Rose felt her face burn. She laced her fingers together and twisted them.

"Yes, that. What made you lie?"

"I-I don't know. I thought maybe if you thought Cletus had sent for me, I wouldn't seem so desperate to get married."

"You're desperate to get married? Why?"

"It's because of what's waiting for me in Michigan if I go back."

"What's waiting for you?"

"An unhappy life with Albert Winters, my father's apprentice. I thought maybe if he and my father knew I was married, they wouldn't come after me."

Hazel's mouth dropped open. Just as quickly, she shut it. "Why in the world would they come after you?"

"Don't ask. I've already said too much."

The jingling of harness rings caught Rose's ears. She craned her neck around to look at the door.

"I'll see who it is. Maybe it's the doctor come to check on you." Rising, Hazel walked to the door and opened it.

"Good day," Rose heard a man's voice call.

"Good day to you," Hazel said. Rose twisted her torso around to see who was speaking, but she couldn't see past Hazel's large frame filling the doorway.

"Is the man of the house at home? I have some very fine tools and harnesses I'd like to show him."

"You just missed him. He's out mending fences."

"My dear lady, I also have wares that would suit the gentler sex. Care to have a look?"

"No, can't say that I would."

"Come now, surely there is something that might appeal to your eye. I carry fine dress goods, pots and pans, and—"

"No, thank you," Hazel said, stepping back inside the house and shutting the door.

"Let me beg some grain, hay, or water for my horse," the man shouted.

"He'll leave in a minute," Hazel said, returning to her seat. "Now, where were we?"

Rose opened her mouth to speak; but in the next moment, the door crashed open, and the peddler was grabbing Hazel's arm. "Ah, so there's two of you. Good," he said, with a fiendish smile. "And one of you is hurt," he said, looking down at Rose's foot on the cushion. "Such handsome women."

He bent down, clasping Hazel's face in his large hands. Rose hobbled from the room into the bedroom as quickly as she could and threw open her trunk. Grasping the revolver at the bottom, she limped back into the kitchen to see Hazel's arms flailing as she tried to push the man off her.

"Stop," Rose yelled, casting aside the pain that seared her foot. "I'll shoot!" she exclaimed, cocking the gun with unsteady hands.

The man stopped kissing Hazel and stood to his full height. "Come now. Put the gun down. Be a good girl," he said, coming around the table toward her.

Rose took a step back onto her bad foot and fired the gun, but she only grazed the man. He grabbed his torn coat sleeve and rushed out the open door.

Jumping into his wagon, he cracked the whip over his horse, who bolted. Turning the wagon around, he rushed off the property.

Rose stood shaking in the doorway of the house. Turning, she gazed at a disheveled Hazel, who was gasping for air. Hurrying to her side, she stroked the older woman's arm. "Did he hurt you?"

"Oh, my heart," Hazel said, clutching her chest.

"Should I go get Harl?"

"How? You can't walk that far."

"Come and lie down in your bed."

"But what about supper?"

"You let me worry about that. My foot's better. Come on now." Helping the older woman to stand, Rose led her into the bedroom and helped her take her boots off and climb into bed.

"A gun!" Hazel exclaimed. "You have a gun. Oh, my heart."

"Shh, just rest for now. We'll talk later."

"But you don't know what to fix for supper."

"I'll figure out something."

In a few hours, when Harl returned to the house, he found Rose limping around the table setting places. He frowned, shrugged off his coat, and pulled off his hat and gloves.

"You shouldn't be on your feet. Where's Mama?"

"Shh," Rose said, placing her finger to her lips. "She's in bed."

Harl cocked his head to one side. "Why's she in bed?"

"We had a little bit of an incident is all."

"What happened?"

"A peddler came and wouldn't take no for an answer."

Harl raced to his mother's door, knocked, and entered.

Mama struggled to climb out of the bed.

"What happened, Mama?"

"A peddler came and burst in on us when I decided not to buy anything from him."

"He tried to kiss your mother," Rose said from the doorway.

"He did what?" Harl asked, balling his fists at his sides.

"But I put a stop to that with my father's service revolver."

"Thankfully, she had that gun, or who knows what that man might have tried? She fired off one shot. That's all it took to make him move—that and a hole in his coat."

"I could have aimed for his heart, but I know how you like your clean floors and didn't want to make a mess."

Mama reached out and grabbed Harl's forearm. She pulled herself up from the bed. Harl stood, his mouth agape.

"I knew I shouldn't have left you two alone for so long."

"Now, it's not your fault. I've never seen this man before and, thanks to Rose, probably won't see him ever again."

Rose smiled. "Supper's ready."

"Thank you. I'm sure you fixed something wonderful for us," Mama said, taking a step forward.

Rose limped back out of the doorway and let Mama pass, followed by Harl, who offered his arm to her.

"Oh, thank you," she said, taking it.

"I don't want your ankle swelling up again," he said.

Rose set the meal on the table and then returned to her chair.

"Harl, would you do the honors? I can't quite think straight," Mama said, folding her hands and bowing her head.

Harl and Rose followed her lead.

"Thank You, Father God, that no one was hurt this afternoon while I was away. Thank You for protecting my mother and Rose. Bless this food to our nourishment and the hands that prepared it. In Jesus' name, amen."

Mama speared some meat on the platter with her fork and passed it to Rose, who took a helping before handing it to Harl.

"What's on your mind, son?" Mama asked.

"Dogs. We should have a couple of dogs on the place. Maybe if we would have had dogs, that man wouldn't have come near you; and they could have alerted me to the stranger's presence with their barking. I'll check around town tomorrow when we go in for church and see if anyone has some for sale."

"That sounds like a fine plan to me," Mama said.

Chapter 9

The next day, the weather was dark and gloomy.

"Looks like snow," Mama observed as Harl helped her up onto the seat beside him on the wagon. He then went around to help Rose climb into the back.

"I don't know. Might be rain, what with the ice breaking up in this temperature rise," Harl said.

"Let's take it nice and easy, anyway," Mama replied.

The drive into town was slow. When they arrived at the schoolhouse church, Harl helped the women out of the wagon by the door before driving his team to a spot without ice in the schoolyard.

Inside, Harl was greeted by his sister, Catherine. "Brother, it's so good to see you," she exclaimed, hugging his neck. "I thought this ice was never going to break up."

Glancing around the room, Harl smiled when he spotted his niece, Clair, sitting between her grandmother and Rose.

"It's good to see you, too, sister. Where's your man?"

"In the backroom praying for the service today."

"Is he treating you and Clair all right? I haven't seen you since you got married."

She nodded and grinned. "Couldn't ask for better."

The door at the front of the room opened, and Samuel Harris stepped out and over to the white, wooden podium.

"You best go find your seat," Harl said.

Catherine hurried down the aisle to where Clair sat. Rose moved over to the edge of the bench when she saw the girl's mother approach. Catherine sat and hugged Clair.

Samuel smiled out at the congregation, Bible in hand. "Is there anyone with a song on their heart today?"

When church ended. Harl stepped outside. He found George Wayright, owner of *The American Bugle* newspaper.

"Wayright," he called.

George turned and smiled when he caught sight of Harl. "You calling me, Harl?"

"Yes, you heard anybody that's got a dog they want to get rid of?"

"I know Paul Richardson's dog just had pups a couple of months ago. They might like to find homes for them."

"Thank you kindly."

Harl craned his neck to see around the crowd. Maybe Mrs. Gladys Richardson, Paul's wife, was in church. Spying her coming out the door, he intercepted her.

Doffing his hat, he smiled. "Sure was a good service today."

"Yes, quite." She craned her neck around to the right and left as if looking for someone or something.

"Are you in need of a ride home?"

"No, my husband will be along shortly."

"I hear your dog had pups."

"Over eight weeks ago."

"Would you be willing to part with a couple?"

"I don't know. I'd better leave that to my husband to decide. Oh, here he comes now."

Harl looked to where she pointed. A scowling Paul Richardson drove his team of draft horses beside them. Reaching out his hand to his wife, he pulled her up beside him in the wagon.

"Word has it you have some pups you'd like to get rid of," Harl said.

"Maybe for a price. How many you want?"

"I'd have to see them first."

"Come on up this afternoon around three o'clock?"

"Will do."

Paul spoke to the horses, and they walked on. Harl stared after them until he felt a tiny hand in his. Looking down, he saw Clair's bright blue eyes looking up at him.

"Hey, Clair, honey," Harl said.

Clair smiled up at her uncle. He picked her up and balanced her on his hip. "Where's your mama?"

Clair pointed. "Over there with Daddy."

Harl swung around and followed her pointing finger to the doorway of the church where Catherine and Samuel Harris stood shaking hands with the last of the attendees. In a few strides, Harl was at his sister's side. "Got someone for you." He smiled as he handed Clair back to her mother.

"You and Mama and Miss Henderson want to come over for lunch?"

"Not today. I'm going up to Paul Richardson's place this afternoon to look at some puppies."

"Puppies!" Clair shouted. "Can I go, too?"

Harl studied his sister's face. "She'd be welcome. You all would be welcome. I'm going up there at three. But you know if she comes, you'll end up with one, too."

Catherine laughed and turned to her husband, who stood listening to the conversation.

"I don't see what it could hurt if we go have a look. Might want one to keep a watch on this one," he said, shaking Clair's booted foot. She giggled and stretched out her arms to Samuel, who drew her into his and kissed her curly, blonde head.

"Mama's got plenty if you have a mind to come for lunch," Harl said.

"No, we couldn't. I have a chicken in the oven. I wouldn't want it to go to waste."

"After you get done eating, come on over, and we'll drive up together to the Richardsons' place," Harl said.

Harl was just wiping his mouth on the cloth napkin in his hand when he heard the jingle of a harness and hoofs plodding through the orchard. "Right on time," he said, rising.

Opening the door, he walked out onto the porch and greeted his sister, his brother-in-law, and Clair. "We just finished eating. Mama and Miss Henderson are going with us." Reaching inside the door, he pulled on his coat, gloves, and hat. "We ready to go, Mama?"

"Just a minute. What's the hurry? I'd like to get these dishes soaking first."

"Here, let me help you," Rose offered.

"No, now you sit still. It'll just take me a minute to pour boiling water over them in the dishpan."

After the dishes were soaking in the water, she walked down the hallway and returned with two coats: one for her and one for Rose.

"Thank you for bringing my coat," Rose said, rising. "I need to get my other boot on. I'll just be a minute."

Limping into Hazel's bedroom, Rose picked up her boot, sat on the bed, and placed it on her foot. She struggled to button it. In the end, she only fastened two of the buttons on the shoe.

"My foot is still swollen," she admitted to Hazel, who stood in the doorway watching.

Standing, she slid her arms into the coat and limped toward the front door, where Harl stood holding it open.

"Now, don't let all this good, warm air out, Harl, honey," Hazel scolded, rushing past him.

He closed the door and helped the women into the waiting wagon at the foot of the steps.

"Careful now," he said, taking Rose's gloved hand. "I'm glad to see that foot isn't bothering you as much now."

"It's definitely a lot better than it was yesterday. It is still not completely healed, but I am able to get along better than I was."

Looking over at Samuel, Harl nodded and climbed up onto the seat with his mother.

"Walk on," he said, jingling the reins. The mules walked forward.

It was a two-mile drive up to Paul Richardson's place. As Harl passed Cletus Tooth's shack, he nodded to Cletus, who had walked out onto the snow-covered, icy dirt patch that was his front yard.

Harl turned to look at Rose, who turned her nose up in the air and faced away from the man who was to be her betrothed.

"Whatcha doing all the way up here?" Cletus called through cupped hands.

"Going to Richardson's place to look at the puppies."

Cletus hurried to catch up to the wagon. Finally walking behind it, he eyed Rose. "You're looking mighty fine today, Miss Henderson."

She turned her head and body away from Cletus.

"What's wrong now? I said you looked fine."

"I don't care for your compliments."

"Ha! Womenfolk!"

Paul Richardson's home was nestled in the next fork up from Cletus's shack. Two barking black dogs ran down the hillside toward the wagon, their tails whipping the air. Paul stepped out onto his porch with his hands in his back pockets and whistled sharply. The dogs ran to him.

"Goodness," Mama said, placing her hand on her heart.

Harl nodded. "Them's some finely trained dogs you got there."

"Yep," Paul said, reaching down and scratching each one behind the ear. "Come on in, and you can see the pups."

Harl helped his mother and Rose out of the wagon. Cletus opened his arms wide to Rose in an effort to help her down, but she refused his offer. When everyone was out of their respective wagons, the party entered Paul's home through the kitchen. Over in one corner of the kitchen sat Paul's boys, Frank and James Richardson, playing with large, black puppies. They laughed as the smallest one fell over its large paws as it lunged for the rag the boys were holding. Paul's wife, Gladys, stepped up beside her husband.

"This here's my wife, Gladys, and my boys, Frank and James," Paul said to Rose.

Gladys smiled at the company. The boys didn't look up but continued playing tug of war with the four pups and the rag.

"Puppies!" Clair exclaimed as she rushed forward to pick up one and hug it. As a reward, the pup licked her face. She giggled.

"Well, when you see a good one, let me know; and I'll pull it out for you."

"What about that one?" Rose asked, pointing to the smallest one.

"He's the runt," Harl said.

"Yes, but he looks so friendly and helpless."

"All right, we'll take that one."

"Better take two. They'll do better in pairs," Paul uttered slowly.

"Then we'll take the little one and the big one," Harl replied.

"Clair? Which one do you like?" her mother asked.

"This one." She giggled. "He's licking my face. I think he likes me."

"How much?" Harl asked.

"Well, I don't rightly know."

"You must have thought about how much you wanted for one. How much for two?"

"I'll take five dollars each."

Harl gasped. "Five dollars?"

"Yep, take it or leave it."

"That's highway robbery!" Cletus, who was standing behind the group, exclaimed indignantly.

"You stay outta this!" Paul roared, pointing a gnarled finger at his neighbor.

Harl looked over at Gladys, who held one hand to her face.

"That's too much, honey. Anyone can see that."

"Well, then, make me an offer."

"I was thinking a dollar for the pair," Harl replied after some consideration.

"And?"

"And a bushel of apples for your trouble."

"You still got apples this time of year?" Paul asked, licking his lips.

"Sure do."

"Where you keeping them apples?" Cletus asked.

"Never you mind. Thing is, he's got 'em! I'll take it!" Paul remarked excitedly as he stuck out his hand.

Harl shook on it, then dug out a coin from his pocket and handed it to Paul.

"I wouldn't have given you such a good deal; but on account of the preacher being here and that bushel of apples you promised, I decided to accept your offer. You can drop it by anytime tomorrow."

Harl turned to see Samuel digging a few coins out of his pocket.

"Now, hold on there, Preacher," Paul said, putting out his hand. "I don't want to go robbing the church. You can have yours."

"I'll pay the same as Harl did," Samuel said, handing over some small coins.

Paul smiled and rubbed his stubbly chin. "Well, if that don't beat all. Never thought I'd see an honest preacher."

Samuel scowled.

"Before you came back from seminary, we had us a traveling preacher who would try and hole up with anyone he could, eat our vittles, and preach us all into Hell on account of me liking a sip of shine every now and then."

"Oh, I see," Samuel said. "Well, that's not me. We pay for what we need."

Paul squinted at the preacher. "You needing anything else? We got some canned goods my woman preserved to see us through the winter. You two gettin' married so suddenly last month, I'm sure your woman didn't have time to get anything grown or canned."

"We keep 'em stocked," Mama said.

"And what we don't have, we buy," Catherine said.

Paul nodded slowly. "You want me to carry your pups out for you?" he asked, turning to Harl.

"No, I can manage."

"Now, wait a minute," Cletus said. "I wanna get me a dog, too. I'll take the one that's left."

"What with?" Paul asked.

"I'll take it on credit; and as soon as the mash is ready, I'll bring some up."

Catherine and Mama gasped.

"What? A man's got to have a job, don't he?" Cletus said. "I'll be needing me a guard dog around the place."

Paul snickered. "Deal," he said, sticking out his hand. Cletus shook it and snatched up the last puppy.

When both women were settled in Harl's wagon, he went back for his pups and placed the squirming dogs in the back of the wagon with Rose, who giggled as they fell over onto her dress hem. She rubbed each one's belly and smiled up at Harl. He returned her smile and gaze.

Samuel's wagon pulled away first. Harl waved in a high arch over his head, and Samuel returned his gesture.

Turning back to Rose, Harl said, "You're going to have your hands full helping me train these dogs."

"What about sending me back home?"

"I don't think you really want to go." Looking up at his mother, who had turned around to watch the playful pups, he said, "We don't mind having you around, anyway. Do we, Mama?"

"It's been real nice having another woman at home again," Mama said.

Harl stepped up on the wheel hub and into the front of the wagon. He sat next to his mother and smiled at Rose over his shoulder. Releasing the brake, he spoke to the mules to walk on.

Chapter 10

Over the course of the next few days, Rose's ankle grew stronger and stronger. One morning, Rose stood at the woodburning stove, frying bacon in a cast iron skillet with the attentive puppies at her feet, when Hazel came into the kitchen.

"What's all this?" Hazel asked. "Did I oversleep?"

Rose laughed and shook her head. "No, I'm feeling well enough to do my share around here now and thought I'd surprise you."

"Well, you did that, for sure."

Harl walked into the kitchen rubbing his eyes and blinked them at Rose. He did a double-take when he saw who was standing at the stove. Turning to his mother, he asked, "What? Aren't you feeling well, Mama?"

"I feel just fine. She beat me to it is all."

Hazel set plates and silverware on the table. "You wanna go get us some fresh milk?" she asked her son.

"Will do." Taking his coat, hat, and gloves, he hurried out the door.

"Hurry back. I'm baking biscuits, too," Rose shouted as the door shut.

In the barn, Harl eased the door shut and grabbed a clean bucket hanging on a nail outside Brownie's stall. He walked to the back of the barn and threw open the sliding door. He whistled shrilly for the cow. She ran to him out of the herd.

"That's a good girl." He placed the rope around her neck and led her to her stall. When she was settled and munching on hay, he seated himself on the three-legged stool beside her and blew into his cold hands before tugging on her udders. In a few minutes, he had a full bucket of milk. Setting the milk on the other side of the stall, he led Brownie back out into the lot with the other cattle.

"There you go, girl. Go enjoy your friends."

Rose's smiling face interrupted his thoughts. *She certainly is pretty.* Harl scowled. *But she isn't a Christian.* Sure, she had attended church with them, but that didn't make her a Christian.

"Lord, show Rose the way to You," he prayed and dusted his work gloves on his britches as he made his way back to the house with the fresh pail of milk.

As Harl entered the kitchen, Rose turned out a skillet of biscuits fresh from the oven onto a plate. Mama poured the milk into a large pitcher and set it on the table.

The puppies whined and kept sharp eyes on Rose as she set the food on the table.

"Don't you worry none," Mama said to the pups now seated on the floor beside Rose. "We won't forget to feed you once we're done."

After the blessing was said, Rose passed the biscuits and gravy to Harl and then the bacon and waited her turn. She partook once the dishes made their way around the table.

In the distance, a train whistle sounded; and Rose looked at Harl, whose fork was poised between his mouth and the plate. He returned her gaze and set his fork down.

"We knew this day would come. Your ankle is healed, for the most part, and it seems the tracks are clear with this unseasonably warmer weather we've had."

Rose turned her head and scowled. "I know. It's just so sudden. I guess it's time for me to go home and face my father."

"There's no rush. Let's eat, and then I'll help you get your trunk straightened out," Mama said, tears gleaming in her eyes.

The rest of the meal was eaten in silence. When they finished, Mama scraped the rest of the food into two old pie tins and placed it by the door with a pan of fresh water for the pups, who gobbled the food.

"Come on, boys. Let's go for a walk," Harl said as he donned his coat, hat, and gloves and then opened the door. The dogs bounded outside before him.

When he was out of earshot of the house, he prayed, "Father God, it seems that we didn't get much of a chance to witness to Miss Henderson. I sure would like to have her stay on with us, but I know the best thing for her is to go home and straighten things out with her father. Please help her to work everything out and realize how much You love her."

Opening the door to the barn, the dogs followed him inside. He eased the door closed and placed fresh hay in both mules' stalls, along with some grain in their feed buckets. Grabbing a shovel, he scooped the manure and carried it outside to dispose of it. All the while, the puppies bounded after him on his heels. When they got too close to one of the mules, it stamped its foot and sent them running to Harl.

He smiled and reached out a comforting hand to each one. "It's all right. You're all right. I bet you won't be doing that anymore."

After removing the dirty straw from the mules' stalls, he placed fresh straw down and then fed the cattle.

"If only she didn't have to go away, Lord. Is there any chance she'd come back?" He waited and listened in his spirit for a response. None came. Turning, he walked back to the house, the little dogs on his heels.

In the house, Harl walked down the hall and turned into his mother's bedroom where Mama and Rose were finishing placing the last of her dresses in the trunk.

"We're just about done here," Mama said as she turned to look at Rose with tears in her eyes.

"I don't know how I can ever repay your kindness to me. Here," Rose said, opening her purse. She pulled out several twenty-dollar bills. "Will this cover my stay with you?" She tried to hand Mama a twenty-dollar bill.

Mama waved her off. "You'll need that for your trip home."

Harl's mouth dropped open. "Where did you get that money? I thought you were destitute."

"Yes, well, I'm not."

"You let me pay for the room and all? And you had money?"

"Yes, that was very gallant of you. The least I can do is to repay your kindness. Here, take it please." Rose bit her lip and furrowed her brows. "I'm really sorry I lied to you."

"The room didn't cost nearly that much," Harl said, waving away the money.

Mama closed the trunk lid. "We're ready."

Rose held a handkerchief to her face. Her brows and mouth pinched tight.

"Now, don't you worry none," Mama said, moving to Rose's side and putting her arms around her. "You can come back once you get home and get things straightened out with your father."

"Wait a minute. She's not going anywhere until she explains some things. We've got plenty of time before the last train of the day comes through. I think we need to have us a cup of coffee and let Miss Henderson explain herself."

"Explain what?" Mama asked.

"The money, and why she said she'd been left at the altar when she hadn't, and whatever else there is for her to explain."

Rose's eyes brimmed with tears as she turned to Harl. Her face was crimson. "Oh, all right. I didn't mean to . . . to . . . "

"To lie?" Harl asked.

"Yes," she whispered.

"I better get the coffee to boiling," Mama said, leaving the room.

In the kitchen, Harl took his seat at the head of the table. Rose sat next to him and Mama across from her. Harl wrapped his hands around the warm cup of coffee and stared at Rose, who glanced everywhere except at Harl and his mother.

"Anytime you'd like to start, I'm all ears," he said.

Rose took her time doctoring her cup with cream and sugar. Her eyebrows pinched together. "I just . . . I came into some money."

Harl shook his head. "No, no more lies."

Rose looked down at her hands now resting in her lap. Raising one hand, she touched her face.

"I-I borrowed one hundred dollars from my father. I needed the money to get down here and set up a little dress and bonnet shop with Mr. Tooth."

"Borrowed?" Harl asked, eyeing her.

"Well, I took it without permission."

Mama's mouth dropped open.

"You mean, you stole it," Harl said, giving Rose a sideways glance before taking a sip of the hot liquid.

Rose pushed the napkin she held up to her face as tears trickled down her cheeks and nodded. "Yes, I stole the money, but I had every intention to pay it back. I wasn't sure how long it would take me, but I was going to pay it back."

Harl shook his head. "And the part about being left at the altar? Why'd you lie about that?"

"I don't know. I had to get away. I thought if my story was sad enough, someone would take pity on me after Mr. Tooth rejected me. Besides, I really was left at the altar a couple of years ago. That's why my father arranged a marriage with his terrible apprentice."

"Ah yes, Mr. Tooth. He didn't send for you, did he?"

"No." She shook her head, scowling. "I wired him and let him know when he could come collect me at the train station. I had money I saved from my work as a milliner that I used to buy my ticket down here. I didn't use any of my father's money for that."

"Finally, we are hearing the whole story," Harl exclaimed dramatically, throwing one hand into the air and sitting back in his chair.

"I really didn't mean to lie, but one lie turned into another and another."

"You didn't mean to lie? That's a lie in and of itself." Harl scowled at her.

"I thought maybe people would forgive me once they knew."

"So, you took advantage of our kindness?"

"No, no, that's really not what I intended to do."

"Now, Harl," Mama cut in, placing her hand on his arm, "what's done is done."

Rose swiped a finger across her cheek. "I'm really so sorry. Can you forgive me?"

Harl's tense shoulders drooped. He looked at his mother, who nodded.

"Yes, we can. We have to. The Bible says that if we forgive, we get forgiveness," Harl said. "I forgive you, but you must return that money to your father the minute you get into town. I guess there's no more to be said as long as you confessed it all."

"I have."

"I'll load your trunk."

"Wait," Rose said as she stood and ran into the bedroom and came back holding a large rock.

"What are you going to do with that?" Harl asked.

"Here, come take it."

Harl stood and walked to Rose. He took the rock from her. Their fingers brushed against each other. Rose gasped and quickly withdrew her hand.

"I thought maybe if I left it here, I could come back and claim it again." Rose lowered her head, and then she raised her eyes to look at Harl.

Mama smiled up at her. "You'd always be welcome to come stay with us."

Rose smiled as tears streamed down her face. "Thank you so much. I'd like that."

Harl, who placed the rock easily on his hip, cocked his head to one side. Harl shifted the rock from one hip to another and gazed over Rose's head. He pinched his brows together and set his mouth.

Rose's chin trembled. "I thought the rock would look nice beside the steps."

Harl nodded slowly and then led Rose and Mama outside and placed the rock on a clear patch of ground beside the steps.

"A little more to the right," Rose said.

Harl moved the rock.

"Yes, that looks good there. What do you think, Hazel?"

Mama nodded. "Now, we just need to get one for the other side of the steps. Maybe you could find another one when you get home."

"And bring it back down with me when I come? Yes, that's a wonderful idea. I'll do it."

"I'll get the mules and wagon ready," Harl said, stiffly. "You all go wait inside."

Harl turned toward the barn, the little dogs at his heels. "We still need to figure out names for you," he said to them.

Inside the barn, Harl harnessed the mules to the wagon, opened the barn doors, and drove them outside and over to the porch. Jumping down, he bounded up the stairs and into the house, past his mother and Rose, who were seated again at the table, and into his mother's room, where he picked up the trunk and placed the noticeably lighter luggage on his shoulder.

"That rock really made a difference in how heavy this trunk was," he said, as he strode out the door. Placing the trunk in the back of the wagon, he went back in for his mother and Rose.

He helped the ladies into the wagon and took up the reins and shook them. The mules walked forward and turned toward the orchard.

"Wait," Rose called. "I want one more look at the house. I wish I had a photograph of it."

Harl paused and turned in his seat. Rose was wiping tears from her face as she looked over at the house. Looking up, she met Harl's gaze. He smiled down at her.

"I'm glad we had such a favorable effect on you," he said.

"Yes, being here was like being . . . home—but not like any home I've ever known."

Mama turned round and patted Rose's shoulder. "You'll always be welcome to be here with us."

Harl and his mother turned back around. Harl shook the reins, and the mules moved forward once again.

When they arrived in town, Harl drove to the train depot. He accepted the money Rose offered for her ticket and headed to the ticket booth to buy a one-way ticket home to Michigan.

He returned in just a few minutes. "Here you are," he said, handing her the ticket.

She smiled through tears as Harl hefted her trunk back up onto his shoulders. Walking around to the baggage area, he placed it down, received a claim ticket from the baggage handler and returned to the wagon for the women.

He helped his mother down first and then took Rose's hand in his as she stepped over the wagon sides and down onto the wheel hub. Harl felt a tingle course up his arm, the arm that held Miss Henderson's gloved hand. He looked into her eyes and smiled, releasing her hand.

"I wish I didn't have to go," she said.

He shook his head. "You know you have to go make things right and then come back and see us."

"I know."

Mama, Rose, and Harl walked into the depot and stood by the fireplace to get warm.

Rose broke away from the group and paced. "What will I say to my father?"

"Tell him you're sorry," Mama soothed.

"Tell him the truth," Harl said.

"He could have me put in jail for stealing so much money."

"He could, but would he?" Harl asked.

"I hope not."

The sound of a train whistle signaled it was coming closer. Harl and Mama stepped out onto the walkway between the train tracks and the depot and watched the train come in. Rose joined them, standing furthest away from the approaching train.

As it slowed and came to a stop, steam poured out from under the train. The trio pressed their backs up against the depot and waited for the people to disembark.

Rose stepped forward and watched as person after person stepped off the train. Jumping back, she gasped.

"What's wrong, dear?" Mama asked.

Harl turned toward Rose. Her eyes were wide with fear.

"It's my father."

Chapter 11

A scowling, short, stout man wearing a black coat over a black suit strode toward them.

"Rose Edith Henderson!" a voice shouted through the throng and steam. The man cut through the steam and came to stand in front of his daughter. Rose's eyebrows were pinched, making her large, green eyes show her fear.

"Father, what brings you all this way, and how did you find me?"

"One hundred dollars missing from my lock box is what brings me all this way, and I finally got it out of the telegraph operator in Chelsea as to where you sent your telegraph. What kind of place is Harrisville, Kentucky, anyway? Why would you want to come to such a terrible place as this?"

"Now, hold on there," Harl said, stepping forward. "This isn't a terrible place. This is where I live."

"Excuse me, sir, but this isn't any of your business," Rose's father said, grabbing her arm. "Come, Rose, we have a train to catch."

Harl stepped around in front of the man and put up his hand. "No, sir, you won't be taking Rose away like this."

Rose's shoulders sagged as if under some unseen weight.

"What concern is it of yours?"

"Rose," Harl said, turning to the lady, "don't you have something you want to give your father?"

Rose opened her purse, dug out the roll of twenties, and placed it in her father's hand. "It's all there, except for the little bit I gave to Mr. Adams for my train ticket," she said, watching him tick through the bills.

"Ah well, that's a good girl. Now, come on, and you can explain yourself to your intended as to why you left him standing at the altar." He took her arm again.

"I left him there because he wasn't right for me. I watched him whip a horse that didn't stand still for shoeing. What do you think he'd do to me if I burned supper?"

"He's not like that. I've never seen him hurt a fly."

"She's telling the truth," Harl said.

"This isn't your business," her father said, squeezing her arm. Rose cried out.

"Father, let me go. You don't want me at home, anyway. Without me there, you and Widow Hampton will be quite happy."

"How did you know we got married?"

Rose gasped. "Did you? Is that why you want me home—to cook and clean for you two?"

"No, you won't be living with us. You'll be living with your intended, who will meet our return train with the sheriff to make sure you make it to your wedding this time." He jerked Rose forward.

"Now, hold on there. She's not going."

"And I say she is." Rose's father looked Harl up and down.

Harl balled his fists at his sides. Rose's father jerked her to his side and walked toward the waiting train.

Rose looked over her shoulder and called, "Help!"

That was all it took for Harl to spring into action. In a moment, he was at her side, wrenching her father's grip off his daughter's arm.

Rose's father struck first. He smashed his fist into Harl's face. Blood spewed from his nose as he returned the punch. Punch after punch, the two men fought as a crowd gathered.

Mama and Rose screamed. Rose ran to Mama, who embraced her.

"Break it up; break it up." The sound of Sheriff Anton Franklin's voice rose through the crowd.

Harl turned to see the sheriff walking toward him just as Rose's father landed another blow on the right side of his cheek.

"I said, break it up!" Franklin yelled, stepping forward.

Both men's noses dripped blood down onto their clean, white shirts. Harl swiped his forefinger under his nose and grimaced.

"You all right, Adams?" Sheriff Franklin asked Harl.

Harl dug in his back pocket and pulled out a clean, white handkerchief. "I'm fine. I've had worse," Harl replied with a grimace.

Sheriff Franklin eyed the stranger in front of Harl. "You're not from around here, are you?"

"Of course, I'm not from around here!" Rose's father spat, scowling.

"What brings you to town, then? Surely, you weren't looking for a fight."

"Certainly not," the man replied, straightening his shirt, "but this man interfered with me taking my daughter home to Michigan with me."

"What's this?" the sheriff asked. "Where is she?"

"Here," Rose called, raising her hand and stepping up to Harl.

"You care to explain what was going on here?" the sheriff asked as he stood waiting with his hands on his hips.

"My father was dragging me away. He wanted me to go back to Michigan with him and marry a man I don't care for."

Sheriff Franklin hooked his thumbs in his vest pocket. "This true?"

"I'm taking my daughter back home to Michigan to her intended."

"Don't seem like she wants to go."

"Oh, she's going all right," her father said, snatching her hand.

"Now, you hold on right there," Sheriff Franklin said, putting a hand on the father's forearm and on Rose's wrist. "We have laws about kidnapping. And if she doesn't want to go with you, that would be kidnapping."

"But she's my daughter."

"That don't mean she is your property to do with as you see fit," the sheriff said. Turning to Rose, he asked, "You want to go with him?"

Rose looked at her father, licked her lips, and swallowed. "No, I don't. I want to stay in Harrisville."

The sheriff turned to her father. "Appears to me that you'll be going back home alone."

Rose's father ground his teeth together and released his hold on his daughter's hand. Rose immediately clung to Harl's side. He placed a protective arm around her shoulders. "Don't think you'll be welcome back in Michigan after this. You've made your choice; now, see it through to the end."

With a huff, he turned toward the train. He patted his breast pocket and spun back around. "I ain't got a ticket," he said. "I can't get on that train."

"Here, take mine," Rose said, handing over her ticket. "I'm sorry, Father. I don't want you to be angry with me. Please forgive me."

Her father breathed heavily through his nose and jabbed a finger in his daughter's face. "I forgive you, but don't let me ever catch you in Michigan!" Turning, he huffed away and back on the train.

"All aboard," the conductor called.

Harl looked down at Rose, who was clutching her purse to her chest. A frown was etched on her face. She looked up at Harl. "I'm so sorry, but it looks like I really am destitute now. Can you forgive me?"

Harl wiped the handkerchief against his nose and checked it. The bleeding had stopped.

"I can." Turning, he looked at his mother. "Can you?"

"Of course I can, honey," Hazel said, stepping forward with open arms. She enveloped Rose in her arms and patted her back as she hugged the woman.

"Besides, if it was the Lord's will for you to be on that train, then you'd be on that train. As it is, you're welcome to hole up with us again."

"Thank you so much— Wait! My trunk!" Rose called to the conductor.

Harl followed him to the baggage car and retrieved her trunk. He pulled out a coin and tipped the man and thanked him.

The three walked to the waiting wagon. Harl set the trunk in the back and then walked around to help his mother up onto the seat and Rose into the back of the wagon.

As they drove back home, Rose chattered. "I'll need to find employment. Do you think one of the dress shops in town would let me have a corner to do up bonnets and hats in? If I had just kept that money, I could have set up a nice, little shop in town; and then you wouldn't have to let me stay at your house. But it wasn't mine to keep, and it was wrong of me to take that money from my father. I know

now I can never return home. I'm so glad I brought that rock with me so as to have a little piece of Michigan here with me. Well, what do you think of that?"

Harl looked over at his mother, who returned his gaze. "Think about what?" he asked.

"Why, setting up in a corner of a shop in town? Do you think someone would let me?"

"I don't see why not," Mama replied.

"Could you introduce me to a dressmaker in town?"

"I could, though I make all my own clothing. Maybe Harl could drive us into town tomorrow, and I'll introduce you to Noralene Fletcher. I've heard tell she's the best seamstress in town."

"Thank you! Thank you so much," Rose exclaimed.

Chapter 11

Rose slept fitfully through the night. She tossed and turned in Hazel's bed. "I will tell Hazel that I can sleep upstairs from now on." She hugged the pillow and smiled as she heard Harl's light snoring echoing in the hallway. She fell asleep, only to be awakened what felt like just a few minutes later by a rooster crowing.

"Might as well get up and tend the fire in the stove," she said.

She dressed in a smart navy blue dress.

In the kitchen, she stoked the embers, poking at them with dry kindling. She soon had a fire going in the cookstove.

She guessed at the measurements of flour, baking powder, salt, butter, and water in a bowl and stirred up dough for biscuits. She kneaded and rolled them out, cutting them into circles using a glass dipped in flour. She greased a cast iron skillet and placed the biscuits in it. Then, she placed the skillet into the oven to bake.

Next, she set the kettle to boiling. Using a coffee grinder, she ground coffee beans and added them to the gray coffeepot on the back of the stove. Pulling the biscuits out of the oven, she turned them out on a plate. Then she fried bacon in the hot skillet and made gravy to go over the biscuits.

Harl rounded the corner of the kitchen doorway. "I don't think it's time to eat just yet." He yawned. "It's only four o'clock in the morning. Mama doesn't get everything going until five."

"I couldn't sleep. Somebody was snoring too loudly," she teased.

"Oh, you heard me then?"

"Your snoring could wake the dead." She laughed.

"I do declare," Hazel said, sliding past her son into the kitchen. "You're as handy as a pocket on a shirt."

Rose laughed. "Thank you. Here, let's sit down and eat while the food is still hot."

"I'll be right back," Harl said, leaving the kitchen and heading toward the sitting room. In a moment, he was back carrying a Bible. "There's something I want to show you."

The three sat at the table, where Rose had set plates, cups, and silverware and bowed their heads. After Hazel prayed, the dishes were passed.

Harl opened the Bible to the Gospel of John chapter three verse sixteen.

"This is one of my favorite verses because it tells us that if we believe in Jesus we won't perish, but will have everlasting life."

Harl read verses sixteen and seventeen and then turned to Rose.

"Have you come to a decision about accepting the Lord in your life?"

Passing the plate of biscuits to Harl, Rose said, "I'm still not sure He'd accept me for all the wrong things I've done."

Hazel passed her the platter with the crispy bacon.

"The Lord'll forgive you if you ask him to. Ain't none of us perfect, even after we accept the Lord into our lives. He keeps on forgiving all our blunders and mistakes, though," Hazel said.

Rose raised her green eyes to meet Hazel's gray ones. Rose smiled and nodded.

"I don't even know how to ask God to be with me."

"Don't you?" Harl asked. "Why it's as easy as anything. It's just like you was talking to us or a good friend. You just tell Him what's on your mind—that you want His Son Jesus as your Savior to forgive your sins and come into your heart—and He will. He's a Gentleman. He waits for us to invite Him in."

Rose bit her lip. "What if . . . what if He doesn't come in? How will I know if He comes in? How will I know if I'm good enough for Him?"

"Ain't none of us good enough. Like the Bible says in Romans chapter five, verse eight, 'While we were yet sinners, Christ died for us.' The Lord knows we are sinners, and He loves us anyway," Hazel said.

"But will he come into my heart?" Rose asked, placing her right hand over her heart.

"He'll come if you ask Him to," Harl replied. "The Bible also says in Romans 10:13 that 'whosoever calls upon the name of the Lord shall be saved.'"

"It all sounds too good to be true," Rose said. "I mean, it's just too easy. It should be harder than just asking God into my heart. It seems like I should have to prove myself worthy of Him."

Harl shook his head, "It is that easy and that hard. You have to bend your pride, but He can help you with that."

"Oh? How?"

"It's a hard thing to admit we need help and that we won't make it to eternity in Heaven with the Lord unless we are willing to bend our will and pride and bring it under the forgiving knowledge of Christ."

Rose licked her lips and looked over at Hazel, who was listening with her head cocked to one side.

"But I don't need help. I'm fine how I am. Yes, I've done bad things in the past. I've lied, stolen, and . . . well, just done some bad things. I don't think God can forgive me if I can't even forgive myself."

"You think you're fine, but you're not. What about eternity? Are you prepared to face the Lord and explain to Him how fine you are?" Harl asked, an edge in his voice.

"Take it easy, Harl," his mother said. "You'll scare her."

Rose finished her breakfast quickly. Placing the fingers of one hand on her temple, she said, "If you will excuse me, I feel a headache coming on."

She stood and placed her empty plate, silverware, and cup in the dishpan to be washed later. Walking to Hazel's bedroom, she stopped and turned around. "Since my ankle is healed, I'd like you to have your room back. I can sleep upstairs from now on." Turning back to the room, she turned the knob and stepped inside.

Lying on the bed, fully dressed, she looked at the white ceiling. "God," she began, "my life hasn't been what it should be. Can you forgive me?" She chewed the inside of her cheek and rolled to her side, listening, as she waited for an answer. She opened and closed her hands as if trying to grasp something. She closed her eyes and was soon asleep.

When she awoke, sunlight was pouring in through the windows at the foot of the bed. Rising with a clear, pain-free head, she adjusted her dress, opened the door, and stepped into the hallway.

Walking into the kitchen, she found Hazel just putting the freshly washed dishes away.

"I guess I timed that just right," Rose said.

Hazel turned and smiled at her guest. "Are you feeling better?"

"Yes, much. My headache is gone."

"Come and take a seat. Let's finish off the coffee from this morning."

Rose pulled two cups off the shelf above the counter and set them on the table with a small pitcher of cream and the sugar bowl.

Hazel poured the coffee and then placed the coffeepot on the back of the stove before sitting across from the younger woman.

Rose doctored her cup with plenty of cream and sugar. Hazel added a bit of cream and sugar to her cup and sipped the hot liquid.

"Seems like there's something on your mind," Rose said, watching Hazel.

"There is," Hazel cleared her throat several times before speaking. "Me and my son were talking after you went in my room. If you are planning on staying on in Harrisville, we'll help you look for employment in one of the seamstress shops in town. We'll introduce you if you like."

"Oh, thank you so much. Any help you can give me would be appreciated."

"We want you to spread your wings and give hat-making a solid try here in town. We're not much into hats, but only because the women around here wear bonnets that they make themselves. Your idea might just catch on."

"And if it doesn't?"

"Then you can find something else to do. You said you were also a seamstress. You might pursue that, too."

"I will need help finding a situation."

"Harl will get word to his sister, Catherine, and Catherine will get word to the seamstresses in town. She and I will introduce you to the two seamstresses, Mrs. Devin Guthrie and Miss Noralene Fletcher. Mrs. Devin Guthrie's name is Bonnie, but don't let her catch you using her first name. She's a proud woman and glad to be married to her man. She wants everyone to know she's a Mrs. Somebody."

"And what about Miss Noralene?"

"Has to work on account of both parents being dead. Died of influenza days apart last year. She's got two younger brothers and two younger sisters to look after and provide for. If I was wanting to set up a hat shop, I'd set it up with her."

"Then there is no need for me to meet Mrs. Devin Guthrie."

"Oh yes, there is. You don't want to be on that woman's bad side. She could make trouble for you—tell folks why they shouldn't be buying hats. No, we'll introduce you to both of them, but we'll just introduce you to Mrs. Devin Guthrie last. Don't want her to get mad."

"How soon will I be meeting them?"

"As soon as Harl finishes the morning chores, he'll hook up the wagon and team; and we'll go see Catherine if you like."

"Yes, I would like that." She drained her cup. "Think I'll go see if I can help Harl with the chores."

"Put your coat on. It's cold out there."

Returning to Hazel's bedroom, Rose opened the wardrobe and pulled out her woolen coat and a pair of calfskin gloves and the hat she had worn at the train station and donned them.

Returning to the kitchen, Rose turned. "How do I look? Warm enough to help with chores?"

Hazel smiled and nodded. "Yes. But maybe a mite too fancy with that hat and calfskin gloves. Here, try on a pair of Harl's old work gloves."

Rose took off the calfskin gloves and replaced them with Harl's oversized work ones.

"No, this won't do," Rose said, removing the gloves. "They're so loose, they'd fall off the minute I started helping with chores."

"If you wear yours, they'll get dirty."

"I'll have to take my chances."

Hazel held the door, and Rose whisked by out into the cold morning. Rose pulled her coat closed and wrapped her arms around her front. Stepping into the barn, she closed the door softly.

Except for the stamping of the mules' feet in their stalls, the barn was quiet.

"Harl? Harl?" she called louder.

"Out here," he called through the open back door of the barn.

Stepping around a fresh pile of straw, Rose followed the sound of his voice, leading her to the open door in the back of the barn. Peering out the door, she saw Harl lifting hay into the feed troughs of the cattle.

Walking through the doorway, she stepped over to him. "What can I do to help?"

Harl turned his head and gazed at her, shooting her a look of surprise. "The chickens haven't been fed yet. You could do that."

"Where's the feed?"

"In the barn. Here, let me finish this, and I'll show you."

Hefting the rest of the hay into the feed troughs of the cattle, Harl turned and walked back inside the barn. He motioned for Rose to follow him and then shut the door.

"Over here. I keep a sack of cracked corn for them," he said, striding toward a large burlap sack. "Here's a small dishpan I put the corn in, then scatter it for the chickens." Looking at her hands, he asked, "Are you going to wear your good gloves to work in?"

"They're all I've got, and yours don't fit."

Pulling a smaller pair of leather work gloves off the shelf above the cracked corn bag, Harl handed them to her. "Put these on. They were my sister's. They should fit."

Rose pulled off her gloves, folded them, and placed them in her coat pocket. She donned the smaller, leather work gloves. "Oh yes, these will do just fine."

Using a metal scoop, Harl scooped cracked corn into the small pan for Rose. Taking the pan from him, Rose's fingers brushed his. She looked up into Harl's eyes and smiled.

Harl gazed down at her. His mouth twitched at the corners. "Once you get done feeding the chickens, go warm up inside while I hitch the mules."

Rose's smile faltered. "All right." Stepping over to the door, she placed her hand on it.

"And don't let the door slam," Harl said. "Please."

"I hadn't planned to." She quietly stepped through the door and out into the barnyard, where she found the chickens pecking and scratching at the hard ground. The ice was gone.

"Here, chick, chick, chick," she called, shaking the pan in her hands. Chickens ran from every corner of the barnyard to her. At first, she tried to scatter the corn using the pan, but that caused the corn to fall in ridges. Instead, she picked up handfuls of the corn and scattered it.

When she finished, she walked back into the barn where Harl was placing the collars on the mules. The dogs were at his feet.

"Come on now, boys, get out of the way," he said.

Rose took off the glove on her right hand and snapped her fingers. "Come here," she called to them. The dogs bounded over to her. Picking them up in both arms, she held the squirming dogs while Harl led the mules out of the barn and over to the wagon.

Rose set the pups down, and they scampered out the door as she pulled the door to the barn closed. She reached down and scratched behind each dog's ear as they waited at her feet. They followed her over to Harl and the mules.

"Almost done here," Harl said, connecting the last of the harness leads to the wagon. "If I was you, I'd change out of those work gloves and put my calfskin ones back on."

"I'll be right back," Rose said. Returning to the barn, she replaced Catherine's old gloves on the shelf above the burlap sack and put her gloves back on.

Rushing out the door, she let it slam. Harl jumped and turned to face her. His eyebrows furrowed, and his mouth was tight. "I told you not to let the door slam. I don't like it. I don't like loud noises, ever since . . . "

"Sorry, it won't happen again," Rose apologized.

Stepping over to the wagon, Rose waited for Harl to stretch out his hand and help her up. "I'll sit in the back on the quilt," she offered.

"I appreciate that."

He stepped into the back of the wagon, around the neatly folded quilt tucked under the shelter of the seat, and moved over to Rose. Holding out his gloved hand, he helped her into the wagon. He held onto her hand a moment longer than was necessary. When she was situated, he jumped down and strode into the house. His mother followed him out, wrapped in a dark blue, woolen coat wearing the hat Rose had given her. He helped her up onto the seat of the wagon, took up the reins, and spoke to the mules, who walked forward toward the orchard.

When they arrived at Samuel and Catherine Harris' home on the outskirts of town, Clair, dressed in a pink frock, and her new puppy ran out the door to meet them.

"Uncle Harl, Grandma," she called, stopping when she saw Rose, who smiled warmly at the child.

Screwing up her face, she pinched her brows together.

"This is Miss Henderson," Harl said. "You remember her from when we went and picked out the puppies don't you?"

Clair smiled. "Yes," she said. Climbing up on the wheel, she peered into the back of the wagon. "You didn't bring your puppies?"

"No, we left them at home," Harl said.

"Oh, Clair! Get down from there. You'll get your dress dirty," Catherine cried, hurrying to help the child down. Brushing off the front of Clair's dress, she looked up as Hazel climbed down. Harl held his mother's gloved hand until she had both feet on the ground. He climbed down and offered his hand to Rose, who accepted his offer of help.

Placing her right foot on the wheel hub, she swung her left leg over and out. Losing her balance, she let go of Harl's hand and fell. Harl, as quick as lightning, grabbed her torso and held it against him to brace her fall. She relaxed in his strong arms, a little smile niggling at the corners of her mouth.

"Thank you, Harl," she said. "You saved me."

"Are you all right?" Harl asked, concern in his voice. His face turned red, and he quickly removed his arms from around her waist.

"Yes, I'm fine," Rose said, straightening her coat and hat.

"Why do I have the pleasure of your company today?" Catherine asked her mother, breaking the awkwardness.

"We—" Hazel started, but Catherine interrupted.

"Let's not talk out here. Come in. Come on, Clair and Sunny." Catherine patted her leg.

Clair and the dog turned and bounded back into the house.

"Sunny?" Harl echoed.

"The dog. Clair named her."

Walking through the open door, Rose looked around her. The light beige-painted foyer held a hat rack with a man's black felt hat. A black umbrella stood against one wall. Off the foyer to the right was a tidy parlor with two overstuffed chairs, a tête-à-tête, and a rocking chair—all upholstered in rich green tones. Two oak tables draped with fringed, white covers and oil lamps stood on either side of the tête-à-tête. Past the parlor, to her right and further up the hallway, was the dining room. A large, oblong, oak table and six chairs stood as the centerpiece of the room. Rose could just make out the edge of a grand, ornate oak buffet in one corner of the room. A door—leading to the kitchen, she suspected—was next to the buffet. Down the hallway to the left was a closed door. *Probably a bedroom.*

Catherine caught Rose's eye as she swung her gaze back to her hostess. Catherine smiled. "What do you think of my home?"

"It's lovely. Just lovely."

"Thank you. I have grand plans for it." Catherine said, leading the way into the parlor.

As Rose stepped into the room onto the plush oriental rug, she gazed around her.

This home, much like Hazel's, was Rose's idea of what a house should be like—comfortable and pleasing.

"Would you like a tour?"

"Yes, that would be nice," Rose said.

Catherine led Rose through her home. Rose drank in every detail from the parlor to the oak buffet to the bedrooms in the back of the house and upstairs. Catherine certainly was a neat housekeeper. Every room Rose entered was spit-spot clean and organized.

Returning to the parlor, Rose saw that Harl sat in one of the overstuffed chairs, while his mother sat across from him in the rocking chair. Clair and the dog bounded over to Hazel.

Clair squirmed up onto her grandmother's lap and started rocking her little body. "Rock me, Grandma."

"No dogs in the parlor," Catherine said, clapping her hands and pointing. "Take Sunny outside and go play in the backyard."

When the child and dog had gone, Catherine gestured to the tête-à-tête for Rose to sit. Catherine sat opposite her in one of the other overstuffed chairs. "Now, what brings you to my home on this fine day?"

"We would like you to get word to the seamstresses in town that Rose here would like to join Noralene and be her hatmaker."

"Oh, what an idea! Are you a milliner then?"

"Yes, I made up my hat and your mother's, too."

Rose removed the hat pin from her hat and handed it to Catherine to examine. Hazel removed her hat as well and handed it to Harl, who jumped up and took the hat to his sister. She examined both hats carefully before handing them back to Harl to redistribute them to Rose and her mother.

"How long have you been a milliner?" Catherine asked.

"I apprenticed with a seamstress and milliner in town for a year." Rose dipped her head. "I was still apprenticing with her when I ran away."

"What's this?" Catherine asked, leaning forward. "Why did you run away?"

Rose clasped her hands in her lap and sighed heavily. "My father was trying to marry me off to his apprentice in my father's blacksmith shop. His apprentice was a wicked man. I didn't want to—*couldn't*—marry him."

Rose watched as Catherine looked to her brother and then mother's faces.

"She can't go home to Michigan," Mama explained. "We're trying to help her get a start down here."

"But why Noralene and not Mrs. Guthrie?" Catherine asked.

"We thought Noralene would be the better choice, since Mrs. Guthrie can be a jealous sort," Hazel said.

"Yes, well, it might be better, then, if Rose were to be a hatmaker for both ladies. Mrs. Guthrie wouldn't like Noralene getting a leg up on her," Catherine stated.

"Hmm, I didn't think of that."

"It might be best to have Rose work at Mrs. Guthrie's place—or at least give her the option of turning her down first."

"What do you think of that, Rose?" Hazel asked.

"I don't know. I'll have to give it some thought after I meet the lady."

"We thought since you were the preacher's wife, you might have some pull with them—and that you could introduce Rose to the ladies."

"I would love to."

"How soon do you think you could introduce me?"

"What about this afternoon? I have some shopping to do in town, anyway. We could go now if Mama could stay and watch Clair."

"Of course."

Rose looked at Harl, who cleared his throat. "I'll drive you if you like."

"It's not that far, and a walk would do us good. Give us a chance to get to know one another better," Catherine said. "You don't mind the walk, do you?"

Rose shook her head. "As long as it isn't far."

Catherine clapped her hands and grinned. "Good, let's go." Standing, she turned to her mother. "There's a pot of soup beans simmering on the back burner and cornbread in the warming oven. If Claire gets hungry, you can give her that."

"Will do."

Rose stood, waiting for Catherine's direction.

"Let me just go get my wrap and basket, and we'll be on our way."

When Catherine returned, she clasped Claire's hand in one of hers. "You be good for Grandma."

"I will."

Catherine adjusted her gloves and turned to Rose. She hooked her arm around Rose's elbow.

"Shall we?"

Rose smiled and nodded.

As they walked, Catherine pointed out various trees to Rose. "Black pine, poplar, dogwood, redbud—come springtime, the hills will be ablaze with color."

"It sounds wonderful. I can't wait until spring. Being from Michigan, I'm used to the cold, but I don't like it very much."

"Oh! Michigan? What is that like?"

"It has rolling, green hills in the spring and maple trees that some people tap for their sap to make maple syrup. It's quite good. It takes buckets of sap just to make one gallon. Mama used to fix pancakes every Sunday morning, and we'd have maple syrup on them. If she didn't have store-bought syrup, she'd make do by boiling down brown sugar in water. That was good, too."

"That's how I make our syrup—by boiling down brown sugar in water. I also add a little bit of vanilla for flavor."

"We have an abundance of ponds and lakes that freeze over in winter, which are great for ice fishing and skating—though that is a sport I do not wish to try. I don't like the feeling of sliding on ice."

"No, I can see your point."

"The hills are great for sledding. That is a sport that I have enjoyed many times since I was a child. There's a big hill where we live in town that draws families from the area with their sleds."

"It sounds lovely, but what about you? Tell me about you."

"I'm twenty-three. I was set to marry a man I didn't love because my father wanted me to. The man wasn't very nice either—well, at least to animals. So, I left him waiting at the altar and skedaddled down here that morning."

"That was a quick trip from Michigan."

"I came by rail, and it took me almost a week to get here what with all the stops at various depots."

"Why did you decide to come here?"

"Oh, you don't know." Rose bowed her head. "I read an advertisement asking for a bride. I had corresponded with the man for a few months before deciding to cut things short and come on down here."

"Who was that lucky man?"

"Unlucky, you mean. Cletus Tooth."

Catherine gasped, stopped, and removed her arm from Rose's. "What a horrid man! Did you know he tried to destroy the schoolhouse when I was the teacher? Or that he spent time in jail for his part in busting out the windows?"

Rose felt her cheeks burn under Catherine's gaze. "I didn't know any of that. Your brother and mother didn't mention it. They only said he was a scoundrel and to be thankful that he decided not to meet me at the station after I telegraphed him my arrival time."

Catherine replaced her arm through Rose's and tugged her along. "Well, they are right about that. He *is* a scoundrel." After a few moments of silence, Catherine asked, "What do you think of my brother?"

"Harl?" Rose felt her face burn. "He's a dear, sweet man. Some woman will be very lucky when she turns his head." Oh, how she wished she could be that woman.

"I saw the way he looked at you in the parlor when you weren't looking. I would say that woman is you."

It was Rose's turn to stop and gasp. She placed her hands on either side of her burning face.

"He looked at me? How?"

Catherine smiled and looped her arms around Rose's elbow. "Let's just say, he's smiling more than I've ever seen him smile. And he's not as jumpy."

"Really?" Rose grinned.

"Yes, really."

A little ahead of Rose and Catherine, an elderly woman handed a large basket up to a handsome man with dark hair. She gripped his hand and stepped into a carriage in front of a large, ornate home.

"Good day, Mother Harris," Catherine called.

The woman reached out a gloved hand and offered it to Catherine. "Good day, Catherine. Who is your friend?"

"This is Miss Rose Henderson. She's new in town. She plans to open a hat shop in one of the seamstress' shops."

"What a splendid idea! Welcome to Harrisville, Miss Henderson. Let me introduce my son, Benjamin Harris."

The dark-haired man tipped his hat and smiled at the pair of women. "Welcome," he said.

"Where are you going?" Catherine asked.

"My son Caleb's wife, Lucy, is feeling poorly. Thought we'd take them some soup for their dinner and see what I can do to help," Mrs. Harris said.

"We don't mean to keep you," Catherine said.

Mrs. Harris smiled. "Thank you, dear."

Benjamin spoke to the horse, and it started forward.

When they were out of earshot, Catherine explained. "That was my mother-in-law. Her sons look similar."

"You were the schoolteacher in town?"

"Yes."

"Why did you stop?"

"Because a married woman cannot teach. Only single ladies may teach. It's the law."

"But so many children are now going without an education because of that law."

"When the board finds a suitable replacement, they'll get school started again. Until then, I've instructed the students to keep reading their books and working the problems as best they can."

"How did you become the teacher?"

"I was voted in on a trial basis by the school board. I went to school for it. Well, I only took a semester of a normal course at Millersburg Female College in Georgetown."

"Why only one semester?" Rose hung on every word.

"Two words: John Reed. My fiancé came home after the war. Well, not right after. He spent some time recuperating in a hospital in Tennessee."

"Oh, he was wounded?"

"Yes, took a shot to his leg." Catherine stopped outside of a shop with rich, green velvet curtains tied back with matching silk ribbons. A white muslin dress was displayed on a wicker body form in the window. "Here we are. This is Mrs. Devin Guthrie's shop." Catherine stepped over to the door and opened it. A bell fastened to the top of the door tinkled.

A short, plump woman with graying hair and wearing a lime green dress strolled out from a room in the back of the shop. The door she came through was framed by identical green velvet curtains tied back with matching silk ribbons. Mrs. Devin Guthrie wore a bemused expression on her face and looked at the women through her eyelashes.

"Welcome to my little shop," Mrs. Guthrie said. Then seeing Catherine, she said, "Oh, Mrs. Harris! This is a welcome surprise. I was wondering when you would find time for a visit. I thought the sermon on Sunday was wonderful, just wonderful. And Rev. Harris delivered it with such gusto."

"Thank you," Catherine said, getting a word in edgewise. "Rev. Harris will be pleased to hear your compliment." Turning to Rose, Catherine said, "Mrs. Devin Guthrie, I'd like you to meet a friend and neighbor. This is Miss Rose Henderson."

Rose felt an overwhelming urge to curtsey but held herself in check waiting for Mrs. Guthrie to speak first.

"My dear." Mrs. Guthrie held out her hand and gazed with half-closed eyes down her nose at Rose. "Any friend of Rev. and Catherine Harris is a friend of mine."

Rose looked at the offered hand and then at Catherine, who nodded her head. Rose shook Mrs. Guthrie's hand. Just as quickly, the older woman snatched her hand back and clapped.

"Now, what can I help you ladies with today?" Mrs. Guthrie stepped around behind a small, glass counter with a display case. Boxes of the finest calfskin gloves lined the display. She picked up a pencil and poised it over a bill of sale book.

Catherine held out her hand to stop the older woman. "We didn't come in to buy anything."

"Oh," Mrs. Guthrie said, disappointment obvious in her tone.

"We came to give you a business proposition."

Mrs. Guthrie smiled and motioned to a sitting area where three overstuffed green chairs and a table sat in the middle of the circle. There was a large, round oriental rug with shades of green throughout on the floor.

The older woman brought her pencil and book and eased herself into a chair.

"Now, what is your business proposition? Wait, first we should have some tea. The kettle is hot. I'll be back in a moment."

Catherine held out her hand to stop her, but Mrs. Guthrie ignored her and rushed out of the room.

Catherine and Rose exchanged glances while waiting for the older woman to return.

"Here we are," Mrs. Guthrie said, holding a tray with a white teapot with tiny, green ivy vines on it, three china cups with the same green ivy pattern, a white sugar bowl, and creamer. A plate of thin cookies sat on top of four small plates with tiny spoons between the plates. Near the chairs sat a potbellied stove. A black kettle puffed steam into the air.

Placing the tray on the table, the older woman smoothed her hair and eased herself into the chair across from her guests. Taking up her pencil and book again, she was poised to write. Tilting her head back and gazing at them down her nose with half-closed eyes, she waited.

Catherine licked her lips. "Rose—er, Miss Henderson—is a milliner by trade. She would like to set up a corner here in your shop and offer your patrons her skills."

Rose held her breath. Mrs. Guthrie's eyes widened, and she dropped her gaze and peered at them over her glasses. "Where are my manners? How would you both like your tea?" She began pouring dark tea into the three cups and passed them out. Holding out the creamer, she offered it to Catherine and then to Rose. Both declined. Holding out the sugar bowl with its delicate-looking spoon, Rose took it and scooped two heaping spoonfuls of sugar into her cup.

Mrs. Guthrie handed them each a plate, which they balanced on their laps, and passed the plate of cookies. Rose took two. Catherine took one. Mrs. Guthrie took one and eyed Rose's plate with two.

After sipping the hot tea, Catherine asked, "Well, what do you think about our proposition?"

Mrs. Guthrie cleared her throat several times, took a gulp of hot tea, and gazed at Rose. "I would need to see a finished product to know if it is worthy of being in my shop. Do you have a sample I might see?"

"Just mine," Rose said, removing it from her head.

Mrs. Guthrie's eyes widened as she took the hat. "You made this?"

"Yes, I used a lot of trim on it, as you can see."

Mrs. Guthrie turned the hat over and over in her hand. "This really is quite exquisite. Could you make up one exactly like this, only in green?"

"I try not to duplicate my hats. I could make one like it, but not exactly. I think each hat should be unique, like its wearer."

"Yes, I see your point," she said, handing the hat back to Rose, who replaced it on her head.

Mrs. Guthrie took a large bite of cookie and a long sip of tea. Setting her plate back on the tray, she asked, "Have you been to Miss Noralene Fletcher's shop yet?"

"No."

"Ah, I see," the older woman tilted her head back and gazed at Rose through half-closed eyes. "Would I have exclusive rights to your designs?"

Rose glanced at Catherine. "What do you mean exclusive?" Rose asked hesitantly.

"Well, I wouldn't want you making hats with just anyone." She sniffed. "I would want your designs to come out of my shop and my shop only," she sniffed.

"All right. Yes, I could do that," Rose said.

"Fine, let me just write up the terms of our agreement in my book; and if you are in accord, we'll both sign it."

"Mrs. Devin Guthrie, we appreciate your quick response, but we wanted to see both shops. Let Rose make up her mind once she's seen them both," Catherine interjected.

"Whatever for? Mine is completely superior to that Miss Noralene Fletcher's shop. Why, she doesn't even have curtains in her windows."

Rose leaned forward and smiled at Mrs. Guthrie. "How soon could you draw up the agreement?"

"Now, that's more like it," Mrs. Guthrie said, chuckling. "It will just take me a moment. More tea?"

"Yes, please." Rose glanced over her shoulder at Catherine, who had a pained look on her face.

Mrs. Devin Guthrie scribbled a few words in the book and handed it and the pencil to Rose, who read it. "I, Miss Rose Henderson, do solemnly swear to work in Mrs. Devin Guthrie's Shop and none other. Signed."

Rose had the pencil poised over the paper ready to sign when Catherine held out her hand. "What about wages?"

"Oh, my dear, I'm giving her space to set up shop here with my clientele. I'm sure she will charge them appropriately."

"But once word of this gets out, wouldn't it be nice to offer her some compensation?"

"Once word gets out, she will have plenty of compensation from my customers and their repeat business."

"Rose? What do you say to that?" Catherine asked.

"I'll sign it," Rose said.

"Yes, but can you abide by it?"

"I will." And with that, Rose signed the paper.

Mrs. Guthrie's smile widened, and she ate the rest of the cookies quickly.

"When should I start?"

"How about tomorrow?"

Rose smiled and raised her teacup to her lips. "All right," she said.

Chapter 14

The next day, Rose was up before the crack of dawn. Her skirt rustled on the stairs as she swooped down them and into the kitchen. She'd have breakfast ready by the time Hazel and Harl got up.

As she passed Harl's room, she heard his soft snoring through the closed door.

In the kitchen, she stoked the embers in the stove and added some dry kindling. Soon, she had a hot fire going. She lifted the coffeepot. It was light. She'd have to add some water to it. A large, gray kettle sat on the back of the stove. Hazel kept it filled with water that simmered all night. Rose wanted fresh water.

Donning her wool wrap, she walked outside with the empty coffeepot in hand. She marched over to the well, let the bucket down, and pulled up fresh water. Dumping half of the contents of the bucket into the pot, she poured the rest back down into the well. A chilly, crisp wind ruffled her hair as she pulled her wrap tighter around her shoulders and neck. With one hand, she held the coffeepot; the other held her wrap tight against her.

When she arrived back inside, Harl was seated at the table reading a wrinkled newspaper. He glanced up at her. Looking back at the newspaper in his hands, he smiled.

"What?" Rose asked, reading his smile as a comment on her appearance. She strode across the room and placed the coffeepot on the hottest spot on the stove. Smoothing her hair, she turned and found Harl studying her. Frowning, she placed her hands on her hips. "Mr. Adams, why are you staring at me so?"

Harl lifted his shoulders and shook his head, ducking behind his newspaper.

Rose stepped over to him and grabbed the paper out of his hands. "What's so funny?" She felt the color in her cheeks rising.

Harl shook his head and grinned. "I was just thinking how nice you look this morning."

Rose smoothed her hair and scowled. "Are you making fun of me?"

"No," Harl said, shaking his head soberly. "It's the truth. Isn't today the day you start at Mrs. Guthrie's shop?"

Rose relaxed. "Yes, it is. Here I was going to surprise you with breakfast, but I'm the one being surprised."

"How so?"

"You weren't supposed to be up yet."

"I always get up this early. Besides, a cold gust of wind woke me. I knew either somebody went out the door or came in. I wanted to make sure everything was fine."

"Oh, I didn't think anyone would notice if I got some fresh water for the coffeepot."

Harl nodded. "Well, I did."

Turning back to the stove, Rose placed a large cast iron skillet on it, dipped her chin, and smiled to herself. *He thinks I look nice.*

Hazel's door opened, and she stepped out fully dressed.

"What's all the commotion out here?"

"Oh, I'm sorry. I didn't mean to wake you, too."

"I felt the door open and thought something was wrong."

"No, nothing is wrong," Rose said. "I just needed fresh water for the coffeepot."

Hazel stepped to the stove and lifted the lid on the large kettle. "You've got plenty of water right here. All you had to do was dip it out."

"But that's been simmering all night. I wanted fresh, cold water for the coffee this morning."

"Suit yourself," Hazel said, replacing the lid.

Rose studied Hazel. "You're not angry, are you?"

"Not at all. Think I'll take a lantern and get us some fresh eggs," she said.

"It's quite chilly out there," Rose said. "Let me go instead."

"All right," Hazel said, handing Rose the empty egg basket and lighting a lantern.

In the chicken coop, Rose carried the lamp and basket in one hand and felt around under the chickens for eggs. Fourteen eggs and several pecks later, Rose returned to the kitchen.

Hazel was standing at the stove turning bacon with a fork.

"Do you want me to do that?"

"No, but you can set the table."

Rose glanced at Harl, who was gazing at her with a smirk on his face.

Furrowing her brows, she pulled plates down off the shelf and set the table around Harl and his newspaper. Noticing the date, she saw that it was two weeks prior.

"Why are you reading an old newspaper, Harl?"

"I didn't get all the way through it last time."

Rose swallowed and blinked at him.

Harl smirked. "Got something in your eye?"

"No," Rose said, placing her hands on her hips.

"Come sit down," he offered.

"I'd rather help your mother dish up the food."

"Almost done," Hazel said. "Harl, put that newspaper away."

Harl folded and tucked the newspaper behind his back in the chair. He ate quickly and then donned his coat, hat, and gloves and whisked himself out the door.

In the barn, Harl fed the mules and brought Brownie in to milk her. He whistled as he worked and thought of Rose. She had stopped lying and was truthful with his sister during their walk into town, which Catherine had relayed to him when they returned.

Rose hadn't seen Miss Fletcher's dress shop. She'd told him she had chosen to work in Mrs. Guthrie's shop without seeing the other one. Mrs. Guthrie could be tough, but Rose could be tough, too. She hadn't gotten this far south without fortitude and knowing a thing or two.

As Harl threw hay out of the second-floor door in the barn down to the waiting cattle, his mind wandered back to Rose; and his mouth crinkled up at the edges. She still hadn't given her life to Christ, though. What would it take for her to bend her strong will and give her heart to the Lord? There was nothing he could think of that would make her do it. All he could hope for was a change of heart and a miracle.

His heart was starting to flutter anytime he was around her, but she wasn't saved yet. How could he be falling for this woman, who refused to give her heart to the Lord? It should be so easy for her to bow her knee and head to the Lordship of Jesus, but why wasn't it? Many people believe that just because they are born in a Christian nation or go to church, they are a follower of Christ; but there's more to it than that. Harl bowed his head and leaned on the pitchfork in his hand.

"Lord, what will it take for Rose to give her life to You? Change her heart and her mind about You and what it means to be a Christian." He raised his face and rubbed at his chin with his work gloves. Looking out at the acres of land he had inherited from his father, he nodded his head and replaced the pitchfork by the door before closing it.

"Oh, Lord, let Rose find You. May she want You." *As much as I want her.* But he didn't dare confess that out loud to himself or anyone else, not even to the mules below him.

"Here," Hazel said, thrusting a basket covered by a linen napkin into Rose's hands.

Rose lifted the napkin and peered inside. A small loaf of bread, a small jar of apple butter, the rest of the bacon from breakfast, and a knife were nestled into the basket.

"What's all this?"

"You'll need something for your lunch, and I know that woman has a hankering for my apple butter or anything sweet. Just wanted you to get off to a good start at your new job."

Rose smiled and cocked her head to one side. "Thank you. Do you think Harl will take me and my trunk into town?"

"Your trunk? Why your trunk?"

"Because that is where I keep the hats I want to make up. I keep loads of supplies in there, along with my dresses and such."

"I think he will. You just go ask him and see if he won't."

Rose buttoned her coat, donned her hat and gloves, and set off for the barn. A strong wind blew between the mountains, causing her to grasp the two combs which held her braided bun into place on her head. Running to the barn, she threw open the door, which caught in the wind and slammed against the barn.

"Harl!" she yelled. "Goodness gracious!" She tugged at the door and pulled it closed behind her. Harl was at her side in an instant.

"I'm so sorry the door slammed. I couldn't help it. The wind took it out of my hands." She fussed with her hair and combs as she tried to smooth stubborn strands of red hair back into place.

Harl grinned. Rose, seeing his face, fumed. "I suppose this is funny to you?"

Harl lowered his gaze and shook his head. "Not particularly. I'm done with the chores if you came to help."

"No, I came to ask you if you would take me into town. I need to take my trunk with me as well because it has all my milliner wares in it."

The corners of his mouth ticked up. "Of course, I would."

Harl eased the door open, holding tightly to the wooden knob. Rose stepped around him and back into the blustery wind. Grabbing the two combs with one hand, which threatened to dislodge from the thick bun again, Rose lifted her skirts a fraction of an inch and ran to the house. Harl ran beside her.

"I don't care how unladylike I may seem right now. I don't want my hair torn to pieces in this wind. Is it usually so windy this time of year?"

"Can be," Harl said, opening the door for her.

"Whew!" Rose stepped over the threshold and into the warm kitchen, where Hazel sat peeling potatoes.

"Goodness!" Hazel exclaimed. "You two look as if some haint is after ya."

Rose looked from Harl to Hazel. "What's a haint?"

Hazel paused her peeling and grinned. "A haint is a spirit that ain't in the ground or one that's not gone on to the great beyond."

"Oh, you mean a ghost," Rose said.

"Yes."

"I'll get your trunk," Harl said, moving past Rose.

As soon as Harl was out of the kitchen, Rose wound her braided bun down. "Would you happen to have some combs I could put my hair up with? I need more than just these two in all this wind."

"Let me see." Hazel rose and went into her bedroom. Rose smoothed her hair and wound it back up into a bun as Hazel motioned for her to come into her bedroom.

In the room, Hazel handed Rose two pretty tortoise shell combs. "I keep these for special occasions. They belonged to my mother. Here, let me."

Hazel pinned Rose's bun with the combs and placed her hands on the younger woman's shoulders. Gazing into the mirror over the bureau, she smiled. "There we go."

Rose touched the now-secure bun. "Thank you."

The two women walked back into the kitchen, where Harl was placing the trunk down by the table.

"All set?" he asked.

"Yes," Rose said. "My trunk should be quite a bit lighter now that the rock is out of it and I've hung my dresses up on pegs in the wall in the upstairs bedroom."

"It is. Let me go get the team ready. I'll come get you when it's time to go."

Rose nodded. Removing her coat, she hung it on a peg next to the door where Harl always hung his. Moving to the table, she sat across from Hazel. "Here, let me help you."

Hazel got up, grabbed a gray enamel pan, placed several potatoes in it, and gave it back to Rose with a knife. The two women sat in silence peeling potatoes, plopping them into a pot with water, and listening to the wind howling around the house.

Rose shuttered. "That wind sounds so forlorn."

"It'll die down after a while. At least, it's not storming."

Harl bounded in the door. "We're ready."

Rose dried her hands on a cotton sack that Hazel pushed toward her. Donning her coat, hat, and gloves, she followed Harl to the wagon. He helped her up into it and climbed up after her. With one hand, she held her hat on her head and, with the other, held onto the seat.

Harl jingled the reins. The mules moved forward. Harl hurried the mules as wind ruffled his hair. The wind didn't allow for much conversation, so they rode in comfortable silence.

When they arrived at Mrs. Guthrie's shop in town, Harl helped Rose down. Rose, carrying the small basket of food, ran ahead of him into the shop to get out of the wind.

"My goodness!" Mrs. Guthrie exclaimed, holding her hand over her heart. "What a day this is. We haven't seen wind like this since the winter of '67."

Harl carried Rose's trunk in and stood waiting.

"Oh, my dear. Here. We'll put it in the back room."

Harl followed Mrs. Guthrie into the room in the back, where he found a clear corner and set the trunk down.

Rose followed. Lining the walls of the back room were bolts of every color fabric. Rose touched the fabric and marveled at the choices. Turning, she looked at Mrs. Guthrie.

"I do love my fabrics. You can never have too many. You never know when someone will come in and want a summer yellow or canary green dress in the dead of winter. Yes, well, that hasn't happened yet, but I pride myself on stocking more exotic hues of fabric than Mr. Grant and his wife, Tippy, at the general store."

"Well, I'll leave you ladies to it then," Harl said, bowing out of the room. Turning back, he asked, "What time should I be here to pick you up?"

Rose glanced at Mrs. Guthrie.

"I would say three o'clock should be fine. It's such a windy day. I don't expect much business," Mrs. Guthrie said. "Unless Uella Perkins stops by. She said she was hankering for some new dresses when I saw her earlier this week at church. Poor thing. Can't buy off the shelf. Has to have her dresses made special on account of her height. Tall as a stalk of wheat and just as thin."

"Yes, well, I'll see you then, Rose," Harl said, doffing his hat. Then he hurried out the door. Rose watched as he climbed up onto the wagon seat and hurried the mules along.

When Rose turned back to Mrs. Guthrie, the woman was smiling. "You've been staying with the Adamses for a while now."

"Yes, it's been a few weeks. They are very nice. Mrs. Adams sent some apple butter, a loaf of bread, and the leftover bacon from breakfast for my lunch."

"Apple butter, did you say?"

"Yes."

"Oh, Mrs. Adams' apple butter is in a class all by itself. What do you say I pour us some tea, and we'll have some?" Mrs. Guthrie's eyes were wide, and her eyebrows arched. She grinned and then looked down her nose at Rose.

"Of course, we can." Rose set the basket on a nearby table while the older woman rummaged through a cupboard under the stacks of fabric for a pretty, green china teapot. Pulling open another cupboard, she took out a small, brown sack and a spoon. She scooped out dark tea leaves and placed them in the pot. Balancing the teapot in one hand, she motioned for Rose to grab two teacups and saucers next to the bag of tea, which she replaced on the shelf.

Rose followed her as the woman marched into the front of the store, where the small potbellied stove stood. Mrs. Guthrie sat down in an overstuffed green chair across from the stove. She motioned for Rose to do the same on the other side of the table.

Rose sat and pulled off her calfskin gloves and placed them in her coat pocket. The heat from the stove was oppressive. She took off her jacket as well.

"You'll find you won't get cold in my shop. No, you won't. I like to keep plenty of wood in my stove at all times. Mr. Guthrie keeps me stocked with wood. He's a good husband."

Rose bit her lip and tried to smile. "Where should I hang my things?"

"There's a few pegs in the back room. Choose one."

Rose took her coat and placed it on a peg.

"You'll find I like to keep my shop neat and tidy," Mrs. Guthrie called. "Do you want to slice the bread, or should I?"

"I will." Rose cut thick slices of bread and smeared ample amounts of apple butter on them. Digging through the cupboards, she found two small plates and placed the slices on them. Returning to the front room, she handed Mrs. Guthrie a plate.

"Oh my. This is a treat," Mrs. Guthrie exclaimed excitedly before taking a large bite out of the apple butter-smeared bread. "Mmm. Tell Mrs. Adams her apple butter is divine—just divine."

Rose hitched up one side of her mouth into a half-smile. "I will." Blowing on the tea in her cup, she sipped carefully.

"So then, tell me about your stay with the Adamses."

Rose sputtered. Regaining her composure, she asked, "What would you like to know?"

"You know, Harl Adams is single," Mrs. Guthrie said, trying to hide a grin behind her tea cup.

"Yes."

"Any sparks flying between you two?"

Rose set her teacup down on the table next to her slice of bread. The audacity of this woman asking such a nosy question! Rose studied the backs of her hands, wondering how she should answer, feeling her face grow warm.

"Well, it's no matter. It's all over town that Mrs. Uella Perkins has set her cap at him for some time now."

"Oh, I didn't know."

"Didn't you? The way that woman looks at him is like a cat looking at a mouse."

Rose wondered what business it was of hers to know that there was another woman besides her who thought about Harl Adams as more than a friend. She opened her mouth to say something, but Mrs. Guthrie cut her off.

"I've been watching Uella at church. She doesn't see me watching, but I see her sneaking sideways glances at Harl Adams, though I have no idea how Mr. Adams feels about her. The poor dear. She lost her husband of three years to influenza last spring. Came through the war without a scratch, only to be cut down in sickness. It's a shame, really. They were such a happy couple. Made for each other."

Rose bit her tongue. She wanted to burst out and tell Mrs. Guthrie to hush; but she didn't dare offend her, or she would jeopardize her position in Mrs. Guthrie's shop.

"Something on your mind?" Mrs. Guthrie asked over the rim of her teacup.

"No," Rose lied. There was plenty on her mind, and what a busybody Mrs. Guthrie was turning out to be. Why she couldn't leave Harl Adams out of the conversation, which was turning out to be more one-sided than she liked, she didn't know. All this talk about her handsome, eligible friend was making her uncomfortable. She glanced up to see a wicked smirk on Mrs. Guthrie's lips.

"You've been staying up at the Adamses' farm for quite some time."

"Just a few weeks. Until my ankle healed."

"Oh yes. You sprained it when you tried to cross the street out front of Garlin Moore's restaurant and hotel. I heard Harl actually took you there himself. Put you up for the night."

Rose's palms were starting to sweat—and not just from the heat of the stove. Mrs. Guthrie was making her uncomfortable. "Where did you hear that?"

"From Garlin Moore, of course. We business owners talk, and it's not every day that a mail-order bride comes to town. You know, with you working here, you might like a change of scenery. If you like, we have a room in our home that we let out. It might be better for business if you moved into town. That way, Harl wouldn't have to drive you in each and every day."

"I hadn't thought of that. You are right. It would be better for me to be in town—closer to the shop so I don't have to rely on Mr. Adams to drive me every day. But how much would it cost me?"

"We could work that out. You'd get room and board and a little stipend on the side, as long as you work for me here and provide my customers with bonnets and such. How does that sound?"

"It sounds wonderful and practical."

Rose saw Mrs. Guthrie eyeing her slice of bread with apple butter.

"I'm really not very hungry. Breakfast wasn't too long ago. Why don't you have mine?" she offered, gesturing to the slice of bread.

Mrs. Guthrie looked down her nose at Rose and then at the bread. "Don't mind if I do."

With Mrs. Guthrie's mouth now full, Rose seized her chance to talk and change the subject. "I certainly hope the people of Harrisville like my hat designs. I could show you a few."

"Mmm," Mrs. Guthrie said and nodded, shoving the rest of the bread in her mouth.

"I'll just go unpack, and then I'll model some of the ones I already have made up."

Mrs. Guthrie raised her teacup as if toasting Rose's idea. Taking her leave from the room, Rose stepped into the back room and over to her trunk.

Lifting the lid, she peered inside at the selection of done-up hats and bonnets. Some of the hats would be too outlandish for a town this small, but the bonnets might strike a chord with the community. She chose a hard-sided pink and tan bonnet with a silk ribbon tie.

Donning the hat, she turned and caught her image in the full-length mirror. Everyone in Chelsea—well, almost everyone—had wanted one of her hard-sided pink and tan bonnets with silk ribbon ties once they saw her sauntering around town in one. Surely, Mrs. Guthrie would approve of her design.

Stepping out from the green-curtained back room, Rose twirled slowly. The loose ends of the bonnet fluttered as she turned. Pulling the ribbons close under her double chin, she tied them into a bow.

Mrs. Guthrie set down her teacup and clapped. "Oh, you are lovely. Just simply lovely. And that is all your creation?"

Rose smiled and nodded, grateful for the older woman's approval of her work.

Mrs. Guthrie held out her hands for the bonnet. Rose untied it and handed it over.

Turning it slowly in her hands, the older woman smiled. "This is some fine work. Very fine work. I think the ladies of this town will greatly admire what you have to offer."

Rose's face glowed with pleasure over the compliment. "Wait, I have more."

"This will be just the thing to place on the dress form in the window. My shop is the only one with such a lovely display, don't you think?" The older woman stood and marched over to the white linen dress on the form in the green-curtained window next to the front door. She carefully placed the bonnet on top of the dress on the neck of the form.

"There," she said, stepping back to look at Rose's handiwork as if it were her own. "I think the ribbons should be tied, though. Don't you?"

"Yes, definitely. I will go get another of my hats to show you," Rose said.

In the backroom, Rose pulled a velvet hat trimmed with feathers from her trunk. Placing it on her head, she cocked it skillfully to one side.

When she stepped back into the front room, Mrs. Guthrie clapped her hands again. "What wonderful wares you have! I wasn't sure about having a milliner in my shop, but you are proving that your bonnets and hats will only complement what I already have or can make. Do come sit down and have some more tea."

Smiling, Rose obeyed. She did not remove the hat from her head but sat and enjoyed a steaming cup of tea.

Mrs. Guthrie raised her cup. "To our lucrative endeavors."

"Here, here."

A few hours later, when the wind had died down, Rose had retired to the back room, where she sat in an overstuffed green chair skillfully sewing a bonnet. Rose felt a gust of wind when the bell over the door sounded, alerting her that someone had arrived. Pausing momentarily, needle poised over her work, she cocked her head to one side, listening.

"Well, bless me," Mrs. Guthrie said. "If it isn't Mrs. Uella Perkins. Miss Henderson, come meet our customer."

Rose stood, placed the hat on the chair, and walked out into the front of the store.

Uella Perkins was tall and thin, just as Mrs. Guthrie had described her. But what Rose wasn't expecting was how pretty she was with her light brown hair, petite nose, and soft gray eyes. Uella wore a heavy, black wool coat over her dress.

"Mrs. Perkins, this is the town's newest resident and milliner, Miss Rose Henderson."

Uella turned toward Rose and smiled. Her teeth were pretty, straight, and white. "I'm pleased to make your acquaintance," Mrs. Perkins said. Her voice was soft and demure.

Rose nodded. "Pleased as well."

"I have some new fabric I want your opinion about," Mrs. Guthrie said. "Let me take your coat."

Uella shucked off her coat into Mrs. Guthrie's waiting arms. No sooner had the coat touched her arms than she was passing it off to Rose. "There are pegs in the back room."

Rose nodded. Taking the coat, she was followed by Mrs. Guthrie and Uella into the back room. Rose placed the heavy coat on a peg and turned to find the women pouring over a navy blue fabric with tiny, pink flowers on it.

"I think this one will suit your coloring very well. It certainly will show off your eyes and the pinkness in your cheeks. You might even catch the eye of a certain bachelor," Mrs. Guthrie said, glancing at Rose, who didn't favor her with a response.

Uella's cheeks grew crimson under Rose's gaze.

Could Mrs. Guthrie be talking about Harl? Rose returned to the chair, picked up the bonnet she had been working on, and continued sewing. She bowed her head over her work, so Mrs. Guthrie and Uella could not see the color rising in her cheeks.

"Thank you," Mrs. Perkins said. "Oh, are you making a bonnet?"

Rose looked up to see Uella walking toward her.

"Yes," Rose said.

"When Mrs. Guthrie makes me up a dress in the navy blue fabric, do you think you could make a matching bonnet to go with it?"

"Certainly, she can," Mrs. Guthrie cut in.

"I would like to have it to wear to church this Sunday—if you can finish the dress in time."

"Of course, I can." Mrs. Guthrie almost sounded hurt. "Besides, I have help now, and I'm sure Miss Henderson wouldn't mind helping me make up the dress."

Rose smiled and nodded; but inside, she seethed. She would have to wear her finest to compete against the likes of Uella Perkins if she wanted Harl's attentions to herself.

Mrs. Guthrie took measurements of Uella's arms, skirt, and bodice lengths; jotted them down on a scrap piece of paper; and nodded to the woman.

"A new dress will be just the thing to . . . "

Mrs. Guthrie smiled wickedly. "Yes. It will be. Would you care for a cup of tea?"

"No, thank you. I have some items I need to attend to at the mercantile. Mrs. Grant sent word that my orders were in."

Turning back to the fabrics, Uella touched a bolt of lovely cream-colored silk. "Maybe the next time I get married, you can work up something in this silk."

Rose scowled as Mrs. Guthrie turned to her. Motioning to Rose, Mrs. Guthrie pointed at Uella's coat and then at Uella, who had her back turned to the women.

Rose jumped up, rushed to grasp the collar of the coat, and hurried to help Mrs. Perkins into it. *The sooner this woman is out of the shop, the better.*

"Thank you," Uella said, buttoning up the front of the coat. "Until Saturday then." She walked out of the back room to the front and out the door. She paused briefly at the front window, looked at the bonnet, and waved to the two women watching her.

Rose and Mrs. Guthrie waved back.

Mrs. Guthrie clapped her hands together. "We have so much to do."

"We?"

"Yes, of course. You'll make her one of your hard-sided bonnets in the blue fabric with the pink roses, and I'll begin work on her dress immediately. What a vision she will be on Sunday."

"Oh," was all Rose could say. Surely, Uella Perkins was no match for Harl Adams's attentions. Surely.

Mrs. Guthrie marched over to Rose's vacated chair with the half-finished bonnet on it, picked up the bonnet, and tossed it aside onto a nearby small table.

Rose's eyes grew wide, and then she furrowed her brows in disgust. "Now, wait a minute," Rose said, her voice rising. "There's plenty of time for me to finish working on that bonnet and the one for Mrs. Perkins."

"No, there isn't. I'll need your help to get the dress ready by Saturday."

Rose glanced around the room until her eye spied a Singer sewing machine in an ornate, oak cabinet. The treadle under the machine looked new, as much of the blackening had not been worn off.

"You have a sewing machine. If you use it, you'll be able to finish in a day or so."

"It doesn't work right. Never has," Mrs. Guthrie said, placing the bolt of blue and pink-flowered fabric on a long table in the middle of the room. She jerked the fabric free from the bolt and laid it out on the table.

"Let me take a look at it. Maybe I can get it working."

"Ha," Mrs. Guthrie scoffed. "Go right ahead. I'll just cut out the pattern for Mrs. Perkins' dress."

Rose sauntered over to the machine and noticed that the spool of thread was wound around the middle part of the machine twice.

Pulling a straight-backed cane chair over in front of the machine, Rose sat and began unthreading the machine.

"Don't do that!" Mrs. Guthrie scolded. "You'll ruin my machine, and it cost Mr. Guthrie a pretty penny this past Christmas."

"Here's the problem. It's threaded twice."

"No, it isn't," Mrs. Guthrie said, peering at the machine over Rose's shoulder. "It couldn't be. Mr. Guthrie followed the directions that came with it."

"Well, it was. Here we are, then. Do you have a scrap of fabric we can test?"

Mrs. Guthrie walked behind the overstuffed chair where Rose had been sitting and pulled out a basket of mismatched fabric scraps. Rose rummaged through the basket and found two blue fabrics. She placed them under the raised presser foot of the machine and then lowered it. Slowly, Rose worked the treadle with her foot while pushing the fabric under the foot and needle. Seeing that the machine was working, she pumped the treadle faster. Holding up the freshly sewn fabrics, Mrs. Guthrie snatched them from her hands.

"My goodness, you are quite handy. How did you know it was threaded wrong?"

Rose shrugged and smiled. "The seamstress I was apprenticed to in my hometown of Chelsea Michigan had one similar. She let me use it to work up bonnets on."

"Oh, the hours you have saved me."

Rose listened to her stomach growl and thought of the bacon still in her basket at her feet. Mrs. Guthrie was humming to herself as she worked cutting fabric.

"If you feel like eating, go right ahead. I'm not hungry."

Reaching down to the basket, Rose lifted the linen napkin and grasped a piece of bacon. After eating, Rose stretched and yawned. "The day has certainly gotten away from us."

Mrs. Guthrie looked up at the clock on the wall. "Goodness gracious me. Is that the time?"

Rose nodded. It was a quarter to three.

"We have worked our fingers to the bone today, and there's no call for that now that my sewing machine is fixed. I suppose Harl Adams will be along soon to gather you."

"Yes." She stretched again and yawned. "If you like, I will spend the night at the Adamses' and bring my things to the shop tomorrow."

"Then we will plan on eating lunch at my home. Is the bonnet ready?"

"Not all the way yet."

"Well, then, you best be gathering your things, and I'll close up the shop. Don't want Mr. Guthrie to have to come looking for me."

Rose placed the bonnet on the table next to the cut-out fabric.

"I'll start sewing the dress tomorrow," Mrs. Guthrie said. "There. I hear the jingle of reins and the sure tromping of hoofs in the street. Mr. Adams is coming."

Mrs. Guthrie hurried over to the peg in the wall that held Rose's coat. Pulling it down, she held it out to her. "Mustn't keep him waiting."

Rose shrugged into her jacket, picked up her hat and placed it on her head, securing it with the hat pin. She grabbed her empty basket and hurried out into the front room just as the door opened. Harl Adams stepped inside. His broad shoulders filled the doorway.

"Hello, Mrs. Guthrie," he said, in a voice smooth as silk.

Mrs. Guthrie smiled. "Hello, Mr. Adams. Come to collect your Rose, then?"

Harl's face turned bright red, and he glanced at the floor. "Um, well, yes," he said, pulling the black felt hat off his head.

Rose swallowed hard as she looked at Harl suddenly out of sorts. He gestured for her with his hat, and she hurried to his side.

"Do you need a ride home, Mrs. Guthrie?" Harl asked.

"Oh, my, no. I only live around the corner, and the walk will do me good. Rose, you might want to mention to him and Mrs. Adams the arrangement we talked about."

Harl and Rose exchanged glances.

"I certainly will," Rose smiled up at the man beside her.

Mrs. Guthrie laughed. "Wait a minute," she said as she went to blow out the lamps in the back and front rooms. "Now, we can leave."

Chapter 16

Harl helped Rose up onto the seat next to him. Even though he wore thick, leather work gloves and Miss Henderson wore calfskin gloves, when their hands touched, electricity shot up Harl's arm. He looked at Rose's face to see if she had felt the jolt, too, but she showed no signs of anything amiss.

Even though the wind had died down from earlier in the day, the temperature had plummeted. Harl pulled the quilt out of the back of the wagon and draped it over their legs.

"Warm enough?" he asked.

"No."

Harl grasped the oilcloth tarp in the back of the wagon and pulled it up and around their shoulders. "How about now?"

Rose shook her head.

Harl placed his arm around Rose's shoulders and rubbed her arm vigorously. "Now?"

Rose laughed as Harl watched her face turn red. Was it delight or embarrassment? "That is much better," she said.

Pulling his arm back around to his side, Harl released the brake and jingled the reins. "Get up there," he said.

Turning his eyes to the passenger beside him, Harl looked for any sign of chill. Rose's legs jiggled under the cover. Harl pulled the oilcloth tarp tighter around them. Rose looked up at him and smiled.

"Thank you," she said through chattering teeth.

"Not at all. We'll be home soon." Harl hurried the mules along. "So, what did Mrs. Guthrie want you to tell me about your arrangement?"

"I had such a good first day with Mrs. Guthrie. She offered me a room at her house. She said I could work for her for my room and board and a little stipend," Rose said. "Then you won't have to take away from your chores around the farm to drop me off and come pick me up. Doesn't that sound wonderful?"

"Oh?" Harl glanced at his passenger.

"She does keep her shop very warm—too warm, in my opinion. But the back room isn't a bad place to work. It's almost comfortable."

"That sounds like a good offer if that's what you want."

"It's not that I don't love living with you and your mother, but living with the Guthries would give you and your mother more space."

Harl stared at the road ahead of them. "Uh huh," he agreed. Changing the subject he asked, "What did you do?"

"I showed off my work. Mrs. Guthrie liked one of my bonnets so well, she put it on the neck of the wicker dress form in the window. Did you notice?"

Harl shook his head.

"Oh, well . . . "

Harl could have kicked himself for missing the fact that Mrs. Guthrie's window dressing had changed, no matter how small an oversight it was. It was important to Rose and should, then, be important to him.

Out of the corner of his eye, he saw Rose turn her face toward him and lean forward.

"Do you know a Mrs. Uella Perkins?"

His passenger seemed to be staring at him for some reason.

He nodded. He was familiar with the woman from church and from having attended her late husband's funeral last year. The widow was always casting glances his way in church. "I know of her," he agreed.

Turning to Rose, he was just about to ask why when he saw her sit back and fold her arms over her ample chest. Had he said something wrong? What had he said? What had made Rose sit back and fold her arms in that way? He couldn't guess. There was definitely something wrong. But what?

"Did I say something wrong, Miss Henderson?"

"Hmph," she sniffed, turning her face away from him.

Harl placed his arm back around her shoulder and squeezed. "I don't know what I said to make you mad, but I'm sorry."

He sat forward to get a better look at her face, but she had turned away from him and was staring up at the sky, which was growing darker by the minute.

"All right then," he said, removing his arm from her shoulder.

"Oh, you can leave your arm there if you want," she said, turning to look at him.

"I thought maybe my arm was causing you to be angrier."

"No, it felt nice."

Harl grinned and slid his arm back around Miss Henderson's shoulders.

"Mmm," she said, leaning against him. "You're as warm as turkey fresh from the oven."

Harl chuckled.

"What?" she asked, sitting up.

"It's just that I've never been told that I was as warm as a turkey fresh from the oven. It's nice to think I can keep you warm on such a cold night."

Rose relaxed and leaned back against him again.

Harl watched as the sun set on the western hills and sighed.

"What are you thinking, Mr. Adams?"

Harl looked down at the woman nestled against his chest and smiled. "How nice this is to be riding in this wagon with you by my side. How thankful I am that the Lord brought you into my life."

Rose sat up and craned her neck around to gaze at Harl. "Why, Mr. Adams, I do believe you are sweet on me."

Harl bowed his head momentarily and then raised his eyes to hers. "Am I?"

Rose giggled and clapped her hands. "Yes, I do believe you are."

"There's no cause for calling out a man like this just because he has his arm around you to keep you warm in the chilly air."

"It's more than that, and you know it." Rose's eyes shown in the fading light.

Harl tucked his head off to the side and smiled to himself. So what if he had feelings for Miss Rose Henderson? It was only natural. She was turning out to be a fine, resourceful lady—and a pretty one, to boot. If only she was would give her life to Christ, then he could pursue her.

"Won't you even look at me, Mr. Adams?"

Harl chuckled and turned his head back to Rose. By now, the sun had set, and it was too dark for her to make out the red color in his cheeks. His secret was mostly safe with him.

"It's just that I wish you would give your life to Christ."

"Whatever for?"

"Because the Lord has a good plan for your life and I'd hate for you to miss out on it. Plus, you can't go to Heaven when you die without trusting Jesus as your Savior."

Rose took his hand and placed it back on her shoulder. "I'm just not sure I'm ready yet."

"Why not?"

"I don't think I've done enough penance yet," she whispered.

"You don't have to do penance to come to the Lord. He paid it all on the cross when He died."

Rose drew in a breath as if she was going to say more but then leaned back against Harl.

"Let's not talk about that now. I want to drink in this night with you."

Harl sighed heavily and let the mules take their leisure walking home through the bare orchard.

When they arrived back at the house, the dogs ran up to meet them. Rose stretched and yawned. "What a day I've had. Oh, I fixed Mrs. Guthrie's sewing machine. She said it wasn't working before, and that was because she had wound the thread around one of the mechanisms one too many times. Now, she will be able to make dresses in no time flat. I certainly am looking forward to working in her shop tomorrow."

Hazel opened the door, and light from the lamps on the kitchen table shed light all around her, casting her momentarily into shadow.

Harl helped Rose down and handed her the empty food basket.

Rose raced up the steps and embraced Hazel. "I have so much to tell you."

Hazel turned and faced the younger woman. "Oh? What happened?"

"Well, Mrs. Guthrie keeps her shop hot, except for the back room, where I sat to do up a bonnet. And guess what?"

"What?"

"She wants me to move in with her and her husband. And I fixed her sewing machine. There was a thread that was wound around a mechanism twice. Once I discovered that and rethreaded the machine, it worked. Now, she'll be able to double and triple her productivity. Isn't that wonderful?"

"Yes, it is," Hazel said, shutting the door and helping Rose off with her coat. "But do you want to live in town with the Guthries?"

"That would keep Harl from having to take me to work and bring me home every day."

"Then if that's what you want, it's a good plan. I seen you and Harl coming up the lane through the apple orchard. You were leaning on him, and it looked as if he had his arm around you."

Rose paused and stared at Hazel. "Yes, I was; and yes, he did. Was that wrong of us?"

Hazel shook her head. "It's just that Harl never got over his old school crush, Nellie Hampton. She and Edgar Richardson ran off and got married the first chance they got when she was only fifteen. He's got a soft soul, that one. I don't want to see him get hurt again."

Rose's lips parted, and her eyes widened. "I really like your son, Mrs. Adams. I would never do anything intentionally to hurt him."

Hazel cast her gaze to the floor and nodded. "I don't think you would, but that's for Harl to decide."

Just then, Harl bounded into the kitchen. The room fell silent at his entrance, and both women looked at him—one with adoring eyes, the other full of unanswered questions.

"What?" Harl asked, gazing from one woman's face to the other. "What did I miss?"

"Not much, son. Did you wash up?" his mother asked.

"Yes, I did."

"Well, then, Miss Henderson, will you please help me get dinner on the table?"

Why had Hazel reverted to using her last name? Was she angry about seeing her and Harl so close? Maybe it hadn't been proper, but Rose liked feeling Harl's strong, warm arm about her shoulders on such a cold evening. Was that so wrong?

She smiled to herself as she placed the dishes on the table that Hazel handed her. What was this new feeling she had deep in her stomach? Was it love for Harl Adams? She was beginning to feel warmth spread through her from her stomach to her hands, but maybe that was because she was handling hot dishes.

Seating herself at her place at the table, Rose spied a look at Harl, who was looking at her with one side of his mouth hitched up into a grin. She sucked in air knowing he had caught her looking at him and glanced down at her hands in her lap.

"Let's bless the food so we can eat," Hazel said, folding her hands under her chin and closing her eyes.

"Dear Heavenly Father, we thank You for this meal and for this day. Watch over us tonight and into tomorrow. In Jesus' name, amen."

Rose glanced up at Harl. He was still watching her, though his cheeks were a bit red. She let out an involuntary giggle but stifled it quickly, pulling her napkin off the table and placing it at her mouth.

Rose noticed that Hazel darted her eyes to her. "I'm sorry. I just thought of something funny," she lied.

"Oh? And what was that, dear?" Hazel asked.

Rose shook her head. How could she tell this woman that she thought she was starting to fall in love with her son? Was she? Is this what love felt like, all warm inside and the feeling of butterflies flitting around in her stomach?

She had felt this way once before when she was younger and thought she was in love with the man who had left her for another woman. Dark days had followed that failed relationship. It had taken her months to recover. He no longer loved her. God had allowed her heart to be trampled under her intended's feet. How had a good God allowed that to happen to her? Was God even good?

Harl watched questions flit across Rose's face. He wondered what was going on inside that pretty head of hers. Had his kind act of placing his arm around her on the cold ride home sent her into a tailspin? That was not what he had intended. He'd like to ask her what was on her mind, but in order for her to tell him, he'd have to have her alone. Maybe when he went out to bed down the mules for the night and feed the dogs, he could ask her in private.

Once the meal was done, Harl stood and strode over to his coat hanging by the door. His mother handed him two metal plates of leftover food. "For the dogs," she explained.

"They'll be mighty glad of it, too," he said. "I'm going out to brush and bed down the mules for the night. Care to join me?" He directed his question at Rose, who jumped up from the table and rushed to put on her coat and hat.

"I would love to."

Harl wanted to help her into her coat, but his hands were full at the moment with the plates for the dogs. "You'll have to get the door," he said.

"I'll get the door," his mother said. "Rose, you put on those work gloves once you get to the barn. I don't want you ruining your good ones."

"Yes, ma'am."

As soon as Mama opened the door, Rose and Harl scooted out it.

"You seemed to have a lot on your mind during dinner," Harl said when they were out of earshot of the house.

Rose opened the barn door, and Harl stepped through it, followed by the dogs, who barked at the smell of the food.

As soon as they were inside, Harl set down the plates beside the door and watched as the dogs wolfed down the contents.

"It's just that . . . " How could Rose tell Harl about her growing feelings for him? What would he think? How would he react? Or would he feel the same? What if he didn't?

"I wish you would tell me what is going on."

"I think. I may be . . . "

"Hold that thought. I'm going to let the dogs out, so they can do their business."

Harl opened the door, and a cold breeze wafted into the barn. He closed the door once the dogs had gone out and turned back to her, kindness and understanding showing in his gaze. Or was that pity? She couldn't tell Harl she was falling in love with him. No, she wouldn't say anything until he said something to her. That was the best way to handle this. Her heart couldn't take any more rejection.

"Oh, it was nothing," Rose lied and looked over at the bag of cracked corn, where Catherine's work gloves sat. "Nothing of importance, I guess."

"It most certainly was something. You seemed to have had a lot of thoughts running through your mind during dinner, and I'd like to hear what they were."

"No, I can't. Don't ask me," Rose said, turning toward the barn door, which the dogs were scratching at, wanting to be let in. She moved to open it, but Harl's hand stopped her.

"I'll get it," he said. "You weren't planning on leaving, were you?"

"Yes, I was. I need to get my things together, so I can move into town with the Guthries tomorrow."

"No, stay. Come keep me company as I brush down the mules."

"All right, but I don't think it's fair that Hazel has to do the dishes herself."

"She'll manage. And it wouldn't hurt for us to have some time together."

"We just had time together, or don't you remember that?"

Harl just shook his head. Picking up a small, empty barrel, he positioned it across from the mules' stalls. "Here you go."

Rose dusted off the barrel top and sat down. She watched as Harl brushed one and then the other mule in silence. What was on that man's mind? She turned her attention to the dogs, who were bedding down for the night on straw in an open stall next to the mules. Was he thinking the same thing she was? Was he falling in love, too? But the man was so quiet with his feelings. She couldn't be sure. To him, maybe she was just a good friend—someone he could talk to about things, though the talking part wasn't going on right now.

"What do you think the Lord thinks of me and the life I've been living?" she asked.

"I know He loves you and wants you to come to know Him like the Bible says in John 3:16: 'For God so loved the world, that he gave his only begotten Son, that whosoever believeth in him should not perish, but have everlasting life.'"

"You make it sound so simple."

"It is that simple and that hard to bow your will to the Lordship of Christ and accept Him into your life as Savior."

When Harl finished, he turned fully to Rose. His face was flushed. Was he thinking of her? She looked down at her gloved hands and smiled. When she raised her head, Harl was standing in front of her. She jumped at his unexpected nearness.

Harl put out his hand. "I didn't mean to scare you." He chuckled. "I . . . " His eyes met hers. The warmth and longing in them was unmistakable. He leaned down toward her.

Suddenly, the barn door banged open. Harl jumped. Hazel stood in the doorway with a grimace on her face. "I could use some help with those dishes, if you don't mind."

Rose's mouth dropped open, and she cocked her head toward Hazel. Closing her mouth, she said, "Right away, ma'am."

Harl backed up. Rose stood and marched out of the barn after Hazel, who was scurrying toward the house.

When Rose looked back at the barn, Harl had already shut the door. What had he almost said to her? Was he going to kiss her? Would she ever know?

Upon entering the house, the dishes were soaking in a steaming dishpan of hot water.

"I'll wash," Hazel said. "You dry." The older woman handed Rose a flour-sack dishcloth and began washing the dinner plates.

Hazel washed in silence, handing the dishes off to Rose, who dried and put them away.

"Is there something on your mind, Mrs. Adams?" Since Hazel had used Rose's surname earlier, Rose felt she should do the same, unsure of the sudden coldness between them.

"Yes." It was several minutes before the older woman continued. "I don't think you are a good fit for my son. I mean, I want him to marry a Christian woman. Are you a Christian? Have you accepted Jesus as your Savior yet?"

Rose took a step back. "No, I haven't."

"I've been praying for a Christian woman to come along for him."

Rose lowered her head. "I understand," she whispered. "Maybe it is for the best that I move in with Mrs. Guthrie. She said I should be in town, so Harl doesn't have to come pick me up or drop me off. He'd have time for his chores."

"I think that is an excellent idea. I have an old carpetbag you could use to tote your things in. I'll get it for you."

Hazel scrambled from the room. In a moment, she was back with a multi-colored carpetbag.

Chapter 11

Rose licked her lips. Taking the carpetbag, she set down the dish cloth. All the dishes were dried and put away. There was no other reason for her to linger in the room. "Well, then, I wish you a good night, Mrs. Adams."

"Good night. I wouldn't pack tonight. Wait until tomorrow morning."

Rose hurried up the stairs to her bedroom on the second level. She placed the carpetbag on the hope chest at the foot of the bed. Sitting on the chair by the window, she let the tears fall. It had all started out to be so promising—writing letters to a man who wanted a mail-order bride had brought her to this lovely little house. And now, she was leaving it for . . . for a new place.

Maybe I should just go home to my father. But how? And would he let me return? He said to never step foot in Michigan again. She did not have any money to buy a train ticket home or to even wire for some to be sent. Her father had been angry the last time they spoke. Returning to Michigan wasn't anything that she wanted. Besides, he had been the reason for her sweet mother's death. How could she return to the household of the man who had caused it? Would her father try to extinguish her life, too, if she went back? She shuddered at the thought of going home to Chelsea. No, there was no going home. Of that she was sure. She would make the best of it here in Harrisville, Kentucky.

Rose slipped off her gown and underthings. She put on her lovely, lacey, cotton nightgown and climbed into bed.

After tossing and turning all night, she awoke a few hours before sunrise. She rubbed her eyes and sat up. Surely, Harl was getting up, too. He'd go feed the animals before having his breakfast.

Rose climbed out of bed and then dressed in her green dress. She wanted to look her best for Harl, even if she was leaving his home.

Swooping down the stairs, she found Mrs. Adams in the kitchen stirring milk gravy in a skillet. Looking around the room, she noticed Harl was not there.

"Where's Harl?"

"Out tending to the animals. Why?"

"I was going to talk to him and ask him if he could take me into town."

"I already talked to him. He'll take you, but he won't be back tonight to pick you up unless we get word that that Guthries don't have a room for you like they said they did."

How did Harl feel about this decision, anyway? They had been interrupted last night before she'd had the chance to ask him. Well, even though she hadn't made it down in time to catch Harl before he went to feed and care for the animals, she'd have a chance to speak to him privately when he took her into town later.

"You ready to eat?"

"Yes."

"I'll dish up the food. You set the table."

Mrs. Adams placed a plate of biscuits, a pitcher of milk, and a bowl of gravy on the table and sat down.

Rose looked at the stove. "Is there coffee?"

"Not yet. Hasn't boiled yet. It will in a little while." Hazel met Rose's glance.

Hazel bowed her head. Rose bowed her head, too.

"Thank You, Lord, for this meal and bless Miss Henderson. Amen." Without meeting her gaze, Hazel passed Rose the biscuits and then the gravy.

Rose took one biscuit, opened it, and laid it on her plate. She spooned milk gravy over it and poured herself a glass of milk. The two women ate in silence.

Sometime after the meal had ended and the dishes were washed and dried, Harl came in. His face was ruddy from being out in the wind.

He looked at the cleared table. "Nothing for breakfast, Ma?"

"Here, fix yourself a glass of milk and get ready to take Miss Henderson to Mrs. Guthrie's shop."

Turning to Rose, she said, "Don't you have some things to take care of this morning?"

Rose glanced from Harl to his mother. "Yes, I do."

Upstairs, Rose carefully folded her dresses one by one and placed them into the carpetbag as tears slid down her face. It was bittersweet to be leaving the Adamses' home. Sucking in her breath, she wiped her tears away and sighed. She was going to a new place with new adventures waiting for her. Picking up the bag, she looked around the room. This place had been such a happy respite for her, just what she had needed at the time.

At the bottom of the stairs, she passed Harl's room. His door stood ajar. She peeked in. Piles of newspapers lined the walls. Why did he keep them? What was that about?

Strolling into the kitchen, she found Mrs. Adams peeling shriveled apples into a metal pan. A ten-dollar gold piece lay on the table.

Pointing to it, Mrs. Adams said, "The ten dollars is for you. I wanted you to have a little money to start your new venture."

"Thank you, Mrs. Adams," Rose said. Taking the coin, she placed it in an inside pocket in her purse.

"Harl will be in shortly, as soon as he has the mules hitched."

"I noticed that he keeps a lot of newspapers in his room."

"Yes, he started collecting and keeping them after the war. I think they give him some sort of peace. He especially likes to reread the ones that covered the war."

"Oh," Rose replied.

"Can I help you with those?"

"No, there's no need. I'm almost done, anyway."

A few minutes later, the sound of Harl's boots on the steps and then porch made Rose turn from his mother to the door.

The door opened, and Harl dashed in. "Ready?" he asked, his face giving away his heart's disappointment.

"Ready."

"Just a minute. Let me wash my hands," Mrs. Adams said.

Rose watched as Hazel washed her hands in the dishwater and wiped them dry on a dishcloth. "Harl, here, help me get my coat on," the older woman said, picking up her coat that was laid across the seat of one of the chairs.

Mrs. Adams then turned to her guest and gestured for her to put on her own coat.

Rose put on the coat, but the collar got tucked under at the back of her neck. Harl reached out to fix it for her, but his mother cleared her throat loudly. Fumbling, Rose adjusted her collar, her cheeks turning pink in embarrassment with how Hazel—Mrs. Adams—was acting. It seemed as though she could not be rid of her guest soon enough.

"Ready?" Mrs. Adams asked. Without waiting for a response, she marched to the door, opened it, and stood waiting. Rose grabbed her hat and placed it on her head. She threaded the hat pin through it and her bun.

Harl walked out first, followed by Rose, who was followed closely by his mother.

Harl helped his mother up onto the wagon onto the seat next to him.

"I'm sorry, I don't believe there is any room up here with us. You'll need to sit in the back."

Harl reached around his mother and pulled Rose up and into the back of the wagon. She felt her cheeks heat.

"Don't worry. I put an extra quilt back here for padding. That way, the ride should be more comfortable."

The ride into town was a quiet one for all parties involved, each lost in their own thoughts.

When they arrived at Mrs. Guthrie's shop, Harl helped his mother and Rose down.

"Wait there," Mrs. Adams said as she walked into the shop.

A few minutes later, Mrs. Guthrie and Hazel came out.

"Rose, I'm so glad you are going to take me up on my offer to stay with me and Mr. Guthrie at our home in town," Mrs. Guthrie said as Harl helped her out of the back of the wagon.

Harl grabbed the carpetbag and turned to face Mrs. Guthrie.

"And only a carpetbag for your things," Mrs. Guthrie said. "You should have had Harl take your trunk home with you yesterday, so your dresses could be properly managed."

"Well, we'll be on our way. Thank you so much, Mrs. Guthrie. Harl, give Miss Henderson her bag. You can empty the contents into your trunk. We'll wait here for the return of the bag, so Harl doesn't have to make a special trip into town to retrieve it."

Rose stumbled into the shop and into the back room, where her trunk sat undisturbed. Opening the lid, she dumped out the contents of the bag into the trunk and let the lid shut.

Walking back outside, she handed the bag up to Mrs. Adams. "Thank you for everything," Rose said. "You both were wonderful."

"You are welcome," Mrs. Adams said.

"Goodbye, Mr. Adams," Rose said. Not waiting for a response, she turned and marched back into the shop.

After Harl and Mrs. Adams had gone, Mrs. Guthrie entered her shop.

"Now, don't you worry about a thing. I discussed with Mr. Guthrie that you would be coming to stay with us, and he is delighted."

"Mr. Guthrie and I have two empty bedrooms, since our boys flew the nest, so to speak. He is keen on having a houseguest again."

Rose managed a weak smile. "That is so kind of you."

"Don't think anything of it. Why, you're doing us a favor. We've talked about letting out those rooms; but to whom, we didn't know. Now, the Lord has answered our unspoken prayers to find us a boarder."

"I do have a little bit of money, but not much. I won't have more until I start selling some hats."

Mrs. Guthrie pinched her lips together as if she had bit into a lemon. "Hush now. I already said you could have the room and your meals and a small stipend in exchange for working for me."

"Mrs. Adams gave me ten dollars to help me out."

"That was kind of her. It'll help you buy more milliner wares for your hats and bonnets."

Rose nodded her head. "Yes."

"Well, then, let's get busy doing up hats and bonnets; and I'll spread the word around town that you are in need of selling your wares, so you won't be destitute. You'll make plenty of money selling what you can and can save a little to get your own place if you want— or you'll go home. But me and Mr. Guthrie are looking forward to having you in our home."

Rose felt her stomach sink. Did Mrs. Guthrie really have to spread the word around town that she might be destitute? What choice did she have? She was at the mercy of Mr. and Mrs. Guthrie's good graces. Home wasn't a place that she could go to anymore, unless she wanted to marry her father's apprentice and feel her father's wrath on her backside. No, it was best that she stayed in Harrisville, husband or not.

"Home really isn't an option for me. You see, my father came to collect me and take me home, but Mr. Adams stopped him. He fought tooth and nail for me to keep me here. There isn't any home to go back to."

"I see." Peering over her teacup at Rose, Mrs. Guthrie smiled. "Harl Adams actually fought your father?"

Rose blew on her tea and nodded. "Yes."

"They certainly took a shine to you. Why the change of heart?"

"She saw me leaning on Harl with his arm around my shoulders to keep me warm when we were coming back to her place last night."

"Oh. Yes, I could see how that might upset Hazel. Harl's her only son, and he's had his heart beat up plenty o' time. He used to be in love with the old schoolteacher, Miss Emma Whittaker, before she ran off to get married. Then there was another woman he was keen on, but she didn't care as much for him as he did for her. She married, too. And then his poor father was shot dead when they were on their way to sign up for the war."

"I didn't know," Rose said, slowly sipping her cooling tea.

"Yes, he was a dear soul before the war. I don't know why no woman has snapped him up. He's turned out shy and reserved. When his father died, it's as if Harl Adams just shut down, as if he didn't have a reason to live. His sister came back, and that seemed to perk him up. And then there was you," Mrs. Guthrie said, turning her full gaze onto Rose's face. "I haven't seen him so engaged with someone since you came along. And he really fought your father for you to stay here?"

"Yes."

"Hmph, there's something to that. The Harl Adams I know wouldn't fight anyone. I think he is sweet on you." Mrs. Guthrie peered over the rim of her cup at Rose, who did not offer her the satisfaction of a response.

Rose took a long sip of the cooled tea before speaking. "Well, that ship has sailed and won't be coming into port anytime soon again."

Mrs. Guthrie put down her teacup and empty saucer with a clatter. "You mustn't think that way. If Harl Adams has set his cap toward you, you can believe that he will find a way for you two to be together—with or without his mother's approval."

"But he loves his mother too much to go against her."

"He does love his mother, I'm sure, but he doesn't want to be a bachelor all his life either. Don't worry. Everything that is supposed to work out will in the end."

"I wish I had your confidence."

"Come now. Let's get to work and put Harl Adams behind us."

Rose drank the rest of the tea in her cup and set it down gently on the table. Rising, she strode into the backroom to the overstuffed chair, where the bonnet for Uella Perkins sat waiting.

Chapter 18

At noon, Rose's stomach growled. Mrs. Guthrie sat at her sewing machine pumping the treadle with her foot. Looking up at the clock on the wall, she raised the presser foot on the machine and allowed the fabric to fall into her lap.

"Looks and sounds to me like it's time for lunch. What do you say we run up to my home? I'll fix us something. We can take our leisure, and you can choose which room you want to stay in."

"All right, but how will I get my trunk up there? It's too heavy for me."

"We'll find someone to tote it for us. My Devin won't be able to because his right arm has been bothering him for some time. Don't you worry now."

Rose nodded and stood. Placing the finished bonnet on the sewing table, Mrs. Guthrie snapped it up and turned it over in her hands. "Lovely, quite lovely."

"Thank you." Rose's stomach rumbled again, and Mrs. Guthrie stood.

They put on their coats. Rose followed Mrs. Guthrie out of the shop and waited as the woman turned the key in the lock. "Can't be too careful. This way," she called over her shoulder as she marched around the shop, through an alley toward the busy main street of town. Across from her was the mercantile.

Rose looked up to see a familiar-looking wagon and a set of mules harnessed to it across the street. Her heart fluttered in her chest. Harl Adams was at the mercantile.

When Rose looked at Mrs. Guthrie, she noticed that she was studying her face.

"I do believe I have a hankering for some of Mrs. Elijah Grant's homemade bread and butter pickles. They are the best I've tasted. They'll be just the thing to put on the table with our lunch."

Rose offered the woman a smile and her arm, which Mrs. Guthrie accepted. Carefully, the women picked their way across the busy street to the mercantile. Rose's heart beat faster with each step. Could they make it into the shop before Harl came out? Would he pause to speak to her?

Entering the shop, Rose craned her head around but didn't see Harl anywhere. Had they missed him? Deep voices sounded in the back of the shop. Rose edged her way toward them, pulled by some unseen force.

One voice stood out to her. It was Harl Adams' deep baritone. Placing her hands on the counter, Rose waited for the men's voices to come near. Harl's voice, sputtered with laughter, came closer. When Harl stepped around the corner of the open door from the back room, Rose sucked in her breath. Harl stopped laughing when he saw her and paused, causing the man behind Harl to run into him. Harl stood firm in place and cast his blue eyes on Rose. The corners of his mouth tugged up into a shy smile as he seemed to drink in her presence.

She smiled, taking in Harl and the new spectacles he wore. She didn't notice the woman behind the counter standing in front of her. What was it that she was saying? Something about what she could do for them? The only thing Rose wanted to do was to stand at the counter and drink in every bit of Harl Adams.

"Rose," he said.

"Hello, Mr. Adams."

Harl grinned sheepishly and pushed the glasses higher up on the bridge of his nose as the small man behind him stepped around him carrying a large bag of flour. Harl moved forward toward Rose and stood near her at the end of the counter. "I was hoping I'd get to see you again," he said.

"You're wearing glasses. Where did you get them?" Rose asked.

"I stopped over at Doc Johnson's office before coming here. What do you think about my new look?" He chuckled.

Rose nodded. "It suits you."

"Doc said they would help with the headaches."

From somewhere behind Rose, a voice spoke. "We could use your help over at the shop," Mrs. Guthrie said.

"Oh?"

"Yes, it's my trunk. We need to move it to Mrs. Guthrie's home."

The sound of crunching paper pulled Rose's eyes away from Harl to the woman behind the counter, who was wrapping a package. She handed it to Mrs. Guthrie, who handed her a coin.

Mrs. Guthrie gestured to the man and woman behind the counter. "Miss Henderson, this is Mr. and Mrs. Grant, owners of the mercantile."

"I'm pleased to meet you," Rose said.

Turning to Mrs. Guthrie, Rose held out her hands for the package.

"I'll take that," Harl said, moving to her side.

Mrs. Guthrie handed it over to him. He offered her his right elbow; and to Rose, he offered his left. They each placed their gloved hands into the crook of one elbow. Harl stepped forward, and the ladies followed.

At the wagon, Harl helped each woman up onto the seat beside him and then climbed in on the other side. "It'll be quicker this way," he explained.

Releasing the brake, he spoke to the mules and eased them out into the busy street. They rode around the block and over to the dress shop, where he parked the wagon.

Jumping down, he asked, "Where's your trunk?"

"Same place as where you left it."

"Stay here," he said. Reaching up, he grasped the key that Mrs. Guthrie gave him and entered the shop. When he returned, he was carrying the trunk.

Placing the trunk in the back of the wagon, Harl hefted himself up onto the seat beside the ladies, released the brake, and set off for Mrs. Guthrie's place.

Mrs. Guthrie was conveniently situated between them, which, of course, was proper.

The Guthries' quaint, white, colonial-style home stood across from Moore's Hotel and Restaurant.

"Here we are," Mrs. Guthrie said, throwing her arms wide when the wagon stopped at the front walkway. "And here is Mr. Guthrie to meet us."

Mr. Guthrie was short and round like his wife; but what she had in pounds, he had in muscle with a solid build. His thick, graying hair was parted sensibly over his left brown eye. His thick, salt-and-pepper mustache and full beard were neatly trimmed.

"Help me down please, dear," Mrs. Guthrie said to her husband, who hurried his steps and put out his hand to steady his wife as she made her descent. She nearly fell into his arms when her foot slipped from the wheel hub, but her husband caught and steadied her.

"Mr. Guthrie, this is Miss Rose Henderson."

Rose turned in the seat and tried to conjure her best smile, even though her eyes betrayed her.

"How do," Mr. Guthrie said, holding out his hand, which Rose reached down and shook.

"Miss Henderson has fallen on some hard times and needs a place to live for the time being until she can get on her feet. And I'm so glad you agreed to have her here with us. It will be such fun."

The amicable man was quick to smile with a warmth that reached his eyes. "Why, of course, she would be welcome here for as long as she needs."

Turning to Rose, Mrs. Guthrie said, "You see, my dear, it will all work out in the end."

"Shall I get her trunk, then?" Harl asked.

"Yes, yes," the older woman said, reaching up and taking Rose's gloved hand.

Rose carefully climbed down. She waited for Harl before she turned with a warm face to her benefactors.

"Now, don't you worry yourself about a thing," said Mrs. Guthrie. "You just come with me, and we'll pick the best room for you."

The pair strolled up the walkway and into the house, followed by Mr. Guthrie and then Harl, who carried Rose's trunk on his broad shoulders.

The home was warm and welcoming and not at all overheated like Mrs. Guthrie's shop. To Rose's left, a cheerful fire blazed in the fireplace. This room must be used as a general sitting room. Overstuffed cream-colored chairs sat in an inviting arrangement around the fire. On one of the ottomans was a newspaper, a bit crumpled, as if hastily discarded.

To her right, a spacious room opened up with stiff-legged, red velvet furnishings stately placed around the room. There was a settee, several straight-backed chairs, and a low table before the settee, flanked by side tables. A fire glared out from a grate in the fireplace.

"What a lovely home," Rose said, turning to her hosts, who showed their appreciation by beaming at her.

"Let's go choose your bedroom while the men talk down here," Mrs. Guthrie said, waving the men into the comfortable sitting room. Harl set the trunk down in the middle of the room. Mrs. Guthrie led the way up the stairs to the second-floor landing. Four closed doors met Rose's gaze.

"Here is the first one," Mrs. Guthrie said, opening a door to their left furthest from the stairs. A full-size bed with a white bedspread sat in the middle of the room against one wall. Two windows looked out at the town. "You'll get plenty of sunshine in the mornings."

Besides the bed, the room was cheerful with Mrs. Guthrie's signature overstuffed furnishings, a desk and chair, a tall dresser, a rocking chair with no arms, and a vanity with a washbasin and pitcher.

The next room Rose looked at had two windows looking toward Moore's Restaurant and Hotel. Again, the furnishings were almost identical to the first room, only the wallpaper showed peacocks lounging in various positions.

"You'll need to keep the shades drawn in late afternoon as it can get quite warm in here in the summer."

"The summer?" Would she still be here in the summer to experience hot afternoons? "I think I'll take the other room."

Mrs. Guthrie nodded as she closed the door. "Yes, if it were me picking, I'd choose the former, too. You'll find the wallpaper is not as busy." She laughed.

Rose hitched up her mouth into a semi-smile. "Thank you so much for allowing me to stay with you. I don't know how I will repay you."

"Pish posh. Don't you worry about it for now. We'll sort it out later when your designs start bringing in customers. Now, let's go downstairs and feed our hungry men."

In the kitchen, Rose and Mrs. Guthrie fried ham, sliced fresh bread, and set out the jar of bread and butter pickles Mrs. Guthrie had bought at Grant's Mercantile.

Rose's eyes wandered to the doorway of the kitchen, hoping to get a glimpse of Harl. She could hear the men talking in the front room but couldn't make out what was being said.

When it was time to eat, Mrs. Guthrie sent Rose to do the bidding. "The table's set and ready."

"Smells good," Mr. Guthrie said. "What are we having?"

"Ham, bread, and pickles."

"Mrs. Guthrie is concise as always," Mr. Guthrie said, eyeing the food sitting in the middle of the table.

"Mr. Guthrie will sit here at the head of the table. I'll sit beside him. Mr. Adams, you take the place opposite Mr. Guthrie; and Miss Henderson, you sit here across from me."

When everyone had taken their seats, Mr. Guthrie bowed his head and prayed. "Thank You, Lord, for this Thy bounty. Bless the hands that prepared our meal. Bless and keep Miss Henderson and encourage her heart. In Jesus' name, amen."

Rose lifted her head and gazed at Mr. Guthrie, who was tucking a linen napkin into his shirt collar. He had prayed that God would encourage her heart. She turned her glistening eyes to Harl. How could her heart be encouraged when it felt as if it would break? Harl would leave for home after the meal, and she would once again be left at the mercy of Mr. and Mrs. Guthrie's kindness. She didn't like to be beholden to anyone, as her father would say.

When would she see Harl again? If only those butterflies flitting in her stomach would stop.

If she decided that Harrisville was not for her and returned home with the money Mrs. Adams had given her, would she be welcome? Not likely, as she remembered her father's rage at the train station when he had tried to drag her onto the train and home. Thankfully, Harl had stepped in and put a stop to it.

Surely, there were more men in the world than just Harl Adams. Yes, yes, there were. There was her old beau, Peter Rhinehart, who had rejected her for another. There was her father's apprentice, Albert Winters, who had beaten the horse and who wanted to marry her— maybe to do the same to her in the privacy of their home. There was Cletus Tooth, who had left after one look at her. And then there was Harl—strong, brave, quiet, deep Harl. Could he be the man of her dreams? Could he be the answer to Mr. Guthrie's prayer for her heart to be encouraged?

"My goodness, dear. You aren't eating anything. Is the food all right?" Mrs. Guthrie asked, worry etched across her face.

Rose nodded her head. "The food is fine. I am just thinking."

"Oh? About what?" Mrs. Guthrie asked, smirking.

"Things."

Mrs. Guthrie darted her eyes at Harl and back to Rose. "What things?"

"Now, now, wife, there's no need to be asking her to reveal her secrets to us. Let her be. When and if she wants to tell us, she will," chided Mr. Guthrie.

Rose cast a glance at Mr. Guthrie. She smiled warmly at him. At least, here was an ally.

Harl couldn't take his eyes off Rose. She looked lovelier than usual in the pretty green dress she had worn to meet Cletus Tooth at the depot. Her lovely red hair was braided in two large braids which wound around her head and were held in place by combs. Little, loose tendrils framed her lovely face. Her peaches-and-cream complexion glowed in the light of the afternoon sun cutting through the sheer curtains in the dining room.

Harl stabbed at the meat on his plate but missed. Catching Rose's eye, he saw her smirk at him. He felt his face grow hot under her gaze. Looking down, he cut the tender slice of ham with his fork and raised it to his mouth. The taste was sweet. He guided his eyes back to Rose, who was spearing a clump of pickles on her plate. Her head was bowed. He couldn't make out her expression. How he wished he could go on studying her, but that would get him into deeper trouble than he was already in. If only the meal could go on and on.

Finishing the contents of his plate, Harl held it up and asked, "That was so good, Mrs. Guthrie. Mind if I have seconds?" Never mind that a hearty lunch was waiting for him back at home. He was content to stretch out their visit as long as possible. Asking and receiving seconds would keep him occupied at the table for a while longer.

"Now, that's more like it," Mrs. Guthrie said with a chuckle as she speared a thick slice of ham and placed it on Harl's plate.

"I sure am enjoying this meal, Mrs. Guthrie," he said, glancing at Rose.

"Yes, I'm sure," she said, looking over at Rose, who continued to pick at her food.

Rose raised her head, looking at Harl. She matched Harl's gaze with her own. Harl's heart leaped as he placed the pickles on his fork. They fell back onto his plate.

Rose raised her napkin to her face, and her eyes squinted. Her body shook. Harl hitched up the side of his mouth in a pleasing smile and speared the runaway pickles with his fork. This time, they made it to his mouth.

He was falling in love with this beautiful woman at his side, but his mother wouldn't approve of him loving a woman who still refused to give her life to Christ. How could he be falling in love with the woman his mother had decided against? He would either have to stand up to his mother or leave Rose be, but the Lord had brought Rose here for him. He was almost sure of it. If only she would give her heart to the Lord, then he could court her properly.

"Harl?" Mr. Guthrie asked.

Harl looked at the man at the end of the table. "I said there's some good ice fishing out on the pond. It's a clear day, and I'm sure the fish will be biting. Would you like to come with me?"

Harl glanced over at Rose, who pushed a pickle around the almost-empty plate. "I would love to, but I've never gone ice fishing. How does one do it?"

Mr. Guthrie chuckled. "Just you wait and see."

Chapter 19

Harl followed Devin out to the barn behind the house. Inside the barn, off to one corner, sat Devin ice fishing gear on a sled.

"We'll take a couple of empty barrels to sit on, a couple of buckets to put our catches in, and the horses' blankets to keep warm. I already cut a hole in the ice. We'll take a dipper out with us to skim off the refreezing ice. That should do."

Harl nodded. He had read about ice fishing in the newspaper many times, but he had never experienced it for himself.

"Let's put your mules in the barn where it's warmer. We'll water and feed them. I'm sure they would appreciate it. We'll only be gone a couple of hours," Devin said.

A couple of hours! I don't have time to be away from home for that long, and I wouldn't want Mama to worry. But I also don't want to be unneighborly.

"I need to send word to Mama of my whereabouts, so she won't worry," he said out loud.

"Let's get the mules situated, and then I'll run over to Garlin Moore's to see if someone from the kitchen can send word to your mother. Why, you may enjoy yourself so much once we get out there that you'll want to stay longer."

Harl grinned. It had been quite a while since he had taken his leisure at anything. The change would do him good.

Harl walked the mules around to the barn and unhitched them.

"Here, I've got a couple of empty stalls. We'll put them in here," Devin said.

Harl led each mule into its own stall. He watered and fed them from Devin supply near his team of draft horses across from the mules. Devin placed hay at the end of the feed trough for each mule. Dusting off his gloves, Devin smiled brightly at Harl.

"I'll cart the sled. Come on; let's go."

Harl wasn't used to walking on ice. He kept slipping and shot his arms out to steady himself.

"This pond is spring-fed," Devin said.

"Yeah, I know it is," Harl said, waving his arms as one of his boots slipped on the ice.

"We're mighty lucky to have this pond in town. Lots of places don't have them. Makes for some good fishing, though, if you know how to do it."

"Uh huh."

"Ah, here's the hole I dug. Had to use an axe to chop through most of it and then a saw for the rest. Come on. Come closer to the hole. You won't be able to fish from way back there." Devin grabbed the two barrels with two short fishing poles off the sled. He placed the fishing gear on the sled and situated the barrels beside the hole as Harl slid up to him.

"Whoa there, Harl. Don't want you to fall in," the older man said, holding out his arm to keep Harl from pitching himself into the hole. "Take a seat."

Harl sat down on the barrel next to Devin and watched as the man took a spool of string, tied a curved hook onto it, placed a bit of what looked to be raw meat on the end of the hook just past the barb, and slid it into the water.

"Now, we wait." Looking up at Harl, Devin asked, "You want me to do one for you? Or do you want to try your hand at it?"

"I'd like to try."

Devin unwound several feet of string, pulled a pocket knife out of his pants pocket, and then handed the roll of string to Harl.

"Be careful with this," he said, handing him a fishing hook. "Don't go stabbing your fingers with it. It's a bear to get out if you do."

Harl tied the fish hook onto the end of the string. Devin unwound several feet of string and cut it off with his knife. He opened a small paper parcel and handed Harl a chunk of raw meat.

"You put this on your hook, and you'll soon have fish jumping out of the water for an easy meal."

Harl hitched up one side of his mouth into a smile. "Thank you." He was careful to place the meat on the hook with the utmost care just past the barb.

"Now, you throw it in, jiggle the line a bit, and wait." Devin demonstrated how to jiggle the line. Just then, Devin's line went taut. "Ooh, I got something." Pulling the line up quickly hand over hand, Devin grabbed the large bluegill that broke the icy surface of the water. He unhooked the hook and placed the fish in the bottom of the bucket. "There's one," he said, his eyes dancing with delight.

Harl jiggled his line and soon had his first catch of the day.

The men took turns reeling in fish after fish. When the bucket was nearly full and a good two hours had passed according to Devin's pocket watch, the men packed up and headed back to the house. Devin pulled the sled behind him, smiling all the way to his home.

At the house, the men stopped off in the barn.

"Here, Harl. You take half of these fish."

"But I didn't catch that many."

"Doesn't matter. You still helped, and the missus doesn't care that much for fish. She'll cook it and eat it, but she doesn't go back for seconds. You take these fish for you and your mother to enjoy."

"All right. Thank you."

Devin poured the fish and some ice into a bucket for Harl. "These'll make good eating, and there's plenty more where they came from. You come out anytime you like. You want help cleaning yours?"

"I would."

Using one of the benches in the barn, the men worked cleaning the fish. The scraps were thrown into a bucket. "That'd make some good broth if you put it in cheesecloth and let it simmer on the stove. Why, them dogs of yours would go crazy for a nice, hot meal of fish scraps."

"I'll see if Mama feels like cooking up the remains when I get home. Thank you for that outing. I enjoyed myself, but the livestock has got to be tended to now. I better be getting home."

Devin stood and went into one of the stables to walk out one mule as Harl brought out the other one. In a few minutes, Harl had his mules hitched back up to the wagon.

Rose came out onto the porch and waved at him. "It was good seeing you, Mr. Adams."

"My pleasure, Miss Henderson."

With that, he set off for home.

As he drove, he recounted the day's happenings. Meeting Rose at the store in town had been the highlight. He had hoped that he would catch a glimpse of her and planned to drive by the dress shop to do just that, but the Lord had seen fit to bring her to him.

He knit his brows together. Why? What was the purpose? His mother was obviously against the match—all because she didn't think her a fit wife for her son. Miss Henderson had never once told them that she had given her life to Christ, but had she? Things like that are sometimes a private matter that one keeps quiet in their heart.

Harl remembered his own experience at turning his life over to Christ. He was a boy of about ten. His parents had always taken him to church, and he heard the Gospel message of Jesus' death on the cross for the world's sins and our need to accept Him as our Savior, but sin was something only bad people did. He wasn't a sinner—at least, he did not think so at the age of ten. So, he put off giving his heart to the Lord by not repeating the words that the traveling preacher had said as to how to accept the Lord into his life.

It was as easy as that and as hard, until one night when a rather rambunctious thunder and lightning storm had Harl scared half to death. He didn't want to die without giving his life to Christ, so he spoke the words the preacher had said to pray if a body wanted to accept the Lord and not face damnation in Hell fire.

It was a simple prayer. "Father, I confess I'm a sinner in need of saving. I believe Jesus died for my sins on the cross. I give my heart to Your Son, Jesus, to cleanse me of my sin and take me to Heaven when I die. Amen."

When he prayed that prayer, his heart seemed to open wide with gladness. The storm raging outside of their home didn't matter. All that mattered is he knew he had accepted Christ as his Savior, and Heaven was his promise when he died. He didn't need to fear this or any other storm now that his heart was settled with Christ.

He smiled to himself, thinking back to when he had told his parents what he'd done and the joy that had shown on their faces. His father had patted his back while his mother hugged him and cried tears of joy.

For the next several weeks, his father had told anyone that would listen to him that his boy had accepted Christ as his Savior. Those who went to church and had already received Christ were overjoyed at the news and clapped young Harl on the back and welcomed him to the family. Those who were not churchgoers seemed to scrutinize his father's words. Did they not comprehend that Harl now had a place in eternity with Christ while theirs was uncertain? Harl couldn't be sure.

Placing his foot up on the wagon box in front of him, Harl contemplated what he would tell his mother about his day. He had planned to go visit Rose at the dress shop, but she and Mrs. Guthrie had saved him the trip by showing up at the mercantile.

There was no reason to lie to his mother and leave out the part about seeing Rose. She had been the real reason he was in town today. Going to see Doc Johnson for a pair of glasses and buying supplies for the homestead was just an excuse to get him into town and in close proximity to her. Surely, his mother would understand.

When Harl pulled up in the yard of his home, his mother opened the door and stepped out onto the porch.

"You were gone so long, I thought you got lost. Thought I'd have to send out a search party," she teased. "And you got a pair of glasses, too."

Harl laughed. "Yep, I went and saw Doc Johnson, and he fitted me with a pair of glasses. Said they'd help with the headaches. What do you think?"

"They suit you, but can you see straight with them?"

"A lot better than before. I ran into Mrs. Guthrie in town. She invited me over for lunch, and then I went ice fishing with Mr. Guthrie."

Hazel placed her hand on her jaw. "You saw Miss Henderson, then?"

"Yes, but not on purpose," he lied. "She and Mrs. Guthrie came into the mercantile while I was there."

His mother had a look on her face as if she had eaten a bad piece of meat.

Harl swallowed hard. "Sorry, Mama. I meant to see Miss Henderson when I was in town today, and the Lord worked it out that I was able to."

Hazel grimaced. "I've been praying for a good Christian woman to come into your life to be your wife, honey. I don't want you taking up with someone who doesn't know the Lord."

Harl looked at the ground and sighed heavily. "I better get the mules put away and tend to the livestock."

Turning the mules, he headed for the barn. Sliding the doors open, he climbed back up in the seat and, with the dogs running alongside, entered the barn. When he climbed down from the wagon, the dogs were right there with him. They wagged their tails and seemed to smile up at him as they bounced up and down before him.

"There're my good boys. What have you been up to today, eh?"

Harl slid the barn door closed and placed his hand on it for a moment before moving off to tend to the mules. As he worked, his thoughts turned back to what his mother had said. She wanted a Christian woman for him. He understood her reasoning, but Miss Henderson was so close to accepting the Lord. It was only a matter of time. What would cause her to bow her head to the Lordship of Jesus and give Him her heart? He didn't know, so he prayed.

"Lord it is no coincidence that you brought Miss Henderson here to us. I pray she comes to know you and gives her heart to you soon. In Jesus' name, amen." His breath came out in cold white clouds. How could he be used by the Lord to help bring Miss Henderson to Christ? He silently raised his hands in surrender to the Lord as he whispered, "Help me help her."

He unhitched the team of mules, led them into their respective stalls, refilled their water buckets at the well, and placed feed in their troughs. Next, he moved on to feed the cattle. Brownie was the last one he tended. He led her to a stall, milked her, and set her out to pasture again. All that was left was to take his catches to his mother, which he cleaned and rinsed in well water. He threw the scraps to the dogs, who gobbled them up.

When he reached the house toting a bucket of milk and the freshly cleaned fish, his mother was back inside the kitchen stirring something on the stove.

"I brought us some fresh fish for supper," he said, pushing his glasses up higher on the bridge of his nose.

"Oh, how nice! It's been ages since we've had fresh fish. I'll bread them and fry them up."

Harl placed the bucket of fresh milk on the sideboard and tilted the bucket of fish for his mother to see.

"And you already cleaned them. Thank heavens."

Harl smiled. "You want me to set the table?"

"No, I'll do that." Hazel stirred flour, salt, and pepper into a mixing bowl with some of the fresh milk. "So, how was Miss Henderson?"

Harl studied the back of his mother's head before answering. "She seemed well. The Guthries have taken a liking to her."

"That's good." Hazel set a skillet on the hot stove and added some lard to the pan. She waited for it to melt before adding strips of battered fish to it. The fish sizzled when they hit the pan.

"I enjoyed going fishing with Mr. Guthrie. He said for me to come on back anytime I like, and we'd go again. I can get us fresh fish all winter."

Hazel turned and faced her son with a pained look on her face. "I don't think that is a good idea."

Harl jerked his head to one side. "I don't see why not."

"I don't want you seeing Miss Henderson; and if you are up at the Guthries', you'd be more likely to run into her than not."

Harl's brows pinched together, and his mouth sagged into a frown. "I've never known you to be uncharitable toward anyone. Why now? And why with Miss Henderson?"

"Has she given her heart to the Lord yet?"

"I don't think so, but I don't know."

"If not, then she's just not right for you. I don't want you starting something you won't be able to finish," she said, throwing one hand in the air.

"Won't be able to finish? Why? Because she hasn't professed Christ as her Savior to you?" Harl's blood pressure was starting to climb.

"Yes, about that," Hazel said, turning back to the stove.

"What about that? She's changed, Mama. She's going to church now."

Hazel shook her head. "Just because she goes to church doesn't make her a Christian, son. You know that."

Harl could feel his heart beating faster. His face felt hot. They'd never had an argument over anything. Why now? Did his mother see or know something about Rose that he didn't?

"I know that, but people come to Christ in all different ways. Some come quietly and some boldly. Just because her conversion experience doesn't fit into what you think it should be doesn't make her a non-Christian."

Hazel dished up the fish onto a platter and added more lard to the pan and more strips of fish. "I just don't want you going and getting your heart broken again."

"What makes you think Miss Henderson would break my heart?"

"She doesn't seem to be the staying type."

Harl's jaw twitched as he watched his mother spear the fried fish and place them on the platter on the sideboard. "She would have been the staying type if you hadn't chased her off."

Hazel gazed at the ceiling. "I don't want to keep talking about it. She's fine where she is, and that is that. Let's not fight about it." Hazel turned with the platter and placed it on the table. She moved the hot pan to the side of the stove, where it could cool. Grabbing plates and utensils, she set the table.

"You want milk?" she asked.

"Yes."

Hazel poured milk into glasses and set them on the table by each place setting. "I cooked up some stew, too, before you came in." She dished up stew into two bowls. One she gave to Harl; the other she set by her place. Lastly, she placed a loaf of fresh bread and a plate of butter on the table and then took her seat. Folding her hands in front of her and bowing her head, she asked, "Would you say the blessing?"

"Father God, we thank You for this food that we have received at Your hand. Bless it to the nourishment and strength of our bodies. And I pray for Miss Henderson that she may come to know You in a way that is pleasing to You and evident to us. In Jesus' name, amen."

Harl watched as his mother's head shot up as he prayed for Miss Henderson. Their eyes locked, and she frowned.

"And, Lord," she prayed, "bring a good Christian girl into my son's life. Amen."

"One that meets with your approval?"

"Yes."

Harl sighed. "Pass the fish please."

Chapter 10

After Harl had gone, Rose walked back inside and donned her coat. "Are we ready to return to the shop?"

"I think so. Mr. Guthrie will keep the fish outside until we get home tonight. Then I'll cook them. I better tell him to cover the bucket with something, or he'll have every barn cat on this side of the town trying to snatch our dinner out of it."

Just then, Mr. Guthrie entered the kitchen. "Did you remember to cover that bucket?" his wife asked. "I don't want the barn cats stealing any of our dinner."

"Yes, Mama. I did. It's safe in the tack room closet in the barn."

"Did you wash up?"

"Yes, why?"

"You still smell like fish."

"Well, that can't be helped."

"Take a bar of my lye soap and a bucket of warm water from the stove and do some scrubbing please."

Mr. Guthrie's eyebrows knit, and his mouth turned down at the corners. Obediently, he grabbed a bar of white soap off the side cupboard. He filled a bucket with water from off the side of the stove and headed back outside.

"Now, we're ready," Mrs. Guthrie said, grabbing her coat.

As they walked, Rose noticed Mrs. Guthrie stealing sideways glances at her. "What is it?"

"Oh, nothing. Well, it's just that you've been quiet ever since Harl left. I can't help but wonder if there might be something blooming between you two."

"Not if his mother can help it."

"Mrs. Adams? Why, what has she said?" Mrs. Guthrie stopped, turning to Rose.

"Harl's mother made it very clear that she doesn't want me to see her son. Apparently, I'm not right for him."

"Why ever not?"

"Because I haven't given my life to Christ."

Mrs. Guthrie's brows knit together. "That is a private thing between you and the Lord. Just because you aren't falling down in repentance in the aisle of the church every Sunday doesn't mean your relationship with the Lord isn't decided."

"Maybe that's what she wants."

"What?"

"Me to fall to my knees and beg God to forgive me and give me a new life in Christ."

"Let's move on. People are starting to stare. Ah, here we are." Mrs. Guthrie walked through the alleyway, turned the corner to her shop, keyed in, and stepped over the threshold.

Two women hurried into the shop behind them.

"Oh, Mrs. Guthrie, thank heavens," said the taller of the two women. She was flanked by a shorter woman.

Turning, Mrs. Guthrie asked, "Mrs. Lovely, whatever is the matter?"

"Where have you been? My Susan needs her mail-order wedding dress fitted. Would you just look at the monstrosity they sent us?"

Mrs. Lovely turned her head to peer at Rose. "And who is this?"

"Oh, forgive me. Iva Jean Lovely, this is my new milliner, Rose Henderson. You should just see what she can do with a bonnet."

Mrs. Lovely eyed Rose suspiciously. "Yes, but is she any good with a needle?"

"Just look at this bonnet," Mrs. Guthrie said, returning from the window display.

Mrs. Lovely touched the bonnet tentatively and nodded. "Well, we aren't here about a bonnet. I came straight over here after unwrapping Susan's gown."

Mrs. Lovely thrust the dress into Mrs. Guthrie's hands, still holding the bonnet. "Can you fix it?" Without waiting for an answer, Mrs. Lovely continued, "I told Susan that if anyone can fix this mess, it would be you, Mrs. Guthrie."

The older woman's smile spread across her face. "Why, of course, I can fix this. Come in the back. Miss Henderson, can you please wait out here in case any other customers come in?"

Susan, who seemed to be holding her breath, let out a sigh as the women moved into the back room. Mrs. Guthrie pulled the green drapes closed.

Rose sank into one of the overstuffed chairs and let out a breath. Her thoughts turned to Harl Adams. *What is he doing? When will I see him again? How can I win back his mother's affection?* "Probably by staying away from her son," Rose whispered.

The ladies in the back room spoke quietly, but Rose could make out a few words. "Harl and Hazel Adams . . . Michigan." They must be talking about her. Was that the reason she had been excluded?

What if she returned to Michigan? Where would she go? What would she do to make a living? There was no going back to her hometown of Chelsea—of that, she was sure. Her father and Albert were there waiting for her. She couldn't return—*wouldn't* return—to their clutches.

She listened to the whirl of the treadle sewing machine in the back room.

"There now," Rose heard from the back room. "Try that on. Rose, please come here."

Rose got up and went into the back room.

"What do you think of Susan Lovely's dress?" Mrs. Guthrie asked.

Rose turned toward the woman. She was wearing a dark green dress that fit her curvaceous figure.

"Very nice. It's lovely," Rose said, smiling. "You do excellent work."

Mrs. Guthrie and the other two ladies beamed.

"Yes, she does, doesn't she?" Mrs. Lovely asked proudly.

Susan held the skirt out and turned slowly. "Mama told me if anyone in this town could fix it, Mrs. Guthrie could."

"Quit your twirling, and let's get you out of it. Don't want anything to happen to it before you and Wesley get to the church on Friday."

Mrs. Guthrie pulled the curtains shut with Rose in the room. The ladies lifted the gown over Susan's head and placed it on the back of one of the chairs in the room. Mrs. Lovely helped her daughter pull her dress over her head and button it in the front.

"Now," Mrs. Guthrie said, opening the curtains.

Susan reached for the newly altered dress and folded it. Hugging it to her chest, she turned to Mrs. Guthrie. "Thank you."

"How much do we owe you?" Mrs. Lovely asked, digging through her small purse for a few coins that jingled in the bottom. She held out her open hand with two coins in it.

Mrs. Guthrie said, "That will be plenty."

"We'd love to see you at the wedding Friday," Mrs. Lovely said.

"Here in town?"

"Yes. Pastor Samuel Harris will be officiating."

"I would love to."

Turning to Rose, she asked, "What about you? Care to attend?"

"Yes." Rose had never attended a wedding in the South and wondered if it was like the ones up North.

"Good. We'll see you Friday afternoon at four o'clock."

"You know, you really should have a new bonnet to match your dress," Mrs. Guthrie said.

Susan turned and smiled at her mother.

"Well, all right, then," her mother said.

"I think this fabric would be charming," Mrs. Guthrie said, pulling out a bolt of green cotton. "How quickly do you think you could have the bonnet ready?" she asked Rose.

"Now that the sewing machine is fixed, I would say an hour."

Rose picked through her wares on a shelf in the back room. She found a template for bonnets. She measured it on Susan's head and made adjustments before cutting the fabric to fit. The women sat in chairs around the room with tea cups in hand and watched as Rose pumped the treadle with her foot. The needle punched its way through the fabric and the hard sides of the cardboard bonnet shell. Adding some green silk ribbon as ties, Rose held up her creation.

"It's perfect," Susan said.

"How beautiful! Susan, you'll be the talk of the town in your gown and bonnet," her mother said. Mrs. Guthrie only nodded.

"We best be getting home. My Wilbur worries so," Mrs. Lovely said, digging in her bag for a few coins. Handing them to Rose, she said, "I hope this is enough."

Rose smiled. "Yes, thank you."

"We've had a lovely time, thanks to you ladies," Mrs. Lovely said.

"So, we'll see you Saturday?" Susan asked.

Mrs. Guthrie looked at Rose, who smiled. "We'll be there."

Mrs. Lovely and Susan headed for the door. Mrs. Guthrie headed them off and opened it for them.

Once they had gone, she turned to Rose and smiled. "Quite a good take for your first job, wouldn't you say?"

"Yes. If we can stay busy, I'll be able to afford to pay you rent."

"My dear, if we can keep up this pace, you can afford your own room in the hotel if you want."

The ladies laughed.

"Now, let's tidy up and head for home. We've had a full day, and we have frozen fish to cook."

When Mrs. Guthrie and Rose returned home, they found Mr. Guthrie hard at work in the barn feeding the animals.

"Where did you say you put the fish?" Mrs. Guthrie asked.

Rose pointed to the tack room door, where a mama cat and her three kittens sat mewing.

Rose laughed. "They're a dead giveaway."

"Shoo now, shoo, Sassafras!" Mrs. Guthrie said, trying to move the cats out of the way with the toe of her shoe as she opened the door.

A kitten rushed by her and sprang at the covered bucket as Rose jerked it out of reach. The kitten plopped onto the floor, paws splayed and with what Rose could only guess was a dissatisfied look on its face.

From behind her, Mr. and Mrs. Guthrie chuckled. "That is one disappointed kitten," he said.

"Not this time, little one," Rose said to the kitten, who had regained its footing. With his tail swishing furiously behind, he left the tack room as Rose shut the door.

Hoisting the bucket up to her shoulder, she was met with very disappointed gazes from the cats.

"How much longer will you be, dear?" Mrs. Guthrie asked her husband.

"I'll be in before you finish frying the fish," he said.

The mother cat and kittens had gathered around Rose's skirt. "We better hurry to the house now, or they'll be climbing your legs."

"There's plenty there," Mr. Guthrie said, weighing in with the cats.

"Oh, all right. If it will keep the peace," Mrs. Guthrie said, pulling the bucket down off Rose's shoulder. She reached under the covering and tossed a slightly frozen filet out to the mother and her babies. "Now, let's hurry to the house."

Rose hoisted the bucket back up onto her shoulder and rushed out of the barn and into the house, flanked by Mrs. Guthrie.

"Made it," Mrs. Guthrie exclaimed breathlessly. Rose turned to see Mrs. Guthrie peering out the window in the door.

Rose laughed.

"Let's get that fish in the kitchen and to frying before they discover where we've gone."

"Are your animals always so energetic?"

"Only when we have fish, which is about once a week. We'd have it every day if my husband had his way."

"So, why don't you?" Rose asked, walking behind the older woman into the kitchen.

"I don't like the smell of fish, and he doesn't do a good job of scrubbing it off his hands and arms."

"Oh," Rose said, placing the bucket on the sideboard cupboard.

"Feel like helping me make a batter for the fish?"

"Of course."

The women worked mixing up a buttermilk batter. One rolled the fish into the batter, then on a plate with flour, while the other one placed it into a hot skillet with lard.

As the women were just finishing up their task, Mr. Guthrie walked in. "Smells wonderful, as always," he said.

"Did you wash up?"

"Yes."

"Fine, fine. Rose, you go wash your hands and set the table, and I'll be out with the fish."

Rose turned to the wooden sink and pumped water into a dishpan. Taking a bar of lye soap, she washed her hands free of the batter. Drying them on a flour sack used for that purpose, she gathered plates and utensils and set the table.

Mrs. Guthrie brought the platter of fish to the table. She took her seat, folded her hands, and bowed her head. Mr. Guthrie followed suit, as did Rose. She was getting used to daily prayers surrounding eating.

"Thank You, Lord, for this food. Bless it to our bodies. And help Miss Henderson fit into her new home in this community. Amen," Mr. Guthrie said.

Help me fit in? Am I not fitting in? What have I done wrong now? When the platter was passed to her, Rose took two filets and placed them on her plate. She cut the fish with her fork and tasted it. "Mmm," she said. "This is very good. It's been ages since I've had fish."

"I'm glad you like it," Mr. Guthrie said.

When the meal ended, Mrs. Guthrie and Rose cleared the plates. There were still a few pieces of fish left over.

"If you wouldn't mind, would you throw that out for the cats? I saw Sassafras peeking through the window during dinner. She's been a good mouser, and I can't deny her a share."

Rose walked through the dining room and smiled when she saw Sassafras on two legs, peering at her through one of the windows.

As soon as Rose walked through the front door of the house, Sassafras and her three kittens surrounded her, mewing. "Yes, all right, then," she said, throwing the fish into the yard for the cats.

She caught a glimpse of the full moon in the clear night sky as the cats devoured the fish. Looking up at the moon, she thought of Harl, and her heart ached. Was he gazing at the same moon as she? What was he doing at that moment? Was he thinking of her? How could she right whatever she had done wrong to offend his mother? Was there any way to get back in her good graces? Harl knew the answer to that, but would he tell her?

Turning, she walked back into the dining room and into the kitchen to help with the dishes.

After they ate, Harl retreated to the barn to tend to the harness—not because it needed tending but because he wanted to get away for a while and talk to the Lord in private.

Standing momentarily on the steps outside the house, he looked up at the full moon. His heart sank as he gazed at it. His mother could be hard-hearted when she wanted to be. She was determined to keep him and Miss Henderson apart, as if she wasn't good enough for him. She *was* good enough. He'd just have to find a way to prove it to her. That was something he'd have to talk to the Lord about in private.

Sauntering down the steps and with the full moon out of his mind, Harl walked to the barn. He found his dogs and threw them the scraps from supper. They devoured it.

Harl checked on the mules, who were still munching away on hay in their troughs. Turning, Harl walked over to the tack room, where he kept his harness. He ran his hands down its smooth sides. The harness was intact. Taking a bucket, Harl walked to the well outside and drew water. Returning to the tack room, he unfastened the harness buckles and placed them at his feet. Taking a rag, he dipped it in the water and wrung it out well. He wiped down the parts of the harness and then worked up a lather using Castile soap.

As he cleaned the harness, he prayed, "Father God, could You please repair Miss Henderson's and Mama's relationship? I like Miss Henderson, and . . . and . . . " Harl studied the stable in front of him. "I'd like her to be my wife, but not if my mother doesn't agree. Miss

Henderson has had her troubles, but I believe they are over now. Please help her come to know You and give her life to You. I want her to know you like Mama and I know you."

What would it take to win his mother over when it came to Miss Henderson? There was a rift there, and Harl didn't know why. With the harness parts completely clean, Harl worked oil into both sides. Once the oil was applied, Harl buckled the harness back together and hung it on the wall.

"Lord, help Mama and Miss Henderson to become friendly again. Help them forgive each other for whatever wrong was done." He shut the door to the tack room and then headed out the barn door followed by the dogs.

When he reached the house, he turned to them. "No, boys, you can't come in here. Mama won't allow it. You'll have to sleep on the porch tonight." Each dog sat down on its haunches. "That's a good boy," Harl said, giving each dog a scratch behind their ears.

Chapter 11

In the morning, Harl was up and in the barn before daybreak as usual. He milked the cow, turned her out to pasture, and fed the herd. By the time he returned to the house, his mother had breakfast on the table. He sat down to scrambled eggs, bacon, gravy, and toasted bread with some of his mother's apple butter.

He hurried through his meal. Then he jumped up from the table and hurried over to the peg with his coat and grabbed his hat.

"Where are you off to in such a hurry?" his mother asked.

Harl glanced back and, without a word, opened the door, letting in the chilly morning air.

He heard his mother gasp behind him. "You're going to see Miss Henderson, aren't you?"

He nodded. "Mama, I believe the Lord brought Miss Henderson here for a reason. And that reason might just be that she is to be my mate one day. I know she hasn't given her life to the Lord yet, but I believe she is close to coming to Christ."

"You know I don't want you to see that woman anymore. She's not right for you. Set your sights on someone else—like Uella Perkins."

Turning, Harl said, "You know I don't cotton to Mrs. Perkins."

"And why not?"

"Because she's scrawny and stares at me in church all the time."

"Now, Harl. She was scrawny when you young'uns were little, but she's turned into a real beauty."

Harl raised his eyes to the ceiling. "Don't 'now, Harl' me. I'm going to see Miss Henderson. Just want to check in on her and make sure she's all right. There's no law against that, is there?"

Hazel placed her hand on her cheek and scowled.

"I thought not. Mama, you've got to let me live my life how I see fit." Stepping outside, Harl closed the door behind him. A smile grew from one corner of his mouth to another. If he could, he would win his mother over to see Miss Henderson for what she was—a fine woman worth loving.

Jogging through the yard with the dogs on his heels, he threw open the barn doors. Gazing at his wagon, he longed for something more modern like a carriage—something that he could be proud to offer a ride in to Miss Henderson, something he'd like to be seen in around town. But a carriage wasn't practical for a farmer like him. He'd have to make do with what he had.

He thought about the other night when Rose was leaning on him for warmth with his arm tucked around her shoulders. He scratched his chin with his gloved hand. Why couldn't he have bought a pair of fine cowhide gloves in town at the mercantile? They would suit him better for a jaunt about town with the woman he was falling in love with. The thought of love stopped him cold in his tracks. Was he falling in love with Miss Henderson? Could she fall in love with him? All he could do was harness the mules, drive them into town, and find out for himself.

Harl worked fast getting the collars and leads on the mules and the mules hitched to the wagon—his plain, old wagon. Would Miss

Henderson mind going for a drive in it? He hoped not. Besides, it was all he had. Hopping up onto the wagon seat, Harl guided the mules and wagon outside. Jumping down, he closed the barn doors and latched them against the wind.

"Feel like going for a walk, boys?" he asked the mules. "Let's go get Miss Henderson and show her the town."

By the time Harl made it into town, Mrs. Guthrie's dress shop was open for business. Setting the brake, he jumped down and opened the door to the shop. The bell above his head tinkled.

"Anybody here?" he called.

Mrs. Guthrie sauntered into the front of the shop, followed by Rose.

"Mr. Adams, how nice to see you. What can we do for you?"

He cut his eyes to Rose, who turned a pleasing shade of pink. "I was just driving by." He looked down at his feet and then raised his head and gazed past Mrs. Guthrie to the woman behind her. "No, I came by to see if Miss Henderson would like a tour of the town."

Rose gasped and smiled.

"It is like I was just telling her: something will work out for her in the relationship area, and here you are. Her knight in . . . well, work clothes."

Harl smiled sheepishly. "I'd be most obliged if you would join me in my wagon and go for a ride around town, Miss Henderson."

Rose scowled. Not at all the response he had hoped for. "What will your mother think?"

"She'll forgive me," Harl said, his mouth twitching into a smile.

The young woman's face shone as she smiled. "If it's all right with you, Mrs. Guthrie, I'd like to go for a drive."

"Why, of course, it's all right with me, dear. You young people go have fun but stay in plain sight of the town. I don't want any busybodies talking."

Rose laughed. Harl offered her his arm, which she accepted.

Stepping out the door, Harl bounded over to the wagon. He helped Rose up onto the seat next to him. Mrs. Guthrie stood on the boardwalk next to her shop door watching.

Harl and Rose's faces beamed their pleasure.

"Here we go. Walk on, boys," he said to the mules as he released the brake. The mules moved forward on the hard-packed dirt of the street. The ice had long since been reclaimed by the earth after a few warm days.

Rose sat close to Harl and tucked her hand around his arm. Harl gazed at her and smiled.

"Do you mind?" Rose asked.

"Not at all. I like it."

The pair drove along the back doors of businesses until they reached the backdoor of *The Daily Bugle*. Harl turned two corners and headed into the busy main street.

"You remember Moore's Hotel and Restaurant?" Harl asked, bobbing his head in the direction of the hotel.

"Ugh, how could I forget slipping and falling when I tried to go see the train schedule for the next day? And then, you came to my rescue once again." She looked up at Harl and saw the faintest breath of a smile creep across his lips.

"I'm mighty glad you fell. It gave you a reason to stay in Harrisville."

Harl felt her hand move up his arm to his bicep. He involuntarily flexed his muscle, which made Rose giggle.

"What?" Harl asked.

"I was just wondering why some young woman hasn't snapped you up into marriage."

"Oh, that. Well, they would have to catch me first; and believe me, they've tried. Seems like the whole town has at one time or another tried to get me hitched to this one or that."

"And?"

"A man don't want to be chased. A man wants to do the chasing."

"And is this the chasing part?"

Harl's face fell. He looked down at the backs of the mules as they lumbered along. Rose could feel the rising tension. She had said something terribly wrong. She didn't expect her flippant comment to hurt Harl's feelings. Oh, why couldn't she keep her mouth shut on such subjects?

"Uh hum." Harl cleared his throat. "Yes, well . . . here's Gage McKee's Bookshop—finest proprietor of books this side of the Cumberland River, or so he likes to say."

Rose looked up at Harl. "I love to read. I should stop in sometime. I see his bookshop is right against Mrs. Guthrie's Dress Shop and is flanked by the alley."

"Yes, there's a lot of riffraff that hangs out in that alley at night, or so I'm told. I wouldn't want you to be out after dark without an escort," Harl said.

"I certainly wouldn't be caught in town after dark. It would be unseemly."

"Yes, I was told that plenty of people enjoy being in town after dark in Marsh's Saloon next door."

"Who is telling you all this?"

"Elijah Grant keeps an eye out. His store's kitty-corner from the saloon, and he says there's quite a lot of troublemakers who come and go out of that place. Speaking of riffraff . . . " Harl jutted his jaw toward the saloon entrance as Cletus Tooth staggered out.

"Well, well, well. If it isn't my loving bride come to watch me walk home," Cletus said, wobbling into the street.

"Look out!" Harl yelled, pulling back on the reins as Cletus stepped in front of Dr. Johnson's buggy, which was speeding down the street.

Cletus looked at Harl and then stumbled in front of the doctor's horse, who reared up and missed crushing Cletus' skull when its massive hoofs came down. The street came to a standstill. Harl set the brake and jumped from the wagon and over to Cletus as the doctor was getting out of his buggy, carrying his black medical bag.

"Are you all right?" Harl asked.

Cletus held his head in his arms. Peering out with one eye open and the other closed, he chuckled. "No damage done."

The doctor, seeing the position of Cletus and that he was not maimed in any way, backed his horse up, giving Cletus a wide berth. The doctor set the brake on the buggy before returning and kneeling beside Cletus.

"Thanks, Doc," Cletus said. "Hey, you almost run me over with that wild stallion of yours."

"You're lucky the doctor has such quick reflexes, or else you would be dead," Harl said.

"Is he all right?" Rose called from her seat in the wagon.

"Yes, he's all right," the doctor called back. "Can you sit up?"

"Why, sure." When Cletus was sitting up, he looked at Rose and smiled. Some of his front teeth were missing. "My loving bride . . . "

"Come on, stand up," Harl said. "And she's not your bride."

Cletus stood and grabbed the front of Harl's clean, white shirt. "Is she yours, then?"

"No," Harl said, holding onto Cletus' arm to steady him as the doctor returned to his buggy.

"Well, if she's not yours, she must be mine. Come here and give me a kiss," Cletus said, wobbling on his feet toward her, making kissing noises at Rose.

"Tsk," she said, frowning. "I seem to remember you rejecting me."

"Oh, now, don't be like that, darling," Cletus said, moving forward as a crowd began to gather.

"I'm not your darling," she said, pulling her exposed boots under her dress.

"You heard the woman," Harl said. "She's not your darling."

"What? You turning her against me?" Cletus asked angrily. Pulling his fist back, he swung at Harl and missed him by a mile. The punch momentarily knocked Cletus off his feet. He staggered back, looking up his nose at Harl. "You stay away from my woman or else."

Harl pulled his head back, glaring at Cletus. "Or else what?"

"You'll see one of these days. You'll see," he said threateningly, turning on his heels and staggering out of the street back onto the boardwalk. He ambled toward home.

Harl mashed his hat back down on his head and strode to his wagon. In a couple of swift movements, he returned to his seat next to Rose.

She threaded her arm around his as he took up the reins and started the mules off again. "The audacity of that man," she exclaimed.

Harl involuntarily flexed his right bicep as Rose clung to his arm. "Pay him no mind."

"You don't really think his threat was real?"

"No. It was the threat of a drunk man, and drunk men don't remember their threats."

Rose smiled at Harl and sat back further on the seat.

"I forgot to point out Doc Johnson's office and home," Harl said, flicking his head back toward the opposite side of the street. "He's over there next to the Mercantile barn in front of the train depot. If ever you are hurt and need help, you just run over to Doc's place, and he'll fix you up."

"Let's hope that I am never in need of him again."

"Down here is Miss Noralene Fletcher's Dress Shop. I hear she's been losing business due to Mrs. Guthrie's getting a milliner working at her shop." Harl grinned down at Rose, who blushed.

"Did you now?"

"You want to stop in and introduce yourself to Miss Fletcher?"

"What would Mrs. Guthrie think? But . . . I am dying to meet the competition, so, yes, let's."

Harl set the brake and jumped down. Turning, he held out his hand to Rose, who descended as if she were a queen. Harl offered his arm to her, and they walked together to Noralene Fletcher's Dress Shop door. In the window stood a dress form with an exquisite gown on it but no matching bonnet or curtains in the window, Rose observed.

When Harl pushed the door open, a little brass bell tinkled overhead, announcing a potential client's presence.

A stately, young woman of about twenty-some years came out of the backroom to greet her customers. She wore a lovely baby blue dress, the color of a robin's egg, with what looked like delicate, handmade lace around the neck of the bodice. Her hair was as black as coal with eyes to match. She smiled when she recognized Harl.

"My goodness! Mr. Harl Adams and Miss . . . "

"Miss Rose Henderson," Rose said.

"Ah, Miss Henderson—the milliner," she said, smiling coolly.

"Oh, you know of me?"

"Yes, I saw Susan Lovely walking around town showing off the bonnet you made her on the arm of her betrothed, Wesley."

"Oh?"

"It was a lovely bonnet. You are just the woman this town needs—someone who can make and adorn hats for our female population."

"I was going to come here and ask about setting up shop in a corner of your business; but I met Mrs. Guthrie first, and she insisted that I set up shop in her store."

Noralene nodded and gestured to four plush, red chairs in the middle of the shop. Harl, Rose, and Noralene sat.

"It's understandable why you would stay at Mrs. Guthrie's shop. She can be quite persistent. Would you care for some tea?"

Harl and Rose waved her off. "There's no need," Rose said. "We aren't staying long. I just wanted to meet you."

Noralene nodded, and her eyes drifted to the backroom doorway.

"Will you be at the wedding this Saturday?" Rose asked.

"Of Susan and Wesley? Yes. I hope Mrs. Guthrie approves of her choice of guests," Noralene said with a smile.

"I hope so, too. Thank you for your hospitality," Rose said, rising. Pausing, she asked, "If you are the best seamstress in this town, why is Mrs. Guthrie making Susan's wedding dress?"

"Oh, that," Noralene said, rising also. "It is because Mrs. Guthrie has a stranglehold on any woman who wants to get married in a nice dress. She was the first to set up shop and is the last word on what is fashionable for a woman to wear to her own wedding. She used to have this shop as her own before she got a better deal on the place where she is now."

Rose nodded. "Thank you. It was very nice meeting you."

"Miss Henderson, Mr. Adams, thank you for stopping by." Then to Rose, she said, "If things with Mrs. Guthrie don't work out, you are welcome here."

"Thank you."

Harl and Rose scooted out the door back onto the busy boardwalk and up onto the wagon.

Rose looped her arm into Harl's as he released the brake. "This has been a nice outing. I'm so glad to have met Miss Fletcher."

"Meeting the competition. Tsk tsk. Whatever will Mrs. Guthrie say about that?" Harl teased.

"I'll tell her if she asks. Do you think she will find out?"

"Oh, she'll know all right. You don't know how gossip can spread in this town." Harl eased his mules out into the busy street. Jutting his chin out, he used it to point toward the livery. "Speaking of competition, there's Henry Fraizer's livery with his blacksmith forge."

Rose turned her head to the right and saw a large, dark-skinned man working the bellows as coals glowed in the forge.

"Across the street is Henry Shoemaker's blacksmith shop." Rose looked around Harl and watched as a man with dirty blond hair hammered away on a piece of glowing metal. Various black, metal implements hung above him on the beams in the shop and on the inside of the doors, which stood open. Rose watched as the man rubbed his arm over his sweaty forehead and brought his hammer down again.

She sat back in her seat but kept her eyes fastened on the man as he worked. She scowled, and her lips worked into a thin line. Harl turned to her and opened his mouth to say something, but he clamped it shut when he saw her expression.

"What's this about?" he asked.

"It's just that I almost married a blacksmith. It's bringing back memories—and not so good memories, at that."

Harl nodded and hurried the pace of the mules. "We've been out on our excursion for a little too long. How about we turn our attention back to Mrs. Guthrie's shop?"

"Yes, let's."

Harl turned onto the street just past the blacksmith's shop. Turning again, he headed past smaller shops to Mrs. Guthrie's dress shop. Harl helped Rose down and walked her to the door.

"Until next time," he said.

Rose giggled. "Until next time," she said. Placing her hand on the door handle, she swung it open.

Harl jumped back into the wagon in a few easy steps, tipped his hat, and told the mules to walk on. When he had turned the corner and was out of sight, Rose stepped into the dress shop.

One of the chairs was turned with its back to the door, and a man sat in it across from Mrs. Guthrie, whose teacup rattled on the saucer as she stared at the man.

"Mrs. Guthrie? Whatever is the matter?"

Mrs. Guthrie raised terrified eyes to Rose. She snapped her head back toward the man, who sat with his hat on his knee—a black, felt hat with three quail feathers in its brim—the hat she had adorned for him. She would know that hat and its wearer anywhere. Albert Winters, her betrothed, was paying her a visit.

"Hello, Rose," Albert said, turning his cold gaze upon her.

Rose swayed, and the room went black.

Chapter 11

When Rose awoke, a crowd had gathered inside Mrs. Guthrie's Dress Shop. Dr. Johnson was among the onlookers.

"That's it. Take your time sitting up now," he said, kneeling at her side.

Rose snapped up into a sitting position.

"Whoa now, not so fast," Dr. Johnson said.

Rose scanned the faces in the room. Mrs. Guthrie stood over her. Her brows were pinched, and she bit her lower lip. Iva Jean Lovely, Susan Lovely, Wesley Robins, and Uella Perkins all stood around her. Shooting her gaze past the onlookers, Rose turned her eyes to the empty chair that had held Albert Winters.

"Where is he?" she gasped, clutching one hand at her throat.

"Where is who?" Dr. Johnson asked, holding her wrist and looking at his pocket watch.

"Albert Winters—that man who was there," she said, jutting her index finger toward the chair he had occupied. "Where is he?"

"He left," Mrs. Guthrie said. "Are you all right?"

Rose felt the back of her head, where a bump was forming.

"I think so."

"Here." Mrs. Guthrie gave her a glass filled with water. Rose took a sip and handed it back.

"Think you can stand up?" Dr. Johnson asked, standing and holding out his hands to her.

"I hope so." Taking his hands, she stood. Rushing to the chair that had been righted to face the chair that Mrs. Guthrie usually sat in, she studied it as if Albert would magically reappear.

"What happened?" Uella Perkins asked.

"She fainted," Iva Jean Lovely said.

"She really should sit down," Wesley said.

Rose waved her hand at everyone and shot into the backroom. No one was there. Rose spun around, throwing herself momentarily into a dizzy spell. Dr. Johnson rushed to her side, grabbed her arm, and steadied her.

Mrs. Guthrie stepped into the backroom. "I ran to get the doctor; and when I got back, he was gone."

Rose staggered over to the chair at the sewing machine and fell into it.

"Who was he? Is that why you fainted?" Dr. Johnson asked.

Rose put her head in her hands. "He was my betrothed, and he's come for me."

"Come for you?" Uella Perkins asked, entering the room.

"Yes, we were to be married a month ago, and I ran away to get away from him."

"And he followed you here to marry you? Oh, how romantic," Uella exclaimed.

Rose turned her gaze onto Uella. "No, it isn't romantic. It's possessive. He can't stand losing me, but I never thought he'd find me here."

"How do you think he found you?" Mrs. Guthrie asked.

"My father told him. He had to have told him once he returned home, and now he's here to take me back."

"Take you back where?" Iva Jean Lovely asked, stepping with her daughter and Wesley into the backroom.

"Back home to Chelsea, Michigan."

"Michigan?" Uella shrieked. "But that's miles away!"

"I know."

"Will you go with him?" Uella asked.

"I hope not," Mrs. Guthrie said, holding out the glass of water to Rose, who took it and drank deeply. "He's not right for her."

Just then, Harl burst into the backroom. "Where is she?" he asked.

Rose raised her hand as the people in the room opened space for Harl to get to her.

"What happened? I was over at the mercantile when George Waywright came in and said someone had fainted at Mrs. Guthrie's shop and was looking for the doctor." Reaching Rose, he asked, "Are you all right?"

Rose nodded. "Yes, I'm fine now. Just as long as he doesn't come back."

Rose bit her lower lip and looked at her trembling hands in her lap. It seemed like ages since she had seen Albert Winters' blond hair and black eyes staring at her. The last time she had seen him was the night before their wedding.

Everything was set. The church and food had been arranged to his pleasure, not hers. They would be wed at the First United Methodist Church on Park Street in Chelsea. It was a lovely, grand church with glorious stained-glass windows. "A perfect setting for a perfect beginning to wedded bliss,"

Albert had assured her. It wasn't a church that either of them attended as both of them were disinterested believers in anything spiritual. What the church represented to her was a lifetime of bondage to a man she did not love. Albert had probably chosen the church for its pious interior and grandiose exterior. Not to mention, it was one of the oldest churches in Chelsea.

Everyone who was anyone in town made an appearance every Sunday in that church. Everyone who was anyone wedded in that church. Even so, nothing could tame Rose's unease the night before what should have been her big day.

She quietly gathered her belongings in an empty trunk hidden in some bushes near the train depot in Chelsea. She had been sneaking items into it all afternoon, beginning with a lovely white rock she had found on her way to the depot with dresses wrapped in plain paper and tied with string. She wanted to look nonchalant. No one would think anything of it—a young woman carrying parcels.

She had even wrapped up her father's service revolver to take with her. Why she had taken the gun he kept in a box beneath his bed, she didn't know. "It was for protection," she had told herself. Protection from what or whom? She didn't dare put a name or a face to what she was protecting herself from. Suffice it to say, if she needed the gun, she would have it.

Lastly, she stole a hundred dollars from the lockbox her father also kept under his bed. She would need the money. She put it and her earnings from her milliner business into her purse, bought a one-way ticket the morning of what was to be the beginning of her wedded bliss, and boarded the train.

She was giddy as the train pulled away from the depot. She tipped a cart boy to fish her trunk out of the bushes and load it into the baggage car. With purse in hand, she was free. She felt as if she was soaring high above the clouds. That feeling of soaring, of getting away with something, came crashing to a halt when she saw Albert Winters' handsome face with his cruel sneer. She had gotten away, hadn't she? She was free to live her life however she pleased, and Albert Winters wasn't part of that life.

"Rose?" It was Harl speaking. "Rose?" he asked more insistently.

"Mmm?" she answered.

"Did you hear me?" Harl asked.

Rose shook her head.

"What do you think of my idea?"

"What idea is that?"

"I'll put you on a train headed to Bell County. There's a little church over there and a family my brother-in-law, Samuel, is friends with that you can stay with."

Rose shook her head and sighed. "He'll just find me in Bell County just as easily as finding me here. Why he waited so long to come for me, I don't know."

"You're not planning on going back with him?"

"What choice do I have? He'll always find me."

Harl grabbed Rose's hands in his big, calloused ones. "No, we can't let him win."

"We?"

"Yes, you and me."

"The only way Albert Winters can be stopped is if he is six feet under with a bullet in his brain."

A collective gasp wound through the group of onlookers.

Harl sat back and pulled the hat off his head. He tossed it on the sewing machine.

"I think you all have seen and heard quite enough," Mrs. Guthrie said, ushering the onlookers out of the backroom. Rose heard the bell at the front door tinkle. A cold gust of wind marked the door's opening. Only Dr. Johnson, Harl, and Rose remained. In a few moments, Mrs. Guthrie joined them again, holding her hand at her throat.

"My dear, you shouldn't say such things," she said.

Rose looked up, fire in her eyes. "Why not? It's true. I'll never be free from him!"

"Yes, but what if something were to happen to him? The whole town'll think it was you."

"What you need is rest," Dr. Johnson piped in, opening his bag. "I'll give you some sedative powder to take when you return to the Guthrie household, and don't leave her home under any circumstances until we can get this Winters situation taken care of."

"I'll take her home," Harl offered. "Wait with her until I can bring the wagon around. I got so addled when I heard someone had fainted that I left my wagon over at the Mercantile."

"I'll close and lock the door to the shop behind you," Mrs. Guthrie offered as Harl retrieved his hat. He and Mrs. Guthrie headed out of the backroom. Again, the bell above the door sounded, and a gust of wind announced the opening of the door. A snap announced the lock was in place.

Mrs. Guthrie returned to the backroom holding her hand at her throat. "What a day this has been!"

Rose shook her head and sipped at the glass of water. A scowl marked her face. "How dare he come all this way thinking he might get me to change my mind about him!"

Mrs. Guthrie rubbed the side of her neck. "Maybe he came to take you home."

Rose lifted her eyes to the ceiling and studied the corner of the room. "Maybe, but he won't be successful," she said defiantly, standing. She walked over to her trunk and threw open the lid. Rummaging around in the bottom of the trunk, she found what she was looking for—her father's service revolver. Pulling it out, she tucked it in the waist of her skirt.

Mrs. Guthrie gasped. "You don't think it will come to that, do you? Mr. Guthrie can protect you. He'll come to the shop everyday if we want him to."

Rose squinted. "Thank you, but I want to make it very plain to Albert that his attentions are not wanted."

"Have you . . . have you ever fired the gun?"

"Yes, when a peddler was harassing Mrs. Adams, I gave him what for," she said, lifting the revolver out of her skirt waistband.

"Oh my. Oh, my dear. Women have no need to carry firearms."

"They do if they have a man like Albert Winters on their trail."

"You don't think he'd try to . . . to force you to return home with him to Michigan, do you?"

"I'm not taking any chances."

Rose walked into the front of the store and looked out the window. She stuffed the gun back into her skirt waistband.

Harl pulled up outside in his wagon. Rose unlocked and threw open the door. She stepped out onto the boardwalk in front of the store and looked to her right and then to her left. Satisfied that no one was lurking, she turned her attention to Harl, who had jumped down off the wagon and offered her his hand. She took it. Electric fire shot up her arm. She scowled at Harl—not because the feeling was unpleasant, but because it thrilled her. And at that moment, she didn't want to feel a thrill.

Mrs. Guthrie followed Rose out, locking the door behind her. Harl helped her into the wagon, too, before he jogged around the mules and climbed on and took his seat. It was a tight fit, but they made it work.

Harl started to turn the mules around, but Rose put her gloved hand on his forearm. "No, I want to take the long way around through town. I want everyone to know I have a gun and let the word spread to Albert to stay away," she said, pulling the revolver out of her skirt waistband and crossing her arms with the gun resting in the crook of her elbow.

Harl nodded once and turned the mules. They headed through town slowly at Rose's command. She frowned and met the surprised gazes of onlookers with a fiery stare and set mouth.

"I think the majority of people are getting the message."

"And what message would that be, Mr. Adams?" Rose asked.

"To not mess with Rose Henderson." He chuckled.

Without removing her gaze from a townsperson, she answered, "And that is precisely what I want them to understand."

"Oh dear," Mrs. Guthrie said.

When they arrived at the Guthrie home, Harl jumped down. He helped Mrs. Guthrie out of the wagon first and then Rose, who still brandished the revolver.

"Put that thing away, will you?" he said.

She allowed a whisper of a smile to cross her lips as she tucked the revolver away into her skirt's waistband.

Mrs. Guthrie led the way into the house, where her husband sat reading the paper in the sitting room.

"I'm so nervous, I don't know what to do," Mrs. Guthrie said, wringing her hands.

"Why so nervous?" Mr. Guthrie asked.

"Show him, Rose," she said. But before Rose could pull out the revolver, Mrs. Guthrie blurted out, "She has a gun."

"A gun!" Mr. Guthrie shouted, scrambling to his feet, crumpling the newspaper in one hand. "You have a gun? Why?"

"Her old fiancé came to town," Mrs. Guthrie answered quickly.

"That's no reason to have a gun!" Mr. Guthrie exclaimed. "You brandish a gun when there is real trouble, not for a man."

"Yes, but this man is trouble with a capital T," Rose said. "You don't know what he is like. He came here to persuade me to return to Michigan with him, and he won't be successful."

"Certainly not," Mr. Guthrie said.

"I think you are in good hands, Miss Henderson," Harl said. "I better get back to Mama and the farm."

"Of course, you need to get back to the farm. Your chores are waiting. Don't you worry about a thing. I'll take care of the ladies," Mr. Guthrie said.

"We'll be all right," Rose said.

"Yes, and I'll drive them into town and stay with them and bring them back at the close of the day."

Harl nodded and donned his hat. "It may be a while before I can get back into town. My chores . . . well, I have things that need tending to every day."

"I understand," Rose said. "Thank you for bringing us home."

The muscles in Harl's jaw tensed, showing his disappointment. How he wished that his mother would relent, so he could bring Rose back to the farm and have her close to him. Knowing that she was in town with the Guthrie family made his stomach churn. He had the cattle to look after, a couple of sows, the dogs, the orchard, and his mother.

"I better get going while it is still light out," Harl said in answer to Rose's thanks. "Keep the doors and windows locked." With that, Harl headed out the door. He waited for Mr. Guthrie to lock it behind him before he leaped into his wagon and headed back out of town for home.

Chapter 23

When Harl arrived home, Hazel was sitting on the porch in a straight-back, cane-bottom chair waiting for him. She wore a heavy, black, wool jacket; gloves; and a hat. Over her lap was draped a crazy quilt. From her shivering form, it looked like she had been waiting a long while for him.

"Where in tarnation have you been?" She didn't wait for an answer. "I had to feed the cattle and your dogs and the chickens and the pigs, and collect the eggs, and milk the cow, and make lunch that went cold, and make dinner that is likely burned—all because you wanted to spend time in town?"

Harl turned his head away from his mother in answer to her question. Walking the mules over to the barn and out of earshot of his mother, he opened the doors and led the mules inside, where he unharnessed them and put them in their stalls with plenty of hay and feed. He rubbed them down with an old cloth and decided to brush them tomorrow. Even though his mother had done his chores for him, there was still plenty to do. The dogs jumped up, licking what they could reach of his gloved hands.

"Down, boys, down." He laughed, his heart light. But what about Miss Henderson? How could he keep her safe when his duty was to his mother and the farm? He would just have to trust that the Lord and Devin Guthrie would keep them safe.

Lifting his arms, he placed them on one of the stalls of the mules and bowed his head. "Lord, I pray Your protection and angels would surround Miss Henderson and the Guthrie's and their property. I pray no evil plan would prevail against them. Help them. Guide them. Keep them safe. I trust them to Your care. In Jesus' name, amen."

When Harl lifted his head, he turned to see the dogs sitting beside the stall watching him with sobering, brown eyes. "I'll just have to trust that the Lord'll take care of them," he said to the dogs. They stood, wagging their tails, seemingly excited that his soothing voice was speaking to them. "You boys be good now and settle down for the night," Harl said, stepping out the barn door.

Harl looked over to the house. Lamplight glowed in the window in the kitchen. His mother was no longer sitting on the porch. He swallowed, sure he'd get an earful when he walked into the kitchen.

Sure enough, as soon as he opened the door, his mother, who was standing at the stove, turned and started in on him. "Had to do the chores myself. It's been years since I've had to throw down hay for the cattle and give them grain to eat—years!"

"And you did a wonderful job of it. There wasn't anything left for me to do, except feed and put away the mules for the night."

"You spent all day in town? And left me the work to do?"

"I spent most of the day with Miss Henderson. Do you forgive me?"

Hazel turned her back to Harl and dished up a plate of something off the stove. When she turned back to him, her scowl was gone. "Of course, I forgive you. I just don't want you neglecting your duties around here when you are gallivanting all over the county with that woman." She set the plate on the table and sniffed.

Harl sat, picked up the fork at his place setting, and began eating. After chewing and swallowing the food in his mouth, he replied, "We weren't gallivanting all over the county, Mama. I was merely looking out for her."

Hazel scowled again and placed her hands on her hips. "Looking out for her? Why does she need looking after?"

"She's in trouble. Her old beau came into town and may try to take her back home to Chelsea, Michigan."

Hazel dropped her hands off her hips, and her face softened. "You mean, that man who whipped the horse for not standing still when he was trying to shoe it?"

Harl nodded, his mouth full of food.

"Oh, that poor girl." Hazel lifted one hand to her throat.

"Mama, couldn't we have her stay with us again? Show her some Christian love and kindness and protect her from what is coming? That way, I wouldn't have to run into town every day, hoping and praying she was all right, and could stay and get my chores done."

"But she wanted to live in town and stay with the Guthries."

"I'm not so sure that is the best place for her now," he said.

"It's up to Miss Henderson what she decides to do, but yes. She would be welcome to stay here again."

His mother sat at the table and watched her son eat the rest of his meal.

He'd have to pray for the Lord's will in all of this. With all the work he had to do, he'd wear himself thin trying to keep up the farm and keep an eye on Rose for her safety. He could do it—of that, he was sure—but he'd need help around the farm, and he knew just the men for the job. He'd speak to them in the morning.

In the morning, he announced his plan to his mother. "I'm going up to Liver Mountain to hire me some workers for the farm. I can't work the farm and keep an eye on Miss Henderson," he said.

"I was wondering when you were going to break down and hire someone. It's about time," his mother said, turning the bacon in the pan as bread toasted on the stove. She fried plenty of eggs for herself and Harl, dished up the items onto two plates, and set one before her son and one at her place.

Seating herself at the table, she added pepper to her eggs.

"You really think Miss Henderson is in trouble and would do better back here with us?"

"Yes, I do."

His mother touched her hand to her face and studied her son's eyes. "Well, if it means that much to you, we can let her come live with us again."

Harl jumped up from the table, causing his mother to throw her hands in the air in surprise. He stepped around the table and hugged his mother and kissed her plump cheek, something he hadn't done since the day his father's body was brought back to the farm.

"Oh, Mama! Thank you!" he exclaimed, kissing her cheek again and again as if emphasizing his point. "Can I go get her?"

His mother laughed and caught her son's face in her hands before he could plant another kiss on her cheek. "Not yet. You need to eat your breakfast, do your morning chores, find those men you want to hire, and then go get Miss Henderson."

Harl returned to his seat, his face flushed with excitement. He wolfed down the contents of his plate and then hurried out to the barn to complete his chores.

When the chores were done, he backed the mules out of their stalls and hitched them to the wagon. Throwing open the barn doors, he guided the mules, pulling the wagon, out into the growing morning sunshine. His first stop of the day would be up to Liver Mountain, where the Williamses and Clyde Haskell lived.

The way up the mountain had not been improved over the few months since he had driven up there. The roads were still deep gullies filled with rocks. He eased the mules around what he could and slowed their pace considerably. When he topped Liver Mountain, several ramshackle houses stood leaning to one side or another. Children playing outside in the hard-packed dirt stopped their play to watch the approaching wagon and driver.

Harl headed to Ezra Williams' home first. As the wagon neared, Ezra came out onto the hard-packed dirt in front of his place. He waved his hand when he saw Harl.

"Mr. Harl, what brings you up this way?"

"Hello, Ezra, ma'am, Jonah, Zillah, and Micah," Harl said as each person gathered in front of the wagon. "I'm in need of some helpers around my farm."

"Whatcha hoping them helpers can do?"

"They need to climb into the hayloft and throw hay down to the cattle and feed the chickens, pigs, mules, and dogs."

"Hmm," Ezra said. "I don't know about climbing no ladders, but I could do everything else. I ain't no spring chicken no more," he said, laughing. "Now, Hezekiah and Aaron might be of more help to you, but

Aaron works at the livery most days. Even so, it might be good to ask him and see what he says. You know when school will be commencing again? My children's been missing learning under Mrs. Catherine."

"I'm not sure. That's for the school board to decide. Perhaps it will start up again once they find a qualified, single teacher."

Harl raised his hat and moved the wagon on to the next cabin. Hezekiah, his wife, and their daughter, Ruthie, were already standing on what was their front lawn. Aaron was not with them.

"Mr. Williams, you remember me?" Harl asked when he was within earshot of Hezekiah's shack.

Hezekiah's face spread into a wide, toothy grin. "Why sure, I remember you. You's the best payer of any white man I ever worked fer."

Harl smiled. "How would you like to earn some more money?"

"Just tell me how," Hezekiah said, stepping forward.

"I need help around my farm."

"You got winter apples that needs picking?" he asked, laughing at his joke.

Harl shook his head and grinned. "No, I've got a farm that needs tending to while I help a lady in distress."

Hezekiah pushed his felt hat up on his head. "That lady in distress wouldn't be Mrs. Hazel, would it? 'Cause my Esther here can tend to her while we tend the farm."

"No, nothing like that. I just need an extra set of hands around the place. Think you could persuade your boy, Aaron, to come with you and help?"

"He's working down at the livery, but he might enjoy a change of pace. I'll ask him when he comes home tonight. What about your neighbor, Clyde?"

"I don't know. You'll have to ask him."

"Think you can be down at my place this afternoon in time for evening chores?"

"Yes, sir."

Harl eased the mules over the uneven, hard-packed dirt patch to the front of Clyde and Lucy Haskell's place.

Before he had time to stop the mules, the Haskells were standing outside their shack's door.

"We heard you coming," Clyde said.

Nancy, Rachel, and Rebecca all gathered around the mules' faces and petted their cheeks and noses. As they fawned over the mules, Harl spoke. "You needing a job, Clyde?"

"I can always use extra money, Mr. Harl. What did you have in mind?"

"I can no longer manage my farm alone, and I'm looking for some good workers to help me with it."

"You want me to come work for you again?" Clyde asked, a smile warming his face.

"Yes, it will require you to climb up on a ladder and get into the hayloft to throw down hay to the cattle below. You aren't afraid of heights, are you?"

"Me? Nah. I'd be happy to help you."

"Thank you. Can you be at my place this afternoon in time for the evening chores to be done?"

"Why, sure."

"I'll see you then," Harl said." Turning to the girls standing in front of the mules, he tipped his hat and said, "Excuse me, ladies."

Their father, Clyde, waved them over. "You leave them mules be and come on back in the house. I'll see you this afternoon, Mr. Harl."

"I like your mules. They's nice," Nancy said.

"I wish we could ride them," Rebecca said.

"Now, hush. Mr. Harl got better things to do than that," Clyde said.

Harl raised his hat and set off for town.

When he reached the Guthries' place, Mr. and Mrs. Guthrie and Rose were eating breakfast. Mr. Guthrie unlocked and opened the door for Harl.

Pulling off his hat, Harl stood at one end of the dining room table.

"You look like the cat that ate the canary," Mrs. Guthrie said. "What's the secret you are holding so tight, you look like you could bust?"

"Welp, once you all finish breakfast, I'd like Rose to pack up and come home with me."

Rose's mouth fell open. "You want me to go home with you? Why? I'm quite happy here."

"Mama and me want you back at our place, so I can keep watch over you and the farm."

Rose sucked in her breath. Mrs. Guthrie clapped her hands. "See, didn't I tell you the Lord would provide for you?"

Rose nodded and then paused. "Oh, my trunk is upstairs. I'll need my trunk."

"Not a problem. I'll head up there after you eat."

"Won't you join us, Mr. Adams?" Mrs. Guthrie said.

Harl waved one hand in the air, while the other one held his stomach. "I couldn't eat a morsel more. I already ate."

"Well, at least sit down with us," Mrs. Guthrie said.

"That I will," Harl said, pulling out a chair.

After Rose finished her meal, she stood and cleared her place. Mrs. Guthrie held out her arm to her. "You don't want to keep your man waiting, now, do you?"

Rose felt her cheeks warming at Mrs. Guthrie's words. "No, but we should do the dishes before we leave. I don't want to have to scrub them later."

"Leave them to me. I'll wash them. Besides, you are going home with Harl, and you won't have to worry about dirty dishes in the sink here anymore. Now, scoot."

Rose returned her dishes to her place and then hurried from the room.

Mrs. Guthrie gathered all the dishes and walked into the kitchen, leaving Mr. Guthrie and Harl alone.

"Seen the newspaper this week?" Mr. Guthrie asked, finishing his cup of coffee and pouring more. He offered the pot to Harl, who declined.

"Haven't had a moment to read it. Why?"

"Looks like the school board took out an advertisement for another teacher to fill Mrs. Harris' place."

"They'll be hard-pressed to find someone to fill the post. I wish they would just allow my sister to continue teaching."

Rose bustled into the room. "The trunk is upstairs, but the rest of my things are up at the store," she said.

"You ready, then?" Harl asked, standing.

"If you'll go get my trunk, please."

"I'll show you to her bedroom," Mr. Guthrie said, rising.

"Yes, let me check on Mrs. Guthrie. She'll have to go with us to unlock the store." She hurried from the room.

Harl followed Mr. Guthrie. When he returned, he was carrying Rose's trunk on his shoulder. Rose and Mrs. Guthrie stood waiting in the foyer.

"Ready," Mrs. Guthrie said, donning her coat, bonnet, and gloves.

Rose threw on her own coat, hat, and gloves and exclaimed, "I'm so excited to be going home with you again, Mr. Adams."

Harl's mouth jerked up into a smile as he led the way to the wagon.

When they reached the store, Harl jumped down and helped Mrs. Guthrie out of the wagon. "You wait here," he said to Rose.

"Oh no, I'm coming with you," she said. Harl helped her down.

Inside the shop, Rose rushed into the back room and gathered her wares.

"Here we go. We'll put these in my trunk," she said, handing the various items to Harl, who headed for the door, followed by Rose.

"I think in light of what has happened that you stay with the Adamses on their farm and don't leave their farm for any reason."

"Not even to come to work at your shop?"

"Especially not to come to work. I can't protect you, and Mr. Guthrie doesn't want to spend all his time in a women's dress shop."

"All right, but what about customers who want fancy bonnets and hats?"

"I'll send them to you."

Rose nodded and followed Harl outside. Placing the items in the trunk in the back of the wagon, Harl helped her up onto the seat.

Jogging around to the other side, he climbed on board, waved to Mrs. Guthrie, and released the brake. Rose sat close.

As they came through the bare orchard, Hazel stood on the porch watching their approach.

Harl pulled up alongside the porch and jumped down. He walked around the mules to the side of the bench, where Rose sat and helped her down.

Standing at the foot of the stairs, Rose opened her mouth to say something, but Hazel cut her off.

"I know things didn't end well for you the last time you were here," Hazel said. "I just want you to know that I've asked the Lord for forgiveness for my un-Christian-like actions. I hope you can find it in your heart to forgive me, too."

Rose smiled up at the other woman. "Yes, of course I forgive you."

Hazel's face lit up in a wide, warm smile as she opened her arms.

Rose strode up the steps and collapsed into Hazel's arms. So many past feelings swelled up in Rose. She thought of her own dear mother, so much like Hazel. A tear stung her cheek.

"Well now," Hazel said, patting her back. "You're welcome here, and all is forgiven. Come on in, and let's get you settled."

By the time the afternoon chores were ready to be done, Clyde, Hezekiah, and Aaron had arrived at the farm.

"Sure was quite a walk getting here," Hezekiah said. "Any chance you could give us a lift home when the time comes?"

"Yes, I will," Harl agreed.

"What would you have us do?" Clyde asked.

"Let's go muck out the stables to start," Harl said. "I'll only need one person for that."

"I'll do it," Aaron said, reluctance in his voice. "It's what I always did down at Mr. Frazier's Livery."

"And a mighty fine job you done of it, too," Hezekiah said, placing a gentle hand on his son's shoulder.

"The other two can carry water and throw hay out of the loft down to the cattle."

"I'll get their feed ready. Aaron, you feel like feeding the mules and dogs?"

"Sure," the boy answered.

When all the chores were done and the mules hitched, Hazel came out with two large mason jars of apple butter.

"Here now," she said, speaking to Hezekiah and Clyde, "you take this apple butter with you as part of your payment."

Hezekiah and Clyde smiled. "Thank ya," Hezekiah said.

Clyde removed his hat and nodded. "That's mighty kind of you, Mrs. Adams."

"We've got more than we can eat in a winter. I wanted to share the Lord's goodness with you men."

As his mother retreated into the house, Harl counted out coins to each man. "Let's get on board the wagon and head for home," he said.

After returning to the farm, Harl put the mules into their cleaned stalls, gave them some feed, petted the dogs, washed up at the well, and then walked into the house. Mama and Rose were putting the finishing touches on dinner, and Mama was humming a hymn.

Rose thought of the ten dollars Hazel had given her. She'd return it to the woman after the dinner dishes were done. She wanted to make peace with her past, and that was a good way to begin.

She looked at Harl, who seemed to be enjoying his food. Could this man be the one for whom she had been destined? Did she believe in destiny? How could she believe in something that she couldn't see? Much like God. Did He still care about her? She had stopped praying; but now that Albert was in town, maybe she should start it up again. It couldn't hurt.

The morning of the wedding of Susan Lovely and Wesley Robins dawned brighter and warmer than usual. The sky was a bright blue with long ribbons of white clouds—a perfect day for a wedding.

"There'll be a dinner at the restaurant after the service," Hazel said. "So, we won't have to worry about lunch. I'm taking them an Around the World quilt I made last year. I hope they like it."

As Rose looked on from the doorway of Hazel's room, she watched as Hazel tied a bright blue silk ribbon around the folded quilt.

"It's a beautiful quilt. I think any young couple would love to have it as a gift for their wedding day," Rose said.

Rose leaned back out the door when she felt a breeze. Harl walked in and set his hat and gloves up on the shelf above the peg, where he hung his coat.

Turning, he called, "The wagon's ready anytime you ladies are."

"Ready," his mother called. Picking up the quilt, she carried it into the kitchen and set it on the table. "Would you carry that out to the wagon please, Harl?"

Harl snapped into action. He picked up the colorful quilt; and without putting on his coat or gloves, he ran it out to the back of the wagon.

"I'm not sure I should be going," Rose said. "I don't have a present for the couple."

"You're with us. The gift is from all of those living under this roof."

Rose tugged on her calfskin gloves and then put on her coat and hat. Hazel followed Rose's lead and placed the blue hat Rose had made for her on her head.

"There now. How do I look?" Hazel asked, turning.

Rose cocked her head to one side and smiled. "You look beautiful. The hat is just the right color for your eyes."

Hazel chuckled.

When Harl returned, he put on his coat and gloves and placed the hat on his head when he stepped outside. "You ladies ready?"

"Coming," Hazel said, gesturing for Rose to step out the door first.

"Don't we need to lock it?" Rose asked.

"No need. The farm hands Harl hired will look after it, and so will the dogs." Calling over to the three hired hands, she asked, "You all will watch the house while we're gone, won't you?"

"Sure will," Hezekiah responded.

"You can count on us," Clyde assured her.

Hazel nodded as the dogs bounded toward her. "Don't you jump up on me," she said. "You just stay right where you are."

Hezekiah whistled, and the dogs ran to him. He patted their heads when they reached him. The dogs jumped up and down as he reached into his pocket for something. Pulling his hand out, he gave each dog the contents.

"What are you feeding them?" Harl asked, helping the women into the wagon.

"My wife had some cured sausage that I brung for my lunch. Thought I'd give them some as a reward for coming to me."

"All right. We'll see you after a while," Harl said, waving as he drove away.

When they arrived at the church, Harl swung himself off the bench and then helped the ladies down. Other people were arriving on foot, by wagon, and by buggy.

"Oh, look, Harl," his mother said. "There's Miss Noralene Fletcher and Mrs. Uella Perkins."

Harl darted his eyes to where his mother pointed and saw the women dressed in their Sunday best walking into the church and greeted by Rev. Samuel Harris in the doorway.

A buggy pulled up alongside theirs, and Mr. Guthrie got out and hurried around the horse to help his wife from her seat.

"Hello, Mrs. Guthrie," Hazel said.

Rose raised her hand and smiled.

"Miss Henderson, how are you faring at the Adamses'?"

"Really well," she said.

"May we sit with you inside?" Mrs. Guthrie asked.

"Of course," Hazel said, "but we'd better be getting inside if we want to get a good seat."

The group of women walked up to Samuel Harris and shook his hand. Hazel hugged him and went into the church, while Harl and Devin murmured over by the buggy.

Mrs. Guthrie took a seat on a bench three places from the front. She scowled. "I told Mr. Guthrie we needed to hurry, but he just had to read the last bit of news in the paper. Tsk."

Around them sat townspeople and those who attended the church.

"Looks like they invited the whole town," Mrs. Guthrie huffed. "Well, at least it is warm enough."

The potbelly stove in the room radiated enough heat to keep the attendees warm. Even though the day was beautiful, it was cold.

When everyone was seated, Samuel walked up to the front of the room. Gone were the pulpit and the teacher's desk and chair. The room was bare, except for the empty blackboard at the front of the room. Without turning to the crowd, the reverend looked at the watch in his hand. He knocked twice on the door in the front of the room.

Wesley Robins, wearing a black suit, opened the door and came out. His dark hair was slicked back and parted in the middle. His face was clean-shaven. He took a place standing next to Samuel.

"If he was there, then I wonder where the bride is," Mrs. Guthrie said in too loud a voice. People in the congregation looked at each other, and a murmur broke out among the guests.

The soft sound of hoofs met Rose's ears. She turned to peer out the window. There, riding in a buggy, was Susan. The bride was coming. "Look, there she is," Rose said, pointing. The crowd careened their heads around to look out the window to where she pointed as the horse and buggy, carrying Susan and a man, neared the church.

Turning her attention back toward Wesley, Rose saw sweat running down his face as he looked out at the crowd, who were now looking toward the door.

Rose craned her neck around when a collective sigh moved through the crowd. She saw Susan standing in the doorway smiling. Her dress fit her well, as did the bonnet Rose had made for her. Rose smiled to herself but turned when she felt someone jab her in the ribs.

"There's your bonnet and my dress. Don't they look lovely?" Mrs. Guthrie whispered loud enough for those around them to hear. Rose turned to Mrs. Guthrie.

"Yes, Susan is lovely," she said.

"That's her father with her on his arm," Mrs. Guthrie said.

There was no music, just the quiet patter of Susan's shoes and her father's soft boots stepping down the aisle. When they reached

Wesley, her father placed her hand in Wesley's, kissed her lightly on the cheek, and joined a woman sitting on a bench at the front.

Wesley joined his intended standing before Rev. Harris. The reverend opened the Bible he was holding and began the marriage service.

After they had spoken their vows, Rev. Harris raised his hands and blessed them.

"May you live long lives. May you not know strife. May you be fruitful. And may you always cleave unto each other." The reverend smiled and gestured for the couple to turn and face the congregation.

"It is my happy pleasure to introduce to you Mr. and Mrs. Wesley Robins."

The congregation erupted into applause, and many shouted, "Congratulations!"

After the applause died down, the father of the bride stood and turned to face the crowd. "You are all welcome to come sup with us at Moore's Restaurant. We have the whole place at our disposal," he said.

"That's Susan's father, Wilbur Lovely," Mrs. Guthrie whispered in Rose's ear. "I hear he's paying for the whole thing."

Rose merely nodded.

Prompted by Rev. Harris, the couple walked up the aisle and out the door. The onlookers followed. By the time Rose, Hazel, and Harl walked outside, the couple was seated in a buggy. Many hands reached up to shake Wesley and Susan's hands and congratulate them and wish them happiness.

"Follow us to the restaurant," Wesley said, turning the buggy around and pointing it toward town.

By the time Harl, Hazel, and Rose arrived at the restaurant, most of the people who had been at the wedding were seated. Garlin

Moore seated them at a table across from the entrance to the hotel. As Rose sat, she caught a glimpse of someone with light-colored hair standing in the doorway of the hotel.

Gasping, she looked again, but the figure was gone.

"What is it?" Hazel leaned over to ask.

"I thought . . . I saw . . . No, it couldn't have been."

"What?" Harl asked.

"I thought I saw Albert skulking around by the hotel door."

Harl turned his head and scanned the crowd. "What does he look like?"

"Blond hair and black eyes. I think he was wearing a black sackcloth suit," Rose said.

"I know what he looks like. We'll keep on the lookout for him. Won't we, Mr. Guthrie?" Mrs. Guthrie asked.

"That we will," Mr. Guthrie said, picking up his napkin and tucking it in his shirt.

When the meal had ended and the presents had all been opened or unwrapped and fawned over by the happy couple, Hazel said, "Looks like the party's dying down. I think it is time to go home."

Harl stood and pulled out his mother's chair and then Rose's.

"Goodbye, Mr. and Mrs. Guthrie," Rose said. "It was nice seeing you again."

"Goodbye, dear girl, and don't you worry about the shop. I'll send any milliner clients your way."

Rose nodded her thanks to the woman and took Harl's offered right elbow while his mother took his left. When they reached the front of the restaurant, Rose hung back. Looking up and down the street, satisfied that Albert was not present, she walked out into the sunshine with Harl and Hazel.

As Harl was helping his mother into the wagon, a cold hand reached around and clamped down on Rose's mouth. She felt something hard and round pushed into her back.

"Don't you scream. Don't you dare scream," a familiar voice whispered in her ear.

Rose's gasp was muffled. Harl and his mother turned to Rose.

Behind the wide-eyed woman stood a blond-haired man with black eyes wearing a black sack-cloth suit. His hand was over her mouth.

"Let her go!" Harl yelled, lunging forward.

Albert moved the gun from her back to her temple where Harl and Hazel could see it.

"Don't you worry. Rose is my problem now. And we're going to take a little walk over to the train station."

When he saw the gun, Harl stepped back.

"That's a good boy." Albert chuckled. "Now, Rose, darling, let's go wait for the train. And don't scream or try to get away from me, or you'll force me to shoot you; and we wouldn't want that, now, would we?"

Rose shook her head.

"That's a good girl," Albert said, moving the revolver down to the small of her back again.

Harl balled his fists at his side. "I can't allow you to take her anywhere," he said.

Albert smiled.

"Don't try me. I would hate for my finger to slip on the trigger and end Rose's life."

"You aren't taking her," Harl said, stepping in the way of Albert and Rose. Albert removed his hand from her mouth but kept the revolver at the ready.

"I say I am. If you try and stop me again, I'll shoot her dead right here because if I can't have her, no one else can either. Isn't that right, darling?" he sneered.

"He's serious," Rose said, her eyes wide with fear. "Don't worry about me." Then lowering her head, but not her eyes, she said, "I left that thing my father gave me in the top drawer of the dresser upstairs."

Harl squinted. What was the thing that her father had given her that was stashed in the top drawer of her dresser?

The sound of a train whistle broke the silence between them. "Our chariot is coming, darling," said Albert. "We are going to go home to Chelsea, and you will consent to be my good, little wife, won't you?"

Rose froze. No, no, she wouldn't. She never would. She would rather die first. Her mind was made up as the train's whistle grew louder.

"Now, don't dillydally, darling, and let's not keep our train waiting."

Rose took a step forward as if to go around Harl, but she turned back to Albert and slapped his face as hard as she could. He staggered backward. Harl sprang into action and pushed Rose out of the way as he lunged at the gun in Albert's hand. A shot rang out, and Harl collapsed into a heap at Rose's feet.

Chapter 15

Rose screamed, "You killed him!"

Hazel scrambled down out of the wagon. "Lord, have mercy on my boy," she cried.

Albert looked at the smoking gun, threw it down, and ran across the street toward the train depot. The gun landed in front of Harl, who lay in a heap in front of Rose. Blood was starting to seep onto his fresh, white shirt, which was visible inside his open jacket.

"Oh, Lord, don't take my boy away from me," Hazel said, kneeling in front of Harl. "Lord, Lord, Lord."

The sheriff, Anton Franklin, ran out of the restaurant and scanned the gathering crowd. "Who did this?" he asked.

"Albert Winters," Rose said, pointing to the depot.

Dr. Johnson hurried out behind Anton. He did not have his black bag with him.

"Goodness," he said. Scanning the crowd, he called to two men. "Help me get him across the street to my office."

Anton, the doctor, and two other men helped carry Harl's limp body across the street to the doctor's office. They burst through the door and placed Harl on top of the examination table in the front room of the office.

"I need to go see if I can find who did this," Anton said, hurrying out the door followed by the two men.

Hazel broke down in tears as she watched the doctor open Harl's jacket and cut his shirt away from the wound. Hazel sank into a chair near the wall and wailed. "Lord, Lord, don't take my boy."

Rose stepped up on the other side of the table opposite the doctor and watched him work.

"Are you able to help me?" he asked.

She swallowed and nodded. "Whatever needs to be done."

"Here, you hold this on the wound," he said, bunching up the pieces of the shirt he had just cut away. As Rose held the cloth against Harl's mid-section, where the bullet had ripped through, she bit her lip and prayed. *Lord, I don't know if You can hear a sinner like me, but I need You. Harl needs You. Forgive me and come into my life. And let Harl live. Please. In Jesus' name.*

A lone tear streaked down one cheek. The doctor grabbed Harl's glasses and pulled them off, setting them down on a nearby table. He rolled Harl onto his side. "Help me get his coat off him." Rose complied. The doctor rolled Harl up onto his other side and threw the coat on a chair nearby.

Harl moaned, but his eyes remained closed.

"It doesn't look like the bullet went all the way through," Dr. Johnson said.

Hazel jumped up and rushed to her son's side. "Harl, you just hold on. The doctor'll fix you up."

Dr. Johnson pulled out instruments from a cabinet and a small metal dish. He set these beside Harl. He pulled Rose's hand and the cloth away from the wound. Using one of the instruments, he plunged it into the hole. In a few moments, he had pulled the bullet free from Harl's side. He placed the bloody bullet into the metal dish.

"He was shot at point-blank range. I would have expected the bullet to have ripped through him. But here it is."

"Will he be all right, Doctor?" Hazel asked, cradling her son's head in her arms.

"He should be. He's not bleeding as bad as he was when we brought him in, so he didn't hit an artery. Thank You, Lord."

"Yes, thank You, Lord," Hazel said, bending as she kissed her son's forehead.

"I'm going to clean and close up the wound now."

Rose stood by watching the doctor's movements as he poured whiskey into the wound. He mopped up the liquid with a clean cloth and then sewed up the wound. Rose looked at Hazel, who had turned her face away.

"All done," the doctor said.

"Is he going to be all right now?" Hazel asked.

"I can't guarantee anything; but I'll keep an eye on him, along with my assistant, who will be in tomorrow."

"Can't we take him home?" Hazel moaned.

"Move him? No, that would not be a good idea."

"I'll stay with him," Rose said. "You go home and get some rest. Plus, you need to tell the farmhands what has happened."

Hazel nodded, tears running down her face. Holding her son's head in her arms, she whispered loud enough for Rose to hear, "Don't you up and die on me like your pa did. Don't you do it. You come on back here." She kissed her son's forehead again and stood to her full height just as Samuel and Catherine Harris burst into the room.

"What's happened?" Samuel asked. "Someone said Harl was shot."

"Yes, he was, but I got the bullet out of him. He should recover."

"Oh, Mama!" Catherine exclaimed, rushing forward with tears in her eyes. "What happened? Did you see who did it?"

Hazel nodded as tears began to flow afresh down her face. She glanced over at Rose.

"It was my old fiancé come to take me home. Harl wasn't about to let him just walk off with me, so he went for the gun Albert Winters was holding and got shot." Rose's bottom lip quivered, but she did not give into the tears she was feeling. She wouldn't. Hadn't she prayed for forgiveness and asked the Lord to be with her? Hadn't she prayed for Harl? Wouldn't the Lord answer her prayers?

She felt a deep sense of peace that no matter the outcome, it would be all right. The Lord was in control.

"Come, Mother Adams, I'll take you home," Samuel said.

"Don't worry, Mama. I'll stay with him," Catherine said, pulling a chair over to sit at the head of the table. She raked her hands through Harl's brown hair and kissed the top of his head. "You keep on fighting. You hear?"

Dr. Johnson offered Rose a chair, which he had pulled up beside Harl. Rose sat.

"I'm going to go clean my instruments. I think Harl's in good care now. I'll be back shortly."

Rose reached up and grasped Harl's hand in hers. His eyes fluttered open, and he looked at her. The faintest hint of a smile played at one corner of his mouth before he closed his eyes again.

"Doctor," Catherine called. Dr. Johnson rushed into the room.

"What is it?"

"My brother opened his eyes! He opened his eyes!"

"That's a good sign, but he lost a lot of blood. Let him rest."

Catherine nodded.

After a couple of hours, Samuel returned. "Catherine, dear, let's go home and get some rest. I'm sure the doctor will send word if anything changes."

Catherine stood and brushed her fingers against her brother's cheek. "You get well, you hear?"

"I'll stay with him," Rose said.

"Thank you so much."

Catherine stepped out of the room and into the waiting arms of her husband.

"You might as well get some sleep, too," Dr. Johnson said to Rose.

"No, I'll sit up with him."

"There's no need. I'll sit up with him."

"This town and Harl need a well-rested doctor. I should be the one to sit up with him."

The doctor threw up his hands. "Suit yourself, but call me if his condition changes." He left the room and returned momentarily with a lit lamp and set it on the cabinet across from Harl. "We shouldn't move him tonight; but tomorrow, we should get him into one of my beds, so he can rest better." Rose nodded.

As the night waned, Rose dozed in and out of sleep. Each time she woke, she grabbed Harl's hand and felt his strong pulse coursing through his veins. Satisfied, she nodded off again.

In the morning, she heard Harl move his feet on the table. Waking, she gazed at his face. His eyes were open, and he licked his lips with a dry tongue. "Water," he whispered.

Rose jumped to her feet and grabbed Harl's hand in hers. "Dr. Johnson," she called, "Harl needs water."

The shuffling of feet told her the doctor was coming. He brought a porcelain pitcher and a glass with him. Pouring the water into the glass, he set the pitcher down and raised Harl's head.

Harl took a few sips of water and shook his head. "That's enough," he said hoarsely. "What happened? I feel as if I've been stomped to death by my mules."

Rose looked at the doctor.

"You were shot," Dr. Johnson said.

"I was? Oh, then, it wasn't a dream," Harl said.

"No, it wasn't," Rose said.

Harl tried to roll onto his left side—the side that had sustained the gunshot wound. He grunted, holding his side.

"Take it slow."

"Doc, if I took it any slower, I'd be dead."

"Come this way to your right side," the doctor said.

Harl obeyed and tried to swing his legs off the table. He grunted again and fell back onto the table holding his left side, where the bullet had entered.

"Did you catch him?" Harl asked.

"Who?"

"The man who did this to me."

"We don't know. The sheriff hasn't returned with word yet," the doctor said.

"Let me have some more of that water," Harl said.

The doctor handed it to him. Harl drained the glass.

Harl looked up at the doctor. "Mighty uncomfortable accommodations, Doc. You got anything better?"

"Yes, I'll let you stay in one of the downstairs bedrooms. Here, let me and your friend help you up," the doctor said placing Harl's arm on his shoulder. He motioned for Rose to do the same. Then picking up the lamp from off the counter, he, Harl, and Rose limped to a bedroom just down the hall from the examination room.

"Here we are," the doctor said, throwing open the door to the room. He led the way inside. The lamp threw oddly shaped shadows up on the walls. The doctor placed the lamp on the high dresser across from the double bed. Two overstuffed chairs stood like sentinels at the head of the bed on either side of it.

Rose threw back the covers and helped the doctor ease Harl down onto the bed. "Shoo, feels like I was stuck with a hot poker that never got withdrawn," Harl said still holding his side.

Rose knelt at his feet and removed Harl's boots and socks. She held the covers up as the doctor helped Harl get his legs into the bed one by one.

"Thank you," he said, grinning at Rose, whose face was cast into shadow. "You, too, Doc."

"You are most welcome."

"Oh, the farm?" Harl asked, turning on his right side.

The doctor put out his hand. "It's taken care of. Your mother went back yesterday afternoon, and I took the liberty of having your mules and wagon walked down to the livery so they could be fed and watered."

"What do I owe you for that?"

"Not anything. It's all taken care of."

"By you?"

"No, by your brother-in-law, Samuel."

Harl nodded and let his head fall back onto the pillow. A deep sigh escaped his lips.

"You rest and don't worry about a thing," the doctor said. "Miss Henderson, are you going to sit up with him?"

"Yes, is that all right?"

"Of course, but I'll leave the door open."

"Thank you," she said, sitting in the chair nearest Harl, whose eyes were closed.

"Let him sleep as long as he can."

"I will," Rose said.

She listened as the doctor's feet pattered down the hall to what she supposed was his room. Rose sank into the overstuffed chair and wished for one of the quilts that now covered Harl. Her shoulders shook, even though she still had on her coat. She unbuttoned it and pulled it tightly around her, trying to block out the cold that seemed to drift into the room like a low fog just below her knees.

Turning to Harl, she watched as his chest fell rhythmically. Her teeth chattered, and she rubbed her shoulders for warmth. As she watched out the window, she saw wispy clouds turning first gray and then pink as the sun began to rise.

She stood and paced the room, trying to warm up her cold legs. Pausing to gaze out the window, she watched as wagons began arriving in town. Her stomach growled. It made such a loud sound that she was sure it would awaken Harl, but he kept on sleeping, snoring lightly.

When she turned to look out the window again, she saw someone skulking around outside of Moore's Hotel. She couldn't quite make out who it was; but the hair color was blond, and the build fit that of Albert Winters. She stepped back from the window, gasping. She lowered the wick on the lamp and then blew out the light.

Standing in the shadows, she caught herself breathing hard. Had Albert seen her? Had he noticed the light just went out in the home of the doctor?

He seemed to be staring her way. Had the doctor locked the door to his office? She couldn't remember. Racing down the hall on the balls of her feet so her boots didn't make a clicking sound on the wooden floor, she ran to the office door and checked the lock. Which way did it go? She tried the door and found it swung open easily. Across the way, a blond-haired man was running toward the open door. She screamed, slammed the door shut, and threw the lock into place. The door rattled. A man's cool voice sounded on the other side of the door.

"Open the door, Rose!"

She screamed again. This time, she put words to her screams. "Dr. Johnson, come quick!"

The doctor ran down the darkened hallway. "What's the matter?"

"Albert Winters is there at the door," she cried out.

"Albert Winters? You mean, the man who shot Harl came back into town?"

"Yes," Rose said, raising her voice. "He's at the door right this instant. He's trying to get in."

"Run down to Harl's room, close and lock the door, and hide under the bed," the doctor said. "Don't open the door for anyone, even me. I thought something like this might happen."

Rose obeyed the doctor's orders and ran to Harl's room, locked the door, set a chair against it, and then crawled under the bed as Harl slept soundly above her.

Rose heard the doctor's bare feet running down the hall and quite possibly upstairs as she heard the creaking of stairs. Then, all grew quiet. She scooted as far under the bed as she could, watching alternatively between the door and the window.

Suddenly, a shot rang out in the morning air, followed closely by another. The sound of the gunfire sounded close. Was Albert trying to shoot the lock open?

A train whistle broke the calm as footsteps were heard running down the hall again. Was it the doctor, or was it Albert? Had he busted his way in?

The sound of knocking on the bedroom door where she hid startled her. "Miss Henderson, it's me. The doctor. Open the door." She knew it was the doctor's voice, but hadn't he said not to open the door to anyone, even him?

Albert's voice sounded outside the window. "Let me in, Rose, or I'll break in."

"Not so fast," another man's deep baritone sounded. It was a voice Rose had not heard before. The sound of scuffling reached her ears.

"Rose, open the door before he breaks in at the window," Dr. Johnson said outside her door.

Scrambling out from under the bed, Rose raced to the door, pausing momentarily to look out the window, where Albert and a larger man were throwing punches at each other's heads and faces.

The door knob rattled. "Miss Henderson!" the doctor exclaimed with a strained voice.

Rose moved the overstuffed chair out of the way and unlocked the door. The doctor grabbed Rose by the arm and pulled her up the squeaking stairs beside him. "Must hide you deeper inside," he gasped as he ran. "Anton, the sheriff, is here. He'll . . . take . . . care . . . of . . . Albert. I fired two shots out the upstairs window to alert him that we needed help. Here. In here," the doctor said, opening a little door through which Rose stepped.

In the room was an old trunk and a few chairs missing the seats, but there was no fireplace. A small four-pane window cast light into the attic's dark corners.

"Can't leave the light. Must not know where you are. Going to help sheriff now. Will lock you in. Hide in the trunk if you hear footsteps," Dr. Johnson huffed out his words.

The doctor extracted himself from the room, closed the door, and threw what sounded like a tiny bolt. Rose stood up, careful to stand in the center of the room so she wouldn't bump her head on the exposed nails in the unfinished, low-steepled ceiling.

The room was colder than Harl's room had been, and her teeth chattered. Walking over to the little window, she peered out. The street was quiet—all except for the train whistle, which broke the silence. A blond-haired man was running up the street toward the train depot. A larger man ran after him. The larger man caught the blond-haired man by his shirt collar. The smaller man spun around and landed a punch directly to the man's nose, which knocked the larger man to the ground. He didn't move. The blond-haired man ran toward the sound of another blast from the departing train whistle, while Dr. Johnson leaned over the larger man, who still did not move.

Rose knocked on the window. The doctor looked up at her. "Is he all right?" she yelled.

The larger man rolled onto his side as blood poured out his nose. He sat and looked up at the window to which the doctor was pointing.

The larger man nodded. The doctor rushed away out of sight of the window.

A few creaking stairs later, the doctor threw open the little door through which Rose had stepped into the attic.

"What happened to Albert? Is that man all right? she asked.

"Albert jumped on the train. It was either that or be arrested. That man down there is Sheriff Anton Franklin, and he'll be fine once I get his nose to stop bleeding."

Tiptoeing into Harl's room, Rose was surprised that he was still snoring as if nothing had happened. "Well," she said with a laugh.

Walking into the examination room, Rose saw the larger man up close. He was wearing a blood-splattered silver star on his brown coat.

"You must be the sheriff," Rose said.

"At your service," Sheriff Franklin said, tilting his bleeding nose in the air.

"Hold this on the bridge of your nose," the doctor said.

"What is it?" Sheriff Franklin asked, not lowering his gaze.

"I put some snow in a cloth. It will help stop the bleeding and the swelling."

The sheriff grunted. Turning his eyes to Rose, he said, "Your fella got away."

"He's not my fella," Rose said hotly. "Do you think he'll come back?"

"Only if he wants to do jailtime for shooting a man and assaulting an officer of the law. Once the doc here's got me fixed up, I'm going to ride up to the train's next stop. See if I can't catch up with him and bring him to justice," Sheriff Franklin said.

Chapter 16

Rose tiptoed down the hallway to check on Harl. He was still snoring softly. Rose paused in the doorway and grinned. Opening her hands, she prayed, "Thank You, Father God, for saving Harl's life and for saving me. I appreciate Your protection."

Harl's eyes fluttered open. She stepped into the room and over to the bed, grasping Harl's hand in hers, and knelt beside him.

"What was that ruckus a while ago?" he asked, rubbing his eyes and then his temples.

"That ruckus was my ex-fiancé giving it one more try at winning me back."

"I take it he wasn't successful." The side of Harl's mouth hitched up into a smile.

"No, not at all. He's on a train headed north."

"Were you praying just now?"

"Yes, I was thanking the Lord for saving you and me."

"You?" Harl asked, letting his eyes close again.

"I asked the Lord to be my Savior and to be with me, and He did. I felt a warmth spread through me like I've never felt before, and I'm at peace. I'm sure that the Lord'll always be there for me."

"And I'll be there for you." Harl's eyes fluttered open and shut. "I need to rest. Is Sheriff Franklin going after that man who shot me?"

"Yes, he'll go as soon as Dr. Johnson fixes his bloody nose."

"Oh good." This time, Harl kept his eyes shut as his head on the pillow turned toward Rose.

Once his bleeding nose stopped, Sheriff Franklin rode like the wind on his horse to the next depot, where he boarded the train. His eyes latched onto the back of the head of the culprit he was after.

Marching up the aisle, he grabbed Albert Winters by the coat.

"Stand up. You're coming with me," the sheriff said.

Albert gasped as he jerked his eyes up at the sheriff. "I ain't going nowhere."

Anton dragged the man off his seat and to a standing position. "And I say you are. March!"

The sheriff maneuvered Albert in front of him. The men walked down the tight aisle as the train lurched forward. All eyes were on them as Albert tried to wiggle out of his coat.

Anton gripped his shoulder harder down to his shirt and skin.

When they came to the doorway, Anton grabbed the man's arm with his free hand and wrestled him off the train onto the platform outside the depot.

"You need any help?" A man's voice sounded behind the sheriff.

Turning, the sheriff saw the train's conductor standing behind him on the step. He wore a concerned look on his face.

"No, thank you. I think I got him." Just then, Albert chose that moment to lunge forward. But Anton's grip was sure.

Walking into the depot, Anton excused himself and cut the line up to the ticket window. "Excuse me," he said to the man behind the counter, "but would you happen to have some rope back there that I could use?"

"Let me check," the man said. Turning from the window, he rummaged around under the counter. "Will this do?" he asked, holding up a length of rope. "We use it for tying up luggage."

"What are you going to do with that?" Albert asked, trepidation in his voice. "I didn't do nothing worth stringing me up for."

Anton took the rope. "Thank you," he said to the man at the counter. Then turning his full attention back to Albert, he said, "Will you be quiet?" The sheriff wound the rope around both of Albert's hands and tied it tight. "There. That should hold you until we get back to town."

When they arrived back to town, Anton walked Albert into the waiting cell in the jailhouse. "This'll be your home until the judge comes through next month."

Albert kicked at the bars on the cell door in response.

"You calm yourself in there."

The corners of Albert's mouth turned down, and he slunk over to the cot in the corner. He lay down and turned his face to the wall.

Several hours after Sheriff Franklin brought Albert back to the jailhouse, the doctor informed Rose and Harl that he had been captured.

Rose shook her head, "Oh thank the Lord."

Harl squeezed her hand as he sat on the edge of the bed.

"Feeling better?" The doctor asked Harl.

"Much. I'd like to go home if that is an option."

The doctor smiled. "Of course, we can get you home, but you need to take it easy. I don't want you doing any farm work for a while. Don't want that injury busting open."

"Don't you worry. I've got farmhands now that can do the work for me."

"I'll go bring your wagon down."

When the doctor left the room, Harl pushed his glasses up higher on the bridge of his nose and pulled Rose close. "Finally, we're going home."

Rose smiled and nodded.

She leaned in closer to Harl as he rubbed her arms. Reaching up, he caressed her face with his hands and pulled her face down to his. He placed a delicate, tentative kiss on her lips. Looking up at her, he whispered, "Is that all right?"

Rose laughed and nodded. "Yes, that is more than all right. It feels wonderful."

Harl reached up and brought Rose's head toward him. He kissed her fervently. She sighed deeply and wrapped her arms around his neck.

"I'm so glad you are better. Now, let's go home."

Epilogue

Several months later, Harl and Rose were strolling through the blossoming apple orchard at his home. The breeze lifted strands of red hair around Rose's face, which she tried unsuccessfully to grasp. Harl smiled and caught a tendril in his hand. He gently placed it behind Rose's ear.

They stood for a moment facing each other as the warm breeze ruffled their clothing.

Rose smiled up at Harl. "I must look a mess. I need to go in and fix these combs."

She turned away from him. He reached out his hand and grasped hers. "No, wait."

Taking a deep breath, Harl held his breath and then blew it out all at once. "There's something that I've been meaning to ask you."

Rose turned back to face Harl. "What is it?"

"Will you consider being my wife?"

Rose gasped and paused before answering. "I would be honored to be your wife, Harl Adams."

The corner of one side of his mouth ticked up. He eased his glasses back up on the bridge of his nose and lowered his head.

Closing the gap between their lips, he kissed her softly. She threw her arms around his neck and kissed him back with unbridled passion.

In the months that followed, Rose and Hazel spent their days planning a wedding. Harl threw out an opinion here and there, but mostly, the women bonded as they discussed flowers and other decorations.

Rose wrote to her father, inviting him to the wedding but not expecting he would come. She was surprised when she received a letter from the town's sheriff informing her that her father and his wife had been tried and convicted for the death of her mother. She was relieved that justice had been served for her mother but also felt a sadness that her father would never be a part of her life. After accepting forgiveness from God for her own sins, Rose found that she was able to forgive her father as well.

When the wedding day arrived, Rose stood admiring herself in the full-length mirror upstairs in her room. The cream-colored silk material she had chosen from the selection at Mrs. Guthrie's dress shop went well with her peaches-and-cream coloring.

Mrs. Guthrie fussed with the hem of the dress, while Hazel placed two more tortoise shell combs in Rose's hair.

Turning Rose to look at her, Hazel smiled at the woman before her. "I'm so thankful to the Lord for bringing you all this way for my Harl. I'm thankful, too, that you gave your life to the Lord. You've turned out to be a fine woman. I'll be proud to call you my daughter-in-law."

Rose hugged her.

"Thank you so much. I'm so glad that you want us to go on living with you."

The pair hugged again.

"Are you sure the hem isn't too long?" Mrs. Guthrie asked.

"No, it's fine. Really," Rose said.

"There now," Hazel said, placing her hands gently on her shoulders. "I'm going to go in the wagon with Harl to the church, and we'll meet you there."

Rose stuck out her hand to Hazel and then to Mrs. Guthrie. "Thank you for everything. I'm honored your son chose me. And this dress is perfect."

"Just one more finishing touch," Mrs. Guthrie said as she arranged a delicate veil on Rose's head. "Let me make sure that Mrs. Adams and Harl leave before you come downstairs."

In a few moments, Mrs. Guthrie entered Rose's bedroom. "They are gone. It's time."

Rose gathered herself together and stepped toward the door, ready to accept her future as Harl Adams' bride.

The End

Love in the Kentucky Hills,
Book One

After Catherine Reed's husband dies, she moves back home in order to accept a new position as the teacher for the town's one-room schoolhouse. Samuel Harris has suffered his own loss and guilt has burdened him ever since. When his old flame comes back to town, he wonders if they can find healing together . . .

For more information about
Greta Picklesimer
and
The Rejected Mail-Order Bride
please visit:

www.gretapicklesimer.com

When Lena Neubauer is sent from Germany to America to help her immigrant brother on his farm and with his young children, she never expects what awaits her in antebellum America. With family honor and devotion propelling her across to an unknown world, Lena soon finds herself stepping into this strange world. After tragedy strikes, Lena finds herself finally at the crossroads and must make a decision that will affect her future—and her family's future—forever.

Sarah Bakker has spent years getting over her love for Michael Thomas. After he went MIA, Sarah thought her heart would never heal. But when he is found alive and returns home, Sarah is thrown together with him to prepare for the town's annual Christmas pageant. Perhaps Sarah will finally find the love she longs for—even if it's only in her dreams.

Sam Anthem has always been a team player, leading his Home Team on secret missions around the world. When he is forced on a vacation, he is introduced to a former covert ops soldier-turned pastor. But the vacation takes a turn when the Home Team comes under attack. As the team fights to stay alive, Sam begins to wonder if there is more to life than just the job. With his life on the line, Sam must decide between the job or his newfound faith and possible love.